Heartbreak U:

Freshman Year

Heartbreak U:

Freshman Year

Johnni Sherri

www.urbanbooks.net

Urban Books, LLC
300 Farmingdale Road, NY-Route 109
Farmingdale, NY 11735

Heartbreak U: Freshamn Year
Copyright © 2024 Johnni Sherri

All rights reserved. No part of this book may be re-
produced in any form or by any means without prior
consent of the Publisher, except brief quotes used in
reviews.

To the extent that the image or images on the cover of
this book depict a person or persons, such person or
persons are merely models, and are not intended to
portray any character or characters featured in the book.

ISBN 13: 978-1-64556-644-1

First Mass Market Printing September 2024
First Trade Paperback Printing April 2024
Printed in the United States of America

10 9 8 7 6 5 4 3 2 1

*This is a work of fiction. Any references or similar-
ities to actual events, real people, living or dead, or
to real locales are intended to give the novel a sense
of reality. Any similarity in other names, characters,
places, and incidents is entirely coincidental.*

Distributed by Kensington Publishing Corp.
Submit Orders to:
Customer Service
400 Hahn Road
Westminster, MD 21157-4627
Phone: 1-800-733-3000
Fax: 1-800-659-2436

Heartbreak U:

Freshman Year

Johnni Sherri

Chapter 1

Franki

Broken in Brooklyn

"Gah damn, shorty," he hissed, dragging out each of his words, as his slow thrusts came to a gradual halt. It was from that final jerk and the low growl he let out against my ear that I realized we were finally done.

As his sweat-covered body blanketed mine, I lay there, feeling almost anesthetized. Eyes glued to the ceiling and my limbs completely weak. We stayed in that position for a while, until the echoes of his loud snoring could be heard around the room. Slowly, I craned my neck to look over at the alarm clock on my nightstand. The bright red numbers told me it was 5:18 p.m.

"Oh, shit!" I muttered, in a panic. Not wasting any time, I pushed his heavy body off mine.

"What's wrong?" he asked, in a daze, his voice strained. Groggy, he struggled to open his eyes wider.

"Nigga, you gotta go. My muva's gonna be home in, like, five minutes," I told him. Every day my mother walked through the front door of our apartment at 5:25 p.m. on the dot.

I shot to my feet, then began frantically searching around the floor for my clothes. I threw his underwear, jeans, and T-shirt at him in the process. Once I was fully dressed and he had everything back on except for the Timberland boots, I glanced over at the clock again. My eyes bugged when I saw that it was now 5:24 p.m.

Suddenly, I heard the sound of my mother's keys in the lock of our apartment door. "Oh my Gawd! She's gonna kill me," I said, panicking, grabbing my head. "Raul, hurry your slow ass up. My muva's coming through the door now," I whispered, as if she could actually hear me.

Skin black as midnight, those gold fronts shining on his teeth, he looked up at me with that set of dark eyes as he put on his boots. "The name's Ramón, shorty, and the fuck am I supposed to do? Hide?"

My heart pounded inside my chest as I looked all around the tiny room, trying to determine the best place for him to go. That was until my eyes landed on the window.

"Franki!" I heard my mother call out from the other room. "You home, baby?"

"Shit, shit, shit!" I pointed toward the window. "Nigga, you just gon' have to jump."

"The fuck!" he said, befuddled, cocking his head to the side. "Shorty, you bugging." After running his hand down his face, he let out a small snort. "I'm too fucking grown for this shit, ma," he mumbled, shaking his head, as he continued to slip on his boots.

With every second that passed, I swore I could hear each of my mother's footsteps as she headed back toward my room. "Franki!" she called out again.

"Coming, Ma!" I yelled, jerking up the window. Instantly, I felt a warm rush of summer air enter my room. After looking down at the eight-foot jump Ramón would have to make, I silently mouthed for him to hurry up.

"You crazy as shit, shorty," he muttered, sliding one leg out the window. As he straddled the windowsill, he allowed his eyes to sweep over me one final time. "Pussy was definitely good, though. When can I see you again?" he said before licking his lips.

Typical New York nigga, I thought.

"Never. I'm heading to college tomorrow, down in North Carolina. Now, beat it!" I said, giving him a little push.

A split second later I heard the loud thud of his body colliding with the ground, Just as I shut the window, my bedroom door flew open.

"Franki, I've been calling you," my mother said, looking around my room. "You all packed up?" Her slanted, Asian-like eyes settled on the suitcases and storage bins that were stacked in a corner.

"Yeah, I'm all packed and ready, ma," I told her, still hearing my heart thumping loudly in my ears.

Suddenly her eyes narrowed, like she was trying to figure something out.

Don't tell me she smells sex in the room!

"Franki, are you sure you're ready to live on your own?" she finally asked.

Letting go a soft sigh of relief, I nodded my head. "Yes, ma. I already told you that I'ma be just fine."

She softly clasped her hands together and held them against the side of her face. "My baby's finally going off to college. I can't believe it."

Her infectious smile returned, and that was when I noticed the fatigue in her eyes. Early signs of wrinkles had just started to show on her smooth dark skin, and traces of silver had appeared at the edges of her hair. She stood there in a standard black-and-white maid's uniform, with old orthopedic shoes on her feet. From her numerous walks to and from the bus stop, the soles had worn down, especially on one edge, causing her lean to one side when she moved.

"I know, I know," she said with her hand up. "I gotta get me some more of these Naturalizers. Only shoes I can work in."

I sighed and rolled my eyes. "Ma, why you still working that job? You the only black woman I know in twenty eighteen that's still willing to be a maid for the white man."

"It's all I know, baby." She shrugged. "My mother was a maid in Brooklyn, your great-grandmother was a maid in Westchester, and her mother was a maid down in Georgia until our family finally migrated up north in—"

"Nineteen thirty-two," I said, finishing her sentence for her with another hard roll of my eyes. It was that same story I'd heard over a thousand times.

"I just don't have anything else to put on my résumé," she admitted. Wincing in pain, she reached down to take the shoes off her feet.

"Well, I ain't gon' be no maid," I mumbled under my breath. I didn't think she heard me, but when she glanced up, the hurt and shame were evident all over her face.

She tried hard to mask it, though, giving me a closed-lip smile. "And I don't want you to be, baby," she said curtly. "Why you think I'm sending you off to college, huh?"

"I know, ma," I said lowly, picking imaginary lint from my clothes to ease through the awkward moment that had suddenly fallen upon the room.

"What you gon' be when you grow up, baby?" she suddenly asked, in the tone of a mother who was speaking to a small child.

"I'ma be a doctor, ma," I said. Our eyes instantly smiled at one another's, like we were making a silent agreement.

Ever since I was a little girl, I had wanted to be a doctor. I remember when I was just five years old, I sprained my ankle playing kickball outside with some of the neighborhood boys. I was in so much pain that I cried until we ended up at Kings County Hospital, smack-dab in the middle of Brooklyn. That was where I met Dr. Warren in the emergency room. She was a tall, beautiful woman with cocoa-colored skin. Wearing green scrubs and white clogs, she looked me over carefully that day. I even remember the X-ray she showed us of my ankle, still perfectly intact.

I watched Dr. Warren's every movement as she worked the ER like she owned it. She immediately fell into the role of superhero for me, with the stethoscope wrapped around her neck and the paper charts in her hand. It seemed as if I, along with everyone else there, was looking to her for help that day. And after all was said and done, I left

Kings County with more than just a sprained ankle, more than just the confirmation that I'd be okay. I walked out with the dream of becoming the first doctor in my family. A black woman doctor.

My entire academic life so far had been filled with nothing but As. Not even a single B marred my perfect record. It was the one thing my mother never had to worry about when it came to me. However, boys were a different story. I lost my virginity early, at the age of fourteen, down in the funky boys' locker room during my freshman year of high school. He was a senior, seventeen years old and our star point guard on the basketball team. *Rakim Shaheed*. I'd never forget his name. Standing at six feet two, weighing approximately 170 pounds, and with skin the color of creamy caramel, that nigga was damn near perfect in my eyes. And although I knew he wanted only one thing, I gave it up with ease after knowing him for only a total of five days.

As if it happened yesterday, I remember feeling that first break of skin and the burning pressure between my thighs. I refused to cry as he tore in and out of me. But it was the lust in his eyes as he dug in deep, like he really, *really* wanted me, loved me even, that caught my attention. Although the feeling was short-lived, in that moment all my pain and hurt seemed to slip away. With the way his strong hands first made contact with my flesh, and the way those big soft lips pressed up against mine, it was unforgettable.

Unfortunately, there was only that one time for Rakim and me, because he ended up being the biggest asshole. He told the entire basketball team what we had done and called me a slut. Although I was totally hurt, I learned an invaluable lesson that day. *Niggas ain't shit.* Yet and still, I found myself on an ongoing search for that same look of want that had filled his eyes that first time. With every guy I fucked thereafter, I longed to see that look. Every time I opened my legs for someone else, it was like chasing my very first high.

Today Ramón was victim number . . . Oh, I don't know. Twelve maybe. I met his roughneck-looking black ass down at the corner store just two hours before. He was tall, with a muscular build and smooth, tatted black skin that sent shivers down my spine. And so he went from getting my number to walking me home and fucking me all in a matter of *two* hours. Sure, I knew I was fast in a sexual sense, but I always made sure to be careful. Not once had I had unprotected sex. I mean, what kind of doctor would I be if I wasn't at least safe and smart when it came to sex, right?

"I'm tired, and we got a long drive tomorrow. Let's just get Chinese tonight," my mother said with a little yawn, pulling me from my reverie.

While smoothing back the messy covers across my bed, I nodded in agreement. "Yeah. That sounds good," I said.

"Let me just change out of these clothes and we'll walk down to New Ming's."

After my mother left, I went across the hall to have a quick wash in the sink. Once I got back to my bedroom, I grabbed my brush off the dresser and held my long black curls with my fist. As I brushed my hair into a ponytail, I glanced at my reflection in the mirror, taking in my brown-sugar skin complexion and my dark, slanted eyes. I was virtually a carbon copy of my mother in her younger years. The only thing my father had gifted me was his perfect set of straight white teeth and his ears. That's right. I said ears. My ears stuck out, a little like an elf's. They used to bother me when I was younger, but now I just pull my hair back and show them mugs off with pride.

Once my mother came out of her room, dressed down in a T-shirt and jeans, we headed out the front door. It was the middle of August, so the evening sun was still hot enough to scorch my youthful skin. As we walked down Sutter Avenue, there were men hanging up and down the block, letting out catcalls in our direction. This was something I had grown accustomed to while trekking the streets of Brooklyn.

Before we could even reach Triumphant, a church along the way, I heard the soft melodies of men harmonizing in the distance. We walked another minute or two, hearing horns honk and tires screech while smelling the car fumes that filled the air. To some, the sight of our filthy streets and cracked-up sidewalks might have been appalling, but to us, Brooklyn was home. The busy sound of the city alone was like music to my ears.

When we finally approached Triumphant Church, three young men came into view, and the sound of their melodic voices grew clear. While snapping their fingers, they sang a gospel song I'd never heard before. Sitting at their feet was a cardboard box full of pamphlets.

Suddenly, one of the young guys who was singing stepped out to get my attention. "Excuse me, Miss Lady."

I slowed my pace and cut my eyes sharply in his direction. He was this light-bright nigga, dressed in what appeared to be a Catholic school uniform. Short-sleeved, button-down white shirt and tight-fitting black slacks. He even had the shiny loafers on his feet. His smooth, angular face was almost pretty like a woman's, and his soft, curly hair was cut low and edged to perfection.

"Gay-ass niggas," I mumbled under my breath. *Pretty niggas that stay in the church, singing and swishing their asses up and down the aisle, are always the gay ones*, I thought.

"Excuse me . . . Miss Lady," he said again. This time, he jogged a couple steps toward us, leaving the other two young men behind. With a pamphlet in hand, he attempted to make eye contact with me.

I put my hand up to stop him in his tracks. "Look, whatever it is, we don't want it, B. Just keep singing and sell that shit to someone else, a'ight?" I snapped, hearing the Brooklyn inflection in my tone.

His head jutted back as his brown eyes narrowed into a stunned glare. From my peripheral, I could see my mother's wide eyes staring at me as well. "Franki! Don't talk to the young man like that," she fussed. Then she softened her expression and spun around to face him. "Here. I'll take one," she said, then took the pamphlet from his outstretched hand.

Just before my mother and I walked away, I caught him licking his full, dark pink lips. Then he let out a small sarcastic snort of laughter. "Ma, Jesus Christ said, 'Do not let your heart be troubled. Trust in God. Trust also in me,'" he preached behind my back.

"Always them gay niggas that be tryna to get me in the church. No thank you," I fussed lowly to myself, walking past him.

"Franki, that's enough! Let it go," my mother said.

"What? It's true, ma," I replied, defending myself with a shrug.

"I know you claim to no longer believe in God. And at your age, I can't make you go to church," she said, holding up both of her hands. "But you will not be disrespectful. Just as those three young men are, *I*, too, am a person of faith. And I am *still* your mother!"

Hearing the oncoming ass whippin' in her tone, I swallowed the comeback waiting on my tongue. Rolling my eyes, I let out a heavy sigh and thought more about her words. It was true, I no longer believed in God. Or at least that was what I told myself these days. Around the age of eight, I lost my father to Rikers Island. And given that I was a Daddy's girl, I was devastated when he left me behind. Although that was only the beginning, from that point on, little by little, my faith seemed to fade.

As a kid, and even now as an adult, I wondered why God had chosen to do that to us. *To me.* When my father went to Rikers, our church shunned us. We were forced to leave our three-bedroom home and go back to the slum apartments on Sutter Avenue. Other than cleaning a few houses every now and then, my mother didn't even have a real job. We struggled every fucking year. Not only that, but my daddy refused to see either one of us while he was doing his time.

It was like every boy or man I came in contact with thereafter was just a useless attempt on my part to fill the void of my father's love. I knew this was most likely why I was so promiscuous. I didn't need a fucking psychology degree to tell me that. But I figured, as long as I was safe, as long as I used condoms each and every time, there was nothing wrong with meaningless sex. *Right?*

Chapter 2

Paris

Milk's Favorite Cookie

In just one more day, I'd be saying goodbye to sunny California and heading to college. Unfortunately, my white mother was forcing me to attend an HBCU, something I'd never even heard of before she mentioned it. "It's your father's alma mater. He would want you to get in touch with your people, Paris," she'd said.

Bullshit! My daddy doesn't give a damn about his people, which is why he married your ass, I remembered thinking.

Nonetheless, the decision had been made without my consent. The tuition check had been mailed, and at nine o'clock tomorrow morning, I was expected to be on a plane headed to Greensboro, North Carolina. It was funny how my mother, who had pushed for this, wouldn't even be there at the airport to see me off. Right now she was vacationing in Spain with her girlfriends, enjoying the last few weeks of summer. This was why I chose to spend my final day here in California at the spa, *alone*. I knew that this college was going to be a life-changing experience for me, and for that, I needed something to clear my head.

Hearing my iPhone vibrate on the table next to me, I removed the cucumber slices from my eyes. "Lisa, be a dear and pass me my phone," I said to the aesthetician. Once she handed it over, I looked down at the screen and saw that it was my best friend, Heather, calling.

"Heather?" I said when I picked up. After putting the call on speaker, I leaned back in the chair and returned the cucumbers to my eyes.

"Like, oh my God!" she squealed. "Paris, please tell me you're not really going to leave me?" Her all-American, blue-eyed, blond-haired California girl accent came through as she spoke in a panic.

I sighed. "Unfortunately, yes. In just eighteen more hours, I'll be headed to North . . . North, ugh." I almost gagged, trying to form the words. "North Carolina!"

"So it's, like, an all-black college or something, right?" she asked.

Having answered this same question for her for the hundredth time already, I found myself getting annoyed. "Yes, Heather," I responded with a deep sigh.

"So, like, will you even get your bachelor's degree there?"

I laughed. "Bitch, you are *so* fucking racist. Of course I'll be getting my degree," I said before I frowned, in deep thought. After what seemed like minutes, I went on. "I mean . . . I think. It is a four-year school." Suddenly I felt unsure.

"You *think*! So you mean you didn't even look them up?" she asked in shock.

"Of course I did," I lied. "It's an HBCU." Feeling the green goop on my face finally harden to a crisp, I lifted my chin to give myself an added dose of confidence. "A historically bonded and accredited university," I stated matter-of-factly.

"Well, that sounds way cool, Par. It's just . . . we're all gonna miss you at Berkeley. I always thought we'd go there together," she lamented.

Hearing her talk about Berkeley, my dream college, caused my eyes to roll. While all my friends were either going to USC or Berkeley, I was expected to attend some god-awful—"ratchet," if you will—school in North Carolina. And all because my mother wanted me to get more in touch with *my people*.

My father, the Honorable Judge David Young, had been a California circuit court judge for ten years. And before he passed away last year, he was one of the most prominent and well-respected black men in our community. For that, I was beyond proud. But he endured a long battle with high blood pressure and heart disease, and a massive heart attack finally took his life.

My father was born and raised in Compton, California. On the wrong side of the tracks, I might add. He was the first in his family ever to attend college. After graduating from North Carolina A&T State University, he went on to study at Harvard Law. Imagine his family's surprise when he brought home my mother, *Becky*. Blond hair, blue eyes, and already four months pregnant with me. Once Grammy passed, my father lost all contact with that side of his family, which meant I rarely interacted with black people other than him. The private school I attended was less than 3 percent black. The country club we were members of was less than 1 percent black. And the beautiful Beverly Hills gated community we lived in was home to only two black people in its entirety: my father and I.

"Like, dude, I'm totally bummed!" Heather said, snapping me out of my thoughts.

"Don't worry. I'll totally come to visit, and you can come visit me too," I said, trying to look on the bright side.

"But isn't your school . . . in the hood?" she whispered.

I shook my head and let out a little laugh. "I'm sure it can't be all that bad, Heather. I mean, it is a historically bonded and accredited university, for God's sake," I cried.

"Oh . . . right!" she said, as though she'd forgotten. "Have you talked to Brad?"

I sighed at just the mention of his name. "No, and I don't plan to either," I quipped.

Brad Andrews had been my boyfriend for the past three years. His thick chestnut-brown hair, bright blue eyes, and perfect set of white teeth could melt any woman's heart. Besides his good looks, he was a charming motherfucker. He could talk his way into a girl's panties within only a matter of minutes. If only he had kept his little pecker in his pants, I thought now. Last month I had caught him French-kissing another girl right outside his house. Didn't take me but .25 seconds to cut his pale white ass off like a pair of blue jeans in the summer.

After hearing the seriousness in my voice, Heather grew silent. When she finally spoke again, she said, "Well, bestie, just say the word and I'm there for a friggin' visit."

"For sure," I told her.

"Peace in the Middle East," she said, using that same lame parting line she'd been using since junior high. She probably had her two fingers up and was making a peace sign.

"Dude! You are so corny," I teased with a little laugh.

Not wanting to end our call, we lingered on the phone for a few more seconds, only sharing silence between us.

"Peace in the Middle East, Heather," I finally said. "I love you."

"Love you too, babe." And with that, she ended the call.

Once my facial was complete and I'd been thoroughly scrubbed down with sugar and honey, I decided to call it a night. It was a little after nine o'clock in the evening when I finally made it home. As I drove my all-white Audi truck up the cobblestone driveway, I took in the sight of our big, lonely house. It was an enormous white-brick mansion featuring twenty thousand square feet of living space, ten bedrooms, and twelve and a half baths, all sitting on a five-acre lot. Indoor and outdoor pool, tennis court, basketball court, you name it. This house had it all. But from the empty driveway to the dark, lifeless windows that reflected the moonlight, that was all it was. *A house.* It hadn't been a home since the day my daddy died, and even before then, I had felt lonely. Not only was I an only child, but my father had also worked extremely long hours and my mother had always hung out with her friends.

After making my way inside, I cut on the lights and disabled the silent alarm. Once I reached my bedroom upstairs, I slapped the light switch on the wall. When the lights came on, my eyes immediately went over to the Fendi luggage collection I had packed in a corner of my room. I sighed on my way into the bathroom. Once I was all showered and dressed for the night, I lay back in my king-size canopy bed. Everything in my room was powder pink, from the curtains and the comforter all the way down to the sheer drapes that hung loosely over my bed at night. My entire room had been designed in Milan, and to say that it was beautiful would be an understatement.

After pulling up the lush covers a tad more, I stretched my arms and let out a small yawn. Just as I reached over to turn my lamp off, I noticed my laptop sitting on the nightstand. "Well, let's just see about this North Carolina A&T," I said to myself.

I knew I should've already done my research on the university, and I probably should have even gone for a visit. But somewhere in my dimwit brain, I had figured that if I didn't show any interest in the place, my mother would finally take the hint. *I guess she showed me.* After I typed "North Carolina A&T State University" in the Google browser and then clicked on the link, the first thing I saw was their cheesy little home page. Black girls with naturally kinky hair and braids, pretending to be engrossed in their schoolwork. Black guys in science labs, and others shown carrying book bags on their backs. Football players with dreads and hats twisted to the back.

"Really, Mom? Ugh!" I muttered, rolling my eyes.

This website, and most likely the university it-self, was in stark contrast to Berkeley's. Berkeley's home page was filled with some of the nation's top graduates and featured a prominent chancellor, dressed in a black cap and gown. The sunniest of California campuses was displayed in the back-ground. I'd be the first to admit that not one black face graced the site's home page, but I was used to that. I was used to not having people that looked like me around, so it really didn't bother me, *I guess*.

Clicking deeper and deeper into the N.C. A&T website, I found myself on the academics screen. I didn't know what course of study I wanted to pursue, which was why I thought my mother was making me suffer. Both she and my father had tried talking me into law school, but I just couldn't see it. *Boring* was the only word to describe the courtroom and our judicial system. I didn't like kids, and teachers didn't make enough money for me, so a degree in education wasn't even an option. After selecting the social work icon, I looked over what the degree entailed. That was a no-go for me too. I could easily admit that I was too selfish and a bit out of touch for a career like that.

Just as I was about to close my laptop and call it a night, my cell phone started to ring. Not recognizing the phone number, I hesitantly swiped my finger across the screen.

"Hello," I answered.

"Hello, darling," my mother said in her usual snobbish tone.

"Oh, hey, Mom."

"I just wanted to make sure that you're all packed up and ready for tomorrow. The car will be there by six to take you to the airport," she said.

Looking over at the six bags of luggage that were neatly stacked in a corner of my room, I let out a deep sigh. "Ready as I'll ever be. I guess," I said lowly, hearing the sadness in my own voice.

"I know you're hesitant—"

"Hesitant!" I shouted, cutting her off.

"Let me finish, Paris," she said sternly. "Now, I know you're not happy about going to North Carolina tomorrow, and I guess I can't really blame you. But know that I'm sending you there not just to honor your father but also to show you a different world. Trust me, you'll thank me later."

"Well, if you are somehow trying to prove a point or show me a different world, as you called it, that's what TVs are for! Sending me hundreds of miles away, without a friend in sight, hardly qualifies you for mother of the year!" I yelled.

Although I was a spoiled brat, I honestly had never spoken to my mother like that before. Her sending me off to some HBCU, against my will, was just the final straw.

"You're just scared, Paris, but this will be good for you. You'll see."

"Well, I'll be eighteen in November. Don't think I won't transfer!" I threatened before ending the call.

I was so furious that my hands were literally shaking. After closing my laptop, I reached over and cut off the lamp. Slipping the pink face mask down over my eyes, I lay back in the bed with the hope of calming myself. What should have been deep inhales and exhales sounded more like huffs and puffs coming out of me. When my breathing settled down, I heard nothing but the sounds of the air-conditioned air blowing through the vents. I childishly kicked off the heavy covers.

"Go to an HBCU with *your* people," I said mockingly, folding my arms across my chest. "Tuh!"

Once I calmed myself down to the point where I could actually begin to fall asleep, I took a few more steady breaths. No matter where I went, my first day of college was going to be a big day for me, and as much as I didn't want to go, I knew my father would've wanted me to. Closing my eyes tight behind the mask, I silently made up a plan in my head. I would go to N.C. A&T only for the first semester, just to appease my mom. After that, I would definitely be transferring to Berkeley.

Chapter 3

Hope

The Non-Mormon Girl

As we parked curbside in front of Holland Hall, I peered out the car window. Freshman students were all spread out across the lush green lawn, hauling luggage, boxes, and bins as they traveled in and out of the dorms. After a sixteen-hour drive from Texas, I finally stepped out of my father's car. Slowly stretching out my limbs, I immediately came in contact with the thick North Carolina humidity. When my father got out after me and jogged around to the back, I heard the trunk pop open.

"Come help get some of this stuff out, Hope," he said.

Pushing my glasses farther up on my nose, I started walking to the rear of the car. "Yes, sir," I said.

Both of us grabbed as much as we could before making our way to my dorm. When we reached it, I allowed my eyes to dart around the lawn in front. I quickly noticed that the freshman girls in this dorm looked nothing like me. Some had long weaves and wigs that flowed down their backs, while others had a more natural look, their hair styled in kinky Afros or wild curls. Stylish skintight clothes were on their backs, and fancy sneakers on their feet. These girls had bodies that were fully grown, with curves I didn't even remember my mother having.

I, on the other hand, was a small-framed, dark-skinned girl from Alto, Texas, a town no bigger than eleven hundred acres. For the past four years of my life, I had kept my hair pressed and styled in a modest bun with Chinese-cut bangs hovering over my eyes. Even on hot days like this, I wore long khaki skirts down to my feet. My shirts always covered everything except for my cross necklace and my lower arms. Courtesy of Walmart, I had on all-white canvas sneakers that were identical to the two other pair I had in my bag. To call myself a plain Jane would just be laughable, as my lack-luster appearance was completely mind-numbing, to say the least. In fact, my nails had never been polished, and at eighteen years old, I didn't even have my ears pierced.

As I lugged my laundry basket up the brick steps of the dorm, I could hear the sounds of my father's labored breathing behind me. My eyes lifted, and I noticed all the old air-conditioning units hanging out the windows. Then I focused on the white wooden front door, which was framed in cement. A sign with slim black letters that read HOLLAND HALL hung above it. When we reached the door, I sat my basket down on the ground and opened the door so that my father could carry some of my heavier items inside. After sticking my leg out to hold the door in place, I picked up the basket once more and followed behind him.

As the first cold breeze from the air-conditioning hit me in the face, I rapidly scanned the front lobby. Girls in all different shades of brown and of all different sizes were scattered about the large space. Somehow, I managed to hear the disapproval in my father's low grunts and groans as we cross the lobby.

"Hope, what floor are you on?" he asked as he approached one of the elevators.

"I'm on the third floor, Deddy," I told him.

When the elevator doors flew open, out came two tall guys. One was a light shade of caramel,

and the other just as dark as me. Both seemed
attractive. They were wearing dirty white football
uniforms, which were obviously padded underneath. Glancing over at their well-defined abs,
which were exposed thanks to the short-sleeved
jerseys they wore, I unintentionally licked my lips.
But before I could even lift my eyes, I heard a low
snort of laughter.

I looked back up and somehow locked gazes with
the dark-skinned one. A smirk, or rather a cocky
curl of the lips, formed on his face. He'd caught
me red-handed. Completely mortified, I tried my
best to hurry up and look away, but not before the
sound of his deep chuckle caught me off guard. It
was manlier than what I was used to hearing from
boys my age. And although he had yet to speak, I
somehow liked the sound of his voice.

"Aye, Meeko," the light-skinned one said, tapping him on arm. "Is that shorty over there?" he
asked, pointing his finger. Before *Meeko* could
answer, the two of them darted past us.

Once my father and I had stepped inside the
elevator, I quickly turned around and looked out
just before the doors closed.

"Aye! Aye, girl!" the light-skinned guy rudely
hollered to some girl in the lobby.

Pulling his fist up to his mouth, Meeko simply
shook his head and laughed. "You stupid, yo."

I rolled my eyes up in my head. "So childish!" I mumbled as the elevator doors closed.

"I thought this was an all-girls dorm, Hope," my father said, sternness in his voice, as he glanced at the floor numbers, which lit up one at a time.

"It is, Deddy. Those boys were probably just here helping someone move in, is all," I explained with a little shrug.

"Mm-hmm," he muttered.

If you couldn't already tell, my father was as strict as they came, and after my mother died five years ago from Graves' disease, his overbearing ways became a lot worse. In high school I didn't go to football games or homecoming dances like most normal teens. I stayed hidden in the house, only watching preapproved television shows throughout the week, studying, and reading books.

In addition to those activities, my father and I spent most of our time in the church. We were both devout members of the United Pentecostal Church, which was why my father preferred that I dressed the way I did. Bible study every Wednesday night, community pantry every Saturday morning, and worship service faithfully every Sunday. I didn't mind church; it was just the nonexistent life outside of the church that bothered me so.

Girls in my high school looked similar to these girls in the dorm, so I'd always stuck out like a sore thumb. I even got bullied from ninth grade all the way through eleventh and was in more fights than I could count. By the time my senior year arrived, I think folks just gave up on me. I wasn't changing and never showed much of a reaction to their crude behavior. Not that I had much choice in the matter, because my father couldn't care less about me fitting in. As long as I was a good *Christian girl* in his eyes, that was all that really mattered.

After getting off the elevator, I took in the sight of all the colorful boards on the walls. There were letters made out of construction paper, with pictures of the girls from the dorm in between. After passing door after door, we finally reached suite 311. I dropped my basket and took out my key before unlocking the door. The closed-off smell of the suite immediately smacked me in the face, and I noticed the painted white cinder-block walls. When I stepped in, I found myself in a small living-room setup, and off in the corner was a galley-style kitchen. The apartment-style dorm suite had four bedrooms and two shared baths. I immediately chose my room, one in the very back.

"You think you'll be okay in here?" my father asked, peering around the room with a look of concern on his face.

Nodding my head, I walked farther into the room. After setting aside my things, I plopped down on the twin-size bed and slid my hands across the smooth plastic mattress. My father walked over to the window and cut the air conditioner on.

Staring out the window at the ground below, he said, "I don't know if I should leave you here by yourself, Hope." I could hear the doubt in his voice.

"Aunt Marlene is just fifteen minutes away, Deddy. I'll be all right," I assured him.

"Yeah, but . . . ," he said, letting his voice trail off.

It was when a dismal silence fell upon the room that I realized my father was actually sad. For the past five years, it had been only he and I. Although he was strict and could be overbearing at times, he was a good father. In the last of my mother's dying days, he had promised to take good care of us both. Now that I would no longer be under his watchful eye, I guess he was getting scared.

"Deddy?" I called out in a low voice.

He peered over at where I sat on the bed before grabbing the back of his neck with his hand.

"Deddy, I promise I'll be all right. You've prepared me for this day. Given me all the tools I need to be successful," I said. Pulling my hands together, my fingers teasing the bottom of my chin, I mulled over my next set of words. "You've taught me right from wrong, Deddy. And you've always kept me straight with the Lord."

He pressed his lips together and nodded, as if he was finally taking in my words.

"I'll be okay without you for a little while. I promise," I said.

His face softened as tears formed in his eyes. "But what if *I* won't be okay without you?" he questioned with a cracking sound in his voice.

I jumped up from the bed and rushed over to him. After throwing my arms around his big, burly body, I squeezed tight and closed my eyes. When I felt him kiss the top of my head, I rested my face against his chest and inhaled the faded scent of his Old Spice cologne. Instantly, I felt the dampness of his shirt press against my cheek.

"Everything will be just fine, Deddy. Just fine."

After bringing the rest of my things inside, my father finally headed back to Texas. I felt a bit torn as I stood on the top step of Holland Hall, watching the low lights of his car grow small. I lingered outside just a few minutes more, swatting away bugs, before heading back inside. Even on move-in day, I could already see that the girls in my dorm had begun to form their own little cliques. Some were sitting around on the couches in the lobby, while other groups were flying past me out the door.

Just as I was about to head back up to my room, I quickly decided that I would go grab a bite to eat before the cafeteria closed. I lifted my wrist, which had my room key and wallet dangling from a coiled bracelet. After making sure my meal card was in there, I shot right back out the door.

The cafeteria was only three buildings down from my dorm, so it didn't take long to get there. As soon as I walked inside, I smelled the aroma of different foods. I picked up a tray and a plate. There was hot pizza, burgers, and fries on the first buffet, but I decided on meat loaf instead. It was what I considered comfort food, and it instantly reminded me of back home.

Sliding my tray down to the register, I gazed out into the large dining hall. Within a split second I was made to feel all of thirteen years old again, scared about which table to sit at among a sea of strangers. After paying and stepping away from the line, I stood frozen in place. My eyes scanned the dining hall for a place to sit, while I silently prayed that a lone table would become available for me. Just as I was about to give up, I finally spotted one.

As I made my way over to the empty table by the window, I kept my eyes trained on it. But by the time I got within three feet of it, I was stopped dead in my tracks. Two pretty girls sat down and claimed it as their own.

"Damn. They stole your seat, huh?" I heard a cocky voice say. This was followed by male laughter.

I looked to my right, and there they were, sitting at a table, the two football players from earlier, along with four other dumb-looking jocks. Quietly, I rolled my eyes.

"We would let you sit here, but we don't fuck with Mormons like that," the light-skinned one said.

"Yo, she ain't Mormon, stupid! Amish, right?" the boy Meeko asked.

Although he wasn't exactly trying to be funny, his whole table found it amusing. Even the snickers of others around us could be heard. Suddenly, I could feel my cheeks start to heat up as I turned to walk away. As I damn near ran for the exit, it felt like God had turned back the hands of time. This was like experiencing my first day of high school all over again.

"Man, you done made that poor girl cry," I heard one of them say from behind me. "Look at her, waddling all fast like a penguin in that long-ass skirt." They all laughed again.

After I entered the cafeteria, I quickly packed my meat loaf and mashed potatoes to go, and then I headed back to Holland Hall. The quiet walk alone was much needed, providing me extra time to think. Although today seemed to be a recap of my life thus far, feeling bullied and out of place, I could only pray my days in college would be brighter. Taking in a deep breath, I looked up and saw only two dimly lit stars in the evening sky. Finding that all-familiar spiritual connection, I momentarily closed my eyes and prayed.

Dear Lord, please . . . please give me strength.

Chapter 4

Asha

The Bad and Bougie

"Girl, that nigga Mark think he's slick. Tried dropping me off last night without running me my money." I had my cell phone up to my ear while I placed the key into the lock and grasped a small bag of groceries. As I opened the door, I pulled my rolling luggage in behind me. "Well, I'm here," I said, letting my eyes roam around the small living room.

"How does it look?" my friend Kiki asked through the phone.

My nose flared at the smell of new paint and at the sight of the plain decor. "Bitch, it'll do, but it ain't all that," I told her, referring to the dorm.

"So why you just ain't stay home with your mama and daddy? They only live, like, fifteen minutes away from campus," she said.

I walked to the first door on my left and peeked my head inside. It was an empty bedroom with an uncovered mattress and a cheap blue carpet on the floor. "And what? Have them control my every move? Shit, I can't be out here tryna snag a baller with my mama all up in my business."

Having already settled on the space, I sat my suitcase and the bag of groceries by the door and made my way over to plop down on the bed.

"Well, have you seen any cuties on campus yet?" Kiki asked.

Flipping my long weave back over my shoulder, I held out my hand to take a look at my new full set. I kept my nails long and pointed at the tips, and today they were painted a pale shade of pink. "I ain't really been looking, but you know a bitch's eyes will definitely be open on the yard this week. Hopefully, I'll run into Jaxon Brown's fine ass."

"So he *is* going there?"

"Yep. I already done checked the roster, boo," I confirmed with a pop of my glossy lips.

Jaxon Brown was the star point guard who'd come out of South Meck High. At just eighteen years old, he had already been featured on ESPN and had been dubbed one of the select few who would eventually enter the NBA draft. I'd been keeping a close eye on him for quite some time, and although I would've rather gone to school out of state, he was one of the main reasons I had decided on A&T. I was going to be the future Mrs. Jaxon Brown if it killed me.

"Well, girl, see if he got a friend," Kiki said with a giggle.

"Bitch, if you wanted a college nigga, then you should have brought yo' ass to college," I said. I placed the tip of one of my long nails between my teeth before I laughed.

"Girl, shut up. College ain't for everybody."

I shrugged my shoulders and rolled my pretty light brown eyes. "Well, enjoy hair school, then, love." I shrugged my shoulders again. "Shit don't hurt my feelings."

"Anyways, I gotta go. Ronnie finna pick me up," she said, sounding like she was on the verge of being mad. She knew I didn't give a fuck.

However, at the mere mention of her older brother's name, I found myself smiling. He and I used to fuck back in the day, when I would spend the night over at her house. Till this day, Kiki's airhead ass still didn't have a clue about it. She was my girl, though. Only one of my friends I had left from high school.

After ending the call, I started unpacking my things. Just about all my shit was name brand, and the pieces that weren't were from high-end boutiques. The funny thing about it was that I actually never paid for any of it. In my mind, that was what niggas were for. Shit, I'd scratch their back, and they'd scratch mine. My parents had always thought that I kept my hair and nails done with the little money they gave me for allowance. But the truth was, I dealt only with niggas who were willing to trick off on me. If you weren't paid, you didn't get laid. Hell, you didn't even get a minute of my time, for that matter.

Just as I was putting one of my dresses on a hanger, a soft knock sounded at my open bedroom door. I looked over and saw this dark-skinned, nerdy-looking girl with glasses standing in the doorway.

"Hi, um . . . I'm Hope. Your new roommate," she said in a mousy voice.

Taking in her long skirt and the cheap-ass canvas sneakers on her feet, I let out a breathy laugh. If every girl on campus looked like her, there would definitely be no competition for a bitch like me. "Oh, hey, girl. I'm Asha," I said, giving her a phony smile.

She placed her hand on the doorframe and hiked her right shoulder. "I think we have two more roommates coming, but so far, it's just you and me," she said.

I stepped inside my closet and placed my dress on the rack. "Where are you from?" I asked, noticing that her Southern accent was quite a bit different than mine.

"I'm from Texas. Where are you from?" she replied.

"Oh, girl, I'm from here. My mama and daddy live just across town," I told her, still speaking to her from behind the closet walls.

"Oh, wow. Well, I guess you'll be able to show us all around."

I stepped out of the closet and saw that her eyes lit up as she smiled, exposing two deep-cratered dimples in each of her cheeks.

"Uh, I don't know about all that, but . . . we'll see," I said.

"You have any brothers or sisters?" she asked, stepping into my room. *See . . .* this nerdy girl was already talking entirely too much for me.

"Yeah, one older brother. He ain't about shit, though. Nigga stay in the streets."

"Oh, yeah," she mused. "I wish I had a sibling. It's just been me and my deddy for the past few years. Well, ever since my mother died."

Oh, hell nah! I know she doesn't think we are finna do a therapy session up in here, when I just met her ass two minutes ago.

"Girl, I'm real sorry to hear that, but look, I gotta make a call right quick," I said, trying to rush her out of my room.

As she was about to leave my room, we heard the front door of the suite fly open.

"Oh dear God, this cannot be it," someone with a snobbish tone of voice could be heard saying in the other room. "And it stinks in here."

Both Hope and I walked out into the living room to see some mixed-looking girl with shades covering her eyes. She was rolling the same Fendi luggage that I'd had my eye on for the past month. The exact same two-thousand-dollar set I had practically begged Mark for, but he had refused. *Bitch*. She had on some short jean shorts that were cut just below where her thick pale thighs began. And the hot pink polish on her toes stood out against the white Michael Kors flip flops on her feet.

As she removed the sunglasses from her face, she shook out her long sandy-brown curls and tossed them behind her back. "This just can't be the right place," she muttered, looking around in disbelief.

"Hey," Hope said, causing the girl's eyes to shift suddenly toward us. "I think you're our new roommate. I'm Hope, and this is Asha," she added, pointing her thumb back at me.

"Three-one-one Holland Hall?" the mixed girl questioned with a look of confusion written on her face.

"Yeah, you in the right place," I told her with a roll of my eyes.

Her eyes swept across the living room once more before she walked a little farther inside. "Oh. Well . . ."

"Here, let me help you with your things," Hope offered. After pushing up her glasses, she took the small Fendi duffel bag from this girl's hand.

"Hospitable, aren't we?" I murmured sarcastically beneath my breath.

"Thanks," the mixed girl said before turning around to look at the white guy who had just entered the suite. Wearing a black suit and cap, he rolled in more bags of luggage behind her. "That's just the driver. He's just helping me bring in the rest of my things."

"Well, there are two bedrooms left. One there." Hope pointed to the door next to mine. "And the one over here."

"It really doesn't matter. I'm going to be here for only four months anyway," the girl said. "Oh, and I'm Paris, by the way," she added, extending her hand.

"Again, I'm Hope." As they shook hands, Hope craned her neck back at me. "And that's Asha over there."

"Hey," I said, pursing my lips, silently hoping that the small greeting I gave came across just as dry as it sounded. Paris simply smiled.

While they ducked into the empty bedroom on the opposite side of the suite, I grabbed the bag of groceries I had placed on the floor. It wasn't much, just a few bottles of water, chips, and some ramen noodles, but it was enough to hold me over until I went to the store tonight. As I started for the kitchen to put my things away, I heard someone else coming through the front door of the suite. My head whipped back until my eyes landed on a brown-skinned girl with naturally curly hair. Judging by the similarities in their features, I assumed it was her mother who was following behind her.

"Franki, where do we need to put all this stuff?" the mother asked.

"I'on know, Ma." She looked over at me. "Aye," she called out.

I placed my hand against my chest. "Y-you talking to me?"

"I mean, I'm looking at you, right?"

My eyebrows shot up at that.

"I'm Franki, and I've been assigned to dorm suite three-eleven," she went on to say, glancing down at a crumpled piece of paper in her hand.

Right off the bat, I didn't like her attitude or the city-girl accent on her tongue. "Welp, it says three-eleven on the door. So I guess that means you've got the right place," I said. Batting my eyes with a phony smile on my face, I spun back around to place my waters in the fridge.

She let out a little snort of sarcasm before mumbling something beneath her breath. As she and her mother moved throughout the suite, I could hear what sounded like a stack of papers being dropped down on the kitchen table. While they went into the bedroom next to mine, carrying bins and mismatched luggage, I went over to grab one of the papers. They were flyers for a party happening later tonight. Someone had just dropped them off and left.

Placing the tip of one of my long fingernails between my teeth, I allowed my eyes to peruse the page. I took in the pretty girl plastered on the front with green strobe lights glowing at her half-naked frame. "Tonight at the Clubhouse," I read out loud. "Ladies get in free before eleven. Featuring DJ Premier."

I was no stranger to the Clubhouse. Hell, I'd been sneaking into that club since I was sixteen, but tonight would be my first time going as a true college student. After hurrying to my room, I grabbed my cell phone off the bed and dialed Kiki's number back.

She answered on the first ring. "Hello."

"Hey, girl, we going to the Clubhouse tonight," I told her. Like I said, Kiki was my only friend, and wherever I went, I made her tag along too.

"Um, okay. What time?"

"Let me see if Mark can get us into VIP. If he can, then we don't have to be there early, but if not, come scoop me around eleven." She already knew that eleven was code for twelve.

"All right, just let me know." She paused. "Oh, hey," she called out, thinking that I was on the verge of hanging up.

"Yeah?"

"What are you wearing?" she asked.

"I don't know. I'm gonna try on a few fits and take selfies before I decide."

"Okay, just let me know. Don't forget," she said.

I rolled my eyes. "Bye."

After hanging up the phone, I rushed over to my closet and combed my fingers through the rack of clothes. As I pulled out my white silk romper, I glanced down at its three-hundred-dollar price tag. Mark had bought it for me just the other day from Saks. As I laid it out on the bed, I heard the sound of laughter coming from one of the other rooms. Releasing a sigh, I quickly suppressed the jealousy I felt from hearing the other girls socializing. Like I said before, I was used to not having any friends.

After plopping down on the bed, I grabbed my cell phone once more. Letting my fingers quickly tap against the screen, I shot Mark a quick text.

Me: Can you get me in the Clubhouse tonight? VIP?

Mark: Depends.

Rolling my eyes, I let go of another deep sigh, then typed back my response.

Me: Okay. I'm on my way.

Chapter 5

Franki

Serendipity's Night at the Club

Since none of us had a car, Paris, Hope, and I took the university's bus across town. It was our first night on campus, and we, or rather *I*, had decided that we all would go out to the Clubhouse. Apparently, there was a back-to-school party happening there tonight, and ladies could get in for free before eleven. I was used to hitting up the clubs back in Brooklyn, so when the guy outside my dorm passed me a few flyers, I knew I'd make my debut. Of course, Hope and Paris hadn't been interested in going at first. I had to talk Paris into it, and then, at the last minute, Hope decided to tag along. I think she just didn't want to be left alone. I tried to invite our other roommate, Asha, but she left before I had a chance, and never came back.

At ten o'clock on the dot, we were all getting dropped off on the corner of Tower Road. I was the first to step off the bus, tugging the white minidress down over my thighs. Instantly, my eyes roamed over my surroundings, and I noticed the raggedy neighborhood sign that read ROSEWOOD beneath a dim, flickering streetlight. Then, suddenly, I heard Paris's bougie ass let out a loud gasp from behind me. Admittedly, this neighborhood was a stark contrast to campus. The sidewalks were lightly scattered with debris, and as I looked farther down the street, I could see a group of men huddling on the corner.

"Oh my God! Where the hell are we?" Paris asked. Her nose suddenly flared and her eyes widened at the sight of our destination.

I craned my neck to look back at her. "What? You ain't never seen the fucking hood before?"

Paris didn't utter a word; she simply rolled her eyes in response. Behind her was Hope, who appeared to be just as scared. She had her arms folded across her chest while she looked around suspiciously through her glasses. I shook my head as I looked her over. She wore her long khaki skirt with a white button-up blouse. She even had those white canvas sneakers on her feet. Both Paris and I had tried to convince her to change her outfit before we left, but she had flat-out refused. She'd said that she was most comfortable wearing what she had on. Taking the hint, Paris and I had decided not to push the subject. Paris, on the other hand, was very stylish. Everything she wore, from the pink romper to the gold heels and accessories, looked very polished and expensive.

"Come on, y'all," I told them.

As we walked down the street, a homeless-looking old man came speeding past us on a bike.

"You know, I think I'm just gonna go back to the dorm," Paris said.

"And just how you gonna get there? What? You gon' stand out here by yourself and wait for the next bus or catch an Uber?" I asked her.

Closing her eyes, she clenched her jaw as the reality of our situation dawned on her. "Fine. Let's just hurry up and get in there," she said.

With our arms linked, the three of us scurried down the darkened street. We passed by a rowdy group of men while we heard dogs barking and babies crying in the distance. After we hooked a left onto Dolley Madison, a bright neon sign that read CLUBHOUSE finally appeared. You could hear the club's music thumping from way outside; however, what surprised me was that there was no line to get in. In fact, the parking lot was damn near empty.

"Are you sure this is the right place?" Paris asked, a look of confusion etched on her face.

I pulled the flyer out from my clutch and read the address out loud. "Yeah, this is it," I said, sucking my teeth. "Man, this shit looks like it's gon' be a bust."

As we made our way over to the front door, I saw a few guys with black fraternity jackets on coming out. They were all laughing and talking among themselves until their eyes finally landed on the three of us.

"Damn," muttered the tall one with dreadlocks, an obvious look of lust in his eyes. "Y'all here for the party tonight?" he asked, rubbing his hands together.

Suddenly, I felt Hope clinging to my arm a little bit tighter. "Yeah. What time does it start?" I asked.

The shorter guy next to him immediately stepped up. "It starts at ten, but people usual—"

All of a sudden, the abrupt sound of the club's door swinging open cut him off. "Aye, man, y'all coming back in here to help or nah?" a guy called from the doorway.

My eyes instantly bucked at the sight of him. *Wait. Is that . . . ?*

I almost couldn't believe it myself, but to my dismay, it was the light-skinned *gay* guy from that church in Brooklyn standing in front of my very own eyes.

He let out a little snort, then licked his full dark pink lips. "Wassup, Ma?" he said to me.

Damn. I had to admit that he definitely looked a lot different than he had yesterday. Long gone were his church boy slacks and the short-sleeved button-up shirt he wore. Instead, he had donned slim black jeans and a black tee and had a simple gold chain around his neck.

"H-hey," I stammered. "Is—"

"So, like, can you guys get us in or what?" Paris interrupted, sounding every bit like a white girl.

"Yeah, y'all come on inside," said the tall guy with the long locs, holding the door open.

As we entered the club, I noticed only a few people sitting around the bar. Although the music was decent, the place was practically empty. I took a seat on one of the barstools, causing both Paris and Hope to follow suit.

"Man, the club scene down here is lame as fuck, yo," I said.

The light-skinned guy from Brooklyn came up behind me and put his mouth up to my ear. "No one comes to the club before eleven thirty," he whispered.

I turned my neck to look back at him. "So then, why are you here?"

"My frat. We're the ones throwing the party," he explained.

My eyes meandered to his black jacket with the Greek letters written in gold. "Uh-huh," I muttered. "So what'd you do? Follow me all the way down here from Brooklyn?"

He smiled, showcasing a bright set of white teeth, then shook his head. "Nah, sweetheart, I go to school out here. I'm a junior," he said.

I rolled my eyes. "Go figure," I muttered.

"Um, excuse me, sir. Bartender," Paris called out, waving her hands to get the bartender's attention. "Can I get an apple martini please?"

I leaned over and nudged her shoulder. "You twenty-one?"

"Pulleasse," she stressed, letting her eyes roll up to the ceiling. She flipped her long curly hair over her shoulder before pulling a driver's license out of her purse. "See, I got a fake ID," she whispered, winking her eye.

I actually think I might like this bougie bitch.

When the bartender brought her drink over, she quickly took a sip from the straw and held up two of her fingers. "Bring two more," she said after swallowing.

The bartender hesitated, giving her a suspicious look, before finally going over to make the drinks. To be honest, I think he knew that we were all underage, but for some reason, he was letting us slide. When he came back over, he set a napkin down on the bar top in front of me, then placed the apple martini on it. He set one up in front of Hope, as well, but she scrunched up her nose and discreetly pushed it away. Before I could get my money out of my purse, *Mr. Light- Skinned* put a fifty-dollar bill in the bartender's hand.

"Aye, keep the change, Chevy," he said.

"Thanks, Josh," the bartender responded with familiarity.

Hmm, Joshua. Of course he'd have a biblical name.

Paris leaned back on her stool in order to cut her eyes over at him as he stood next to me. "You aren't going to have a drink with us?" she asked, almost sounding a bit flirty.

He shook his head. "Oh, nah. I'on drink."

I let out a small snort of laughter. "Yeah, he's into the church," I muttered with a roll of my eyes.

As his eyes narrowed into inquisitive slits, he tapped me lightly on the arm. "Yo, ma, what's the deal with you and church?"

Suddenly the blaring sounds of "Bad and Boujee" by Migos could be heard in the club. Completely ignoring him, I put the martini glass up to my lips and downed its contents all in one gulp. After slamming the glass back down on the counter, I spun around and hopped off the stool. As I made my way to the center of the dance floor, I noticed more and more people starting to pile in. With my arms up high in the air, I began working my hips to the music. I swear, it took less than sixty seconds for some guy to come up behind me and start dancing.

There wasn't a doubt in my mind that I was a very sexy woman with my long black curls and dark, slanted eyes. I was about a size eight, with full C-cup breasts and a wide set of curvy hips. Niggas were practically hypnotized by me. As I bent down to place my hands on my knees, I caught Josh staring at me. Even though he bit down on his bottom lip, there wasn't anything lustful about it. His eyes were completely judgmental. See, that was one thing about me. I loathed self-righteous motherfuckers, and right now, ole boy was giving me that vibe.

While I was out there putting my back into it, I saw Paris dragging a resistant Hope out onto the dance floor.

"Dude, take a chill pill," I heard Paris say. "Like, did we really just come all the way out here to be wallflowers?"

While Paris began twisting her body from side to side like only a white girl could do, Hope just stood there. She pushed her glasses up on her nose, then folded her arms across her chest. Compared to us and the rest of the scantily dressed girls in the club, Hope stuck out like a sore thumb. Reaching out to grab her hands, I tried getting her to move to the beat, but she was too reserved.

"I think I'm just going to go sit back down," she said.

Just as she left to go sit back down at the bar, a long train of guys started stepping through the crowd. They all had on the same black and gold jackets as Josh. And as they strolled to the music, one by one, you could see all their hands going up in the air. They each made the same indistinguishable sign. Hell, I think everyone had seen *Stomp the Yard* before, but never in real life had I seen stepping quite like this. Apparently, I wasn't the only one in awe. Paris damn near bruised my arm with all her constant prodding.

"Look, look," she said with excitement.

At the very end of the line was Josh. For a pretty *church boy*, I had to admit that he had a certain swagger about him. It was a quiet confidence that I couldn't quite put my finger on. Suddenly he stopped mid-stride, leaned back, and released a deep howl from his lungs. All his fraternity brothers in the line in front of him followed suit. As they continued to make their way through, he glanced over at me and winked his eye.

Cocky little bastard, I see.

Before long, the other Greeks began doing their strolls as well. It seemed that just one hour had made all the difference, as the place was now completely packed. Sweat-covered bodies were dancing from wall to wall, with either drinks or fired Black & Milds in their hands.

We stayed on the dance floor all night, working up a good sweat, while Hope continued to sit off to the side. By the end of the night, Paris and I'd had several more drinks, courtesy of a few random guys.

We ended up leaving the club a little after two in the morning. Poor Hope had to practically hold the two of us up as we straggled our way back to the bus stop. When we were almost there, an old black Yukon pulled up beside us. Slowly, the passenger-side window came down, and Josh emerged in the driver's seat. "Aye, let me give y'all a ride back to campus," he said, leaning back with only one hand on the wheel.

I scrunched up my nose and gave him a dismissive wave of my hand. "Nah, church boy. We good," I slurred.

"Franki, dude, you're so killing me! If I have to get back on that damn bus, I swear I might just barf," Paris said.

"Yeah, Franki," Hope chimed in. "At least we won't have to stand out here and wait."

Drunkenly, I sucked my teeth. "Man. Didn't y'all parents teach y'all not to take rides from strangers?"

"Unfortunately, I don't have the kind of parents that actually give a shit about me. Now, come on," Paris urged, pulling me toward the car. She opened the back door and damn near tossed me inside. Hope slid in behind me, while Paris took it upon herself to ride up front in the passenger seat. She craned her neck back and shrugged her shoulders. "I only ride shotgun," she said with a flip of her hair.

As we started to cruise along, I heard Josh turn down the radio. "So did y'all ladies have a good time tonight?"

"Tonight was way cool. Like, I've never actually seen so many black people in one place before," Paris confessed.

Hope let out a little snort beside me.

"Come on, ma. Please don't say dumb shit like that out loud," I told her, catching Josh quietly chuckling to himself from the corner of my eye.

After ten more minutes we were pulling up in front of Holland Hall. Apparently, I was still feeling the alcohol more than Paris, because she and Hope hopped out after thanking Josh for the ride. Sluggishly, I scooted across the back seat and pulled my dress down before finally stepping out.

"Be easy, ma," Josh told me before I shut the door.

With Paris and Hope already out of sight, I lazily threw my hand up in the air and headed for the dorm.

Chapter 6

Hope

Damsel in Distress

Today was my first official day of college, and everything was going absolutely perfectly. My hair had been a bit more manageable this morning when I smoothed it back into a bun, and the pimple on my chin had finally cleared up. Even the sun found a way to shine just right on me during my walk to class. It was now my third class of the day, and I found myself sitting in the front row of Professor Dunbar's philosophy class.

As my eyes scanned the syllabus, I thought back to all the fun the girls and I had over the weekend. It was my first time in a real live nightclub, listening to all kinds of music that I'd never heard before. Then yesterday Paris, Franki, and I went grocery shopping at Walmart, something I had never done without my father. It was also my first Sunday missing church.

Deddy would just die.

It seemed like every day I was living a brand-new experience. Truth be told, I'd never had real friends before, at least not outside church. Franki and Paris were just so worldly, both with their own unique style and accent. And to my surprise, they were both nice to me . . . well, in their own sort of way.

"All right, with that, I'm going to let you guys out a few minutes early. I'll see you back here on Wednesday," Professor Dunbar said.

I gathered my papers off the desk and slid them into my book bag. As I walked out of class and down the corridor, I took in all the flyers that were posted up on the walls. There were apartments for rent, roommates needed, and companies wanting to hire. As I opened the heavy metal door to exit the building, my eyes fell upon the crowd sitting along the short brick wall on the yard. My eyes ultimately landed on the boy Meeko from move-in day. He was sitting in the very center of the herd, talking, with his baseball cap turned to the back. A thin gold chain was draped around his neck, and he wore a loose Nike tank top that showed off his muscular pecs and arms.

Gathered around him appeared to be the same popular crowd from that awful night in the cafeteria. Suddenly I grew nervous, knowing that I'd have to walk past them just to get back to my dorm.

"So then what happened?" I heard a tall, heavy-set guy ask Meeko.

"Damn, nigga. Wait and let me finish my story," Meeko said. Then he licked his lips. "So, look, practice was over, and a nigga was feeling good and shit." He bounced his shoulders and smiled. "So I decided to call shorty up," he said. Then he glanced over at the tall, light-skinned football player whom I'd always seen him with. "Aye, you remember her, Ty? The one I told you was blowing up my DMs. Anyway, I was tryna see if shorty could slide through. She told me to give her about thirty minutes so that her cousin could drop her off. I'm like, '*Bet*,'" he said, licking his lips again. "So thirty minutes later she pulled up on me and—"

"What she look like?" the big guy interrupted eagerly.

"Yo, just hold on and let him tell the fucking story," the light-skinned guy, Ty, snapped.

"So anyway, I see an old . . . looked like an old Fiesta or something." Meeko shrugged. "Some little raggedy car pulling up in front of the dorms. I'm standing by the door, waiting and shit, so finally, I step out on the front porch to meet her. You know, gentlemen shit."

The crowd around him laughed, although again, I don't think he intended to be funny.

"I really ain't even trying to see what baby girl look like, 'cause, shit, I been seeing her er'day on IG." He paused. "I showed you the pictures, Ty, remember?" he asked, looking at his friend.

Ty nodded.

"So right off the top, I noticed that her cousin's little-ass car was rocking from side to side as shorty was trying to make her way out of it," Meeko went on. "Then, finally, I see her big-ass head pop up, and man . . ." Meeko sucked his teeth and shook his head. "Y'all, this wasn't the Beyoncé look-alike, size-eight model chick from Instagram that I'd been talking to. Nah, yo, it's *Precious*, size twenty-eight!" he exclaimed, dramatically waving his hand and shaking his head.

His boys and the crowd around him erupted in laughter.

"Then her cousin's gon' have the nerve to yell out the window, 'All right, Li'l Bit. Call me when you ready,'" Meeko continued, imitating her feminine voice. "I'm like, '*Li'l Bit*? Where?'" he joked while shaking his head. His friends were all folded over, cackling almost to the point of tears. "Man, I took my black ass back inside and shut the fucking door. Tryna catfish a nigga. Fuck that," he told them.

Poor girl, I thought as I began walking past them. Once again, this Meeko fellow and his friends had proven to be real jerks. All of a sudden, I began to hear whispers among the crowd.

"Aye, yo, look," I heard someone say.

I turned around and saw that it was the light-skinned guy, Ty. He was pointing down at my feet. Assuming that he was only making fun of my shoes, I looked down to see that my white canvas sneakers had been stained with blood. I slid my foot out from under my long skirt to get a better look. That was when I saw the red fluid running down my ankle. *Oh God no! It can't be.*

Suddenly, I could feel panic start to settle in. After shifting my book bag over to one arm, I twisted my head around to look at the back of my skirt. Sure enough, there was a bloodstained circle the size of a grapefruit. I was completely mortified. My cheeks instantly burned from embarrassment as I heard the crowd around me begin to laugh again. I looked at the two closest buildings: the one I'd just come out of and the one across the yard. They were both at least forty steps away, so I was just going to have to make a run for it.

"Yo! Er'body, just shut the fuck up!" I heard Meeko's voice suddenly boom from behind me.

As I craned my neck back, I noticed that he was taking off his tank top. His smooth, fudge-colored muscles were exposed all at once. Although I should have been more concerned about my period, I couldn't help but stare. From his perfectly cut wavy black hair to his muscular physique, I had to admit that he was a beautiful young man.

Taking me out of my lustful thoughts, he walked over to me. "Here," he said, then placed the tank top over my head. "Niggas act like they ain't never seen a little blood before," he muttered.

I let my book bag slide down to the ground before putting my arms through his shirt. Surprisingly, it hung low enough to cover up the bloodstain on my butt.

"Thanks," I said.

He picked my book bag up off the ground and swung it over his right shoulder. "You're a freshman, right? Staying in Holland Hall?"

My eyes instantly lit up. *He remembers me.*

"Yes, but I don't think I can make it all the way back over there," I said, looking down at my bloodied shoes. Chewing the corner of my lip, I tried to think of what else I could do. My perfect day had unexpectedly turned into a disastrous one.

With a forward nod of his head, he pointed to a nearby building. "My dorm is closer. I can get you a change of clothes if you want," he said.

Out of nowhere, a tall girl with green eyes, light skin, and short sandy-brown hair walked up. "So, what? You're just gonna take this girl back to your room?" she asked with an attitude.

Meeko gave her a pointed look that spoke of his irritation. "Yo, Jazz, chill out with all that. I'll be right back, a'ight?" he told her.

Then suddenly another girl walked up beside her with a clean maxi pad in her hand. "Here," she offered, handing it over to me.

But before I could even thank her, the tall, light-skinned girl with the green eyes sucked her teeth.

"What? I was just trying to help her out," the other girl explained.

I proceeded to follow Meeko through the yard. The entire way to his dorm, I felt so uncomfortable. The ninety-degree heat was grueling, and I could literally feel the liquid seeping out of me. I kept looking down on the ground to ensure I hadn't left a blood trail behind me. Not only was I uneasy about my period streaming down my leg, but I didn't know Meeko from a can of paint. The first thing my father had told me on the drive here was never to talk to strange boys.

Now look at me.

"What's your name?" he asked as we continued to walk along.

"Hope," I told him.

For some reason, he attempted to suppress a laugh.

"What? What's so funny?"

"Nothing. It just suits you, I guess. All wholesome and pure. My name is Meeko, by the way," he offered.

"Nice to meet you."

After a few more minutes, we reached the brick steps of Pride Hall. It was pretty similar to my dorm, only there were no air conditioners hanging out the windows. Once he led me inside the building, cool air immediately swept across my face. Meeko gave a quick nod of his head, then walked toward the elevator. As I followed behind him, I found myself staring at the thick muscles of his back. They seemed to bounce in delight with each of his strides.

He let me step onto the elevator first, then followed right behind me, only to stand in the opposite corner. The entire ride up to the fourth floor, I remained quiet, in hopes that he wouldn't look at me. I was so self-conscious, feeling that gooey wetness on my socks and in between my tightly squeezed thighs. When the elevator stopped, we got off, and I followed behind him to his room. It was room 409. Inwardly, I laughed at the irony of it, thinking of how Deddy and I had lived by that stuff when it came to cleaning up the house.

"The bathroom's right there." He pointed to a wooden door inside his room. My eyes skimmed across his unmade bed and the empty pizza box that had been left on the floor. "Excuse the mess," he said, kicking around piles of clothes to make a clear path for me to walk down.

"Do you mind if I take a shower? I'll be real quick," I said.

He shrugged, making light of my request. "Do you, shorty. Handle ya' business," he said.

I entered the bathroom and got right out of my clothes. Immediately, I let out a sigh upon seeing the blood that I had gotten on his shirt. As I turned on the shower, I could hear a soft knock on the door. I wrapped my collared shirt around me and cracked the door open only half an inch. Peeking out with just one eye, I saw Meeko standing there with a towel and a washcloth in his hands.

"Here," he said.

I opened the door a little more and reached my arm out to grab the things from his hands. "Do you have any clothes I can borrow?"

He jogged back to his dresser and searched around in his drawers. I watched as he pulled out a pair of boxer briefs, basketball shorts, and a white T-shirt.

"Your underwear?" I questioned, turning up my nose.

He let out a little snort, then said, "Shorty, you gon' need something to hold that pad in place."

My eyes stretched from understanding as I nodded my head. I took the clothes from him and shut the bathroom door so that I could take a quick shower. After ten minutes of washing myself under the hot water, I stepped out and tried my best to rinse the blood from my clothes. Once I was all dressed, wearing his boxers and all, I walked back out into his room.

Meeko was sitting shirtless on the edge of his bed, legs cocked open wide as he texted away on his phone. "You straight?" he asked without looking up at me.

"Yeah," I said lowly. I didn't know why, but I still felt a tinge of shame. "Thank you."

"No problem." He bent down and grabbed a pair of Nike slides from beneath his bed. "Here. You can wear these," he said, tossing them in front of me.

"Thanks." With the wet clothes folded up in my hand, I slid my feet into his shoes. "Do you have a bag I can put this stuff in?"

He looked up at me, then dipped his head toward the dresser. He already had a plastic grocery bag prepared for me. I went over to place my things inside it but left out his tank top. "Um, I tried to wash the stain out of your shirt, but I can take it with me and put it in the wash."

With one hand still typing away, he gave me a dismissive wave with the other. "Just keep it," he said.

"Well, I know you gotta get back to your girlfriend, so, um . . . I'm gonna head on out," I told him.

That must've gotten his attention, because his head jerked back. "Girlfriend?"

"Yeah, the tall girl with the light eyes," I said.

He shook his head. "Nah, Jazz just the homie," he explained, standing up from the bed. Although I nodded, I had no idea what that even meant. "Come on. I gotta meet my boy back on the yard, anyway, so I'll walk with you," he said. Then he slipped a white T-shirt over his head.

We left his room, jumped on the elevator, and headed back outside. As we trekked across campus, I glanced around, taking in just how truly beautiful the scenery was. I admired the lush green lawn with its pink and white dogwood trees, whose flowers would sometimes blow in the wind. I knew it was silly, but the beauty of the place was one of the main reasons I'd chosen this school.

For most of the way, neither Meeko nor I said a word. That was until I was able to spot the yard from a distance.

"I think I'm just gonna go this way," I told him, pointing to another path on the right. Honestly, I was just too ashamed to walk back past the same people who were just making fun of me. Not only that, but I had on all of Meeko's clothes, which practically swallowed my little body whole. I looked ridiculous.

He let out a little snort, as if he knew what the problem was. "What? You don't want nobody to see you wearing my shit?"

I simply shrugged, because I didn't want to lie.

"Well, I mean, you ain't got no problem any other time, wearing that lame shit you be having on, so . . ."

My eyes ballooned. "Just when I was starting to think you were a nice guy."

He laughed and put his hand up to his chest. "I mean, nah, I am a nice guy, but come on, shorty. Them long-ass skirts and them butter cookies you be rocking on your feet . . ." He shook his head. "You can do better than that."

"Wow," I huffed. "You really are superficial."

"Superficial?" His eyes narrowed in surprise.

"Yes, superficial! I heard you back there, talking about that girl that came to see you. And just because she wasn't a size two, you and your friends made fun of her."

He cracked a knowing smile. *A gorgeous smile.* "Nah, I ain't got no problems with big girls. Shid, they need love, too, ya feel me? But that girl, man, she was claiming to be somebody else. Sending me pictures of a whole different broad, pretending like it was her. I can't get with shit like that. If you's a big girl, be confident about your shit. Don't be hiding behind a picture of someone else."

I nodded my head, understanding because, I guess, he was right. "And just in case you're wondering why I dress the way I do, it's because I'm religious. I grew up in the church—"

"Shorty, my muva raised me and my three sisters in the church, no cap. And don't none of 'em dress like that," he declared, cutting me off.

"Well, I was brought up in a devout Pentecostal church where the women keep their hair long and their bodies covered," I retorted.

He cupped his hand around the bun at the back of my head. "So you got long hair, huh?" he asked.

"Yes, it's pretty long. Past the middle of my back." I shrugged.

"That's what's up. You should wear it out some time."

I simply ignored his statement. "So you've got sisters?" I asked.

He let out a small laugh and nodded his head. "Yeah, three of 'em."

"So I guess that's why you didn't freak out when . . ." My voice trailed off because I didn't want to relive the moment by actually saying the words out loud.

"Yeah, I grew up as the only male in the house. Other than when my mother would get a boyfriend." As we approached the bottom of the yard, Meeko placed his hand on the small of my back. "Come on. I guess we can go this way," he said, guiding me in a different direction.

"So where are you from? You talk funny."

He swiped his hand over the top of his head and let out a chuckle. "*I* talk funny?" he said, pointing to his chest. "I'm from Baltimore. Where you from?"

"From Texas."

"Dallas?"

"No, Alto," I told him.

I watched his eyebrows wrinkle. "Never heard of it."

"It's a small town. A place where everybody knows everybody," I explained.

After a few more minutes of small talk, we found ourselves walking up to Holland Hall. "Looks like we're here," Meeko said, scratching behind his ear. If I didn't know any better, I'd say he didn't want to part ways.

"Yeah," I mumbled, realizing that I, too, didn't want our conversation to end.

"So check it, let me get your number so I can call you sometime. Maybe get you to let your hair down," he said, winking his eye.

Thank goodness I had dark brown skin, because I could feel my cheeks growing warm again. "Well, I have a cell phone, but it's only for my father and aunt to call me on," I explained.

"I mean, what Pops don't know won't hurt him, right?" He pulled out his cell phone and tapped the screen.

Against my better judgment, I gave him my cell phone number. Just as I called out the last digit, I saw one of my roommates, Asha, waltzing by. I hadn't seen her since Saturday afternoon, when she first moved in.

"Hey, Asha," I said, smiling and giving her a little wave.

She cut her light brown eyes over at me, then scrunched up her nose before going inside the building.

"Yo, that's your roommate?" Meeko asked.

"Yeah," I sighed.

He shook his head disapprovingly, like he knew something I didn't. "Well, a'ight, shorty. I'ma holla at you later." Then he leaned in close and lowered his voice. "And make sure you keep some extra tampons and shit in your book bag from now on," he joked.

"Ha, ha, ha, very funny," I said with a smile.

"Ah, nice dimples," he said, momentarily studying my face. "But, nah, you be easy."

I watched as Meeko swaggered away from my dorm, stopping every so often to talk to a pretty girl that passed him by. I don't know if it was his good looks and charm or the simple fact that he had come to my rescue today, but either way, I was feeling something I'd never felt before. *A crush.*

Chapter 7

Paris

Dejected, Inspected, and Rejected

After my first full week of classes, I decided that A&T wasn't so bad, after all. Although I was missing my bestie, Heather, like crazy, Hope and Franki actually seemed to be pretty cool. Even my classes were a breeze. I had English 101, Geology 101, and Spanish 201, all subjects I knew I could pass in my sleep. And ever since making an appearance at the club the other night, I even had a few *brothers* with their eyes on me. I'd given my number out more times than I could count over the past six days, and honestly, I was loving the attention.

Even though everything was running smoothly, I still hadn't heard from my mother. She hadn't even called to see if I had made it here and had gotten settled in. Now, I'd never admit this out loud, but the shit was crushing me. My feelings were totally hurt, and I knew the only thing that could possibly help was a little retail therapy. I ended up Googling the nearest high-end stores in Greensboro and came up with only the Four Seasons Town Centre. They didn't even have a Saks. I figured I'd have to start shopping online, but for this day only, I decided to catch an Uber out there.

"So he's in two of your classes?" I asked Heather over the phone. I was walking around the mall with a Dillard's bag in my hand.

"Yes, Par. Like, every morning, at nine a.m., I have to see his stupid little face," she said, referring to my ex, Brad.

"Does he ever ask about me?" I hated even to ask.

"Hmm, well, the first day he did. Asked if I'd talked to you."

I let out a little snort and rolled my eyes. "And what did you say?"

"Uh, duh, bitch! I told him yes. I said that you were out there, totally living your best life," she said dramatically.

My head fell back from laughing so hard. When my eyes regained their focus and I could see in front of me, I noticed some guy damn near breaking his neck to check me out. He was disgusting looking, with a gold and diamond grill in his mouth and tattoos covering his entire neck. Even the flashy jewelry he had on was gaudy, from all the gold and the diamonds glittering around his wrists. My eyes slowly sank, and I saw sagging jeans that barely clung to his waist. The only thing pleasing about his appearance was these bright hazel eyes, a nice contrast to his dark brown skin.

"Ugh. Grody," I whispered, turning up my nose.

"What's wrong?" Heather asked, getting my attention.

As I continued to walk past the guy, who was now following me with his eyes, I put my mouth right up to the phone. "Some ugly wannabe rapper–looking dude is staring me down," I told her.

"Oh," she laughed. "So what's it like? I mean going to an all-black college and all?"

"Hmm," I said, pondering her question. "Well, it's definitely different, that's for sure, but not really in a bad way. Other than the poor living conditions," I told her.

"Are you meeting lots of guys? Black guys?" she whispered, as if it were taboo.

I let out a light laugh. "I've met some, but it's only been a week. I'm really just trying to stay focused on my classes right now and get adjusted to living with three other people."

"Well, when you finally get that big black dick, *please* let me know." She and I both shared a laugh.

"Is that girl Asha still being a bitch?" she asked, remembering that I'd mentioned her the first day we moved in.

"Yep. Total bitch," I confirmed.

Suddenly, I felt a light tapping on my shoulder. I turned around and practically jumped out of my own skin at the sight of the thug who had been gaping at me. Clutching my chest, I tried to calm my racing heart.

"My bad, Mama. I ain't mean to scare you," he said.

Watching his thick brown lips move as he spoke, I could feel my nose starting to flare in disgust. "Ah, Heather, let me call you right back," I said before ending the call. "What exactly may I help you with?" I asked, fluttering my eyes.

He let out a snort of laughter. "Shawty, I just wanted to let you know that you got a beautiful-ass smile. And that body . . ." He bit down on his lower lip, allowing his hazel eyes to hit my frame. "Mm, mm, mm," he uttered with a slow shake of his head.

"Uh, thanks," I said curtly, then turned to walk away.

Gently, he grabbed me by the back of my arm. "So you ain't gon' at least stop and rap with a nigga? I can't even get ya' name?"

After staring down at his hand, which was still on my arm, I let out a deep sigh. "It's Paris," I said, yanking back my arm.

"Nice to meet you, Miss Paris. I'm Malachi," he said, extending his hand. Almost every one of his fingers lit up from a diamond ring.

Reluctantly, I shook his hand with just the tips of my fingers. "Nice to meet you, too, but, uh . . . I have a boyfriend," I lied, attempting to play nice.

"I don't remember asking you all that, Miss Paris." He cracked a half smile, flashing that metal on his teeth. "So you got a boyfriend, huh? Out here spending that nigga's bread, I see." He glanced down at the bag in my hand.

"As if!" I scoffed, feeling my face slowly contort into a scowl. "I have my own money to blow. I don't need someone else's," I said with a flip of my hair. Before my father passed, he'd made sure that my mother and I would be financially set for life. The last thing he wanted was me depending on some man.

He let out a light chuckle, then pinched the tip of his nose. "So where you from? You don't sound like you're from around here."

"California."

"Ah, a Valley girl."

I rolled my eyes. "*Valley girl* is such an eighties term, and no, I'm not from the Valley. I'm from the Hills, if you must know," I told him.

He put both of his hands up in surrender. "My bad, shawty. You talk like a white girl, but that fly-ass mouth you got . . . ," he said, letting his voice trail off. Staring at my lips, he licked his own.

I glanced down at my watch, pretending to be concerned about the time. "Look . . . Malachi, is it?" I said, narrowing my eyes. "I don't mean to be rude, but I really do have somewhere to be."

"Well, shit, I won't hold you," he said, taking a step back. "Stay beautiful, a'ight?" I watched as he strolled away, looking down at his phone as he pulled up the crotch of his sagging jeans.

"Ugh. Yuck." I cringed. Shaking my hand back and forth, I tried to make my memory of his touch magically disappear.

After strolling through the mall for another hour, I caught an Uber back to the dorm. As soon as I entered our suite, I heard a constant knocking on the wall. I walked in farther and peeked my head inside Hope's room. She was lying back on her bed with a pillow over her head, an open Bible on her nightstand.

"Hey," I said.

Hope removed the pillow and sat up on her elbows. "Can you please tell her to stop?"

"Who?"

"Franki. She's in there with some guy," she said, rolling her eyes.

"Some guy?" That was when the light bulb went off inside my head. "She's in there having sex? That's the knocking I hear?"

Dramatically, she nodded her head up and down.

My mouth fell open. "Oh my God," I said with a smile.

"I don't know if I can live like this, Paris. I think I'm just gonna put in a request to move," Hope said.

"Shh," I whispered, putting my index finger over my lips. "Come on."

After grabbing an empty cup from the kitchen, I tiptoed my way over to Franki's bedroom door. Reluctantly, Hope followed behind me with a look of revulsion on her face. I turned toward her and put my finger up to my lips once more in hopes that she would remain quiet. Then I placed the cup up to the door.

"Oh, shit," I heard a male voice say. "Yeah, baby, bounce that ass. Just like that." *Slap, slap.*

I looked back at Hope and stuck my finger down my throat, pretending to barf. She rolled her eyes.

"Oh, fuck, nigga. Oh, shit, I'm about to . . . argh!" Franki's loud scream pierced the thin walls of her room.

"Oh my God," I gasped. "Franki is a pure freak. I had no idea." I burst out laughing.

"It's not funny, Paris," Hope said as she stood there with her arms folded across her chest. "It's disgusting and a disgrace."

"Dude, take a chill pill. It's only sex," I told her, noticing the serious expression on her face.

"Well, maybe to *you*, it's only sex," she mumbled before walking back to her room.

"Hope," I called out to her in a whisper, but she ignored me.

I took a seat down on the little couch in the living room and started to pull out the things I'd purchased from Dillard's. Nothing but two Armani Exchange T-shirts and a Gucci wallet to match my purse. At the sound of Franki's bedroom door swinging open, I lifted my head. Some tall, dark-skinned guy walked out of her room, shirtless. He had on a pair of basketball shorts, with white ankle socks on his feet. In his arms, I could see he was carrying his T-shirt and shoes. Franki was behind him, practically shoving him out of the room.

He craned his neck back and asked, "So when can I see you again?"

"Dave, I already told you that I don't know. I'll call you, a'ight?" she said, damn near pushing him over to the front door. Her curly black hair was all over her head, and she had on a pair of cheerleading shorts and a sports bra.

Once she finally got him out into the hallway, I heard him say, "Well, just promise me you're gonna call."

Frustrated, Franki huffed a deep breath of air, then slammed the door in his face.

"Heartbreaker, are we?" I teased as she walked back into the suite. "Who was that?"

She sucked her teeth. "Man. That was Davion. He plays baseball for the school. Niggas always gotta be so clingy. Just give me the dick and leave. Shit," she fussed, flopping down into the single chair across from me.

"You know you totally sound like a dude, right?"

She shrugged her shoulders. "I mean, I'm just being honest. I'm not looking for no relationship. Just sex. And the sad part about it is, I tell niggas that shit straight from the jump."

"Well, Hope is mad at you," I said.

"For what?"

I smiled. "Because we could hear you and that guy getting it on."

"Well, that's her problem, not mine. Stuck-up ass."

"She is not stuck up—"

"Yeah, you would know," she said, cutting me off.

After giving Franki my middle finger, I said, "But no, really, Hope is just religious. She's probably still a virgin."

"Probably! Nah, she's *definitely* a virgin. But that's all right, though. I can't wait," she said, rubbing her hands together with a crafty smile on her face.

"She's waiting for marriage, I'm sure."

"Uh-huh, that's what they all say."

Suddenly, the sound of keys jingling against the lock of our front door could be heard. Asha entered with several shopping bags in her hands. She had one from Neiman Marcus, one from Louis Vuitton, and even one from MAC. Blowing a large pink bubble with the gum in her mouth, she glanced at us over the Chanel shades covering her eyes. I thought that she was going to speak, but instead, she headed straight for her bedroom.

"Hey, what mall did you go to?" I asked before she disappeared.

She stopped only a few short feet from her bedroom door and removed the sunglasses from her face. "Oh, I do my shopping in Charlotte. I don't buy that cheap shit they have in the malls around here," she said. Then she chomped on her gum.

"Oh, well, next time you go, let me know. I'll ride with," I told her.

"Mm-hmm," she mumbled before going inside her room and closing the door.

Franki rolled her eyes. "Why does she always have to be such a bitch? About every fucking thing?"

"I don't know," I sighed. "I'm starting to get homesick."

"Is your moms coming to homecoming next month?" Franki asked.

I shook my head. "I doubt it. I haven't even heard from her since I've been out here," I admitted shamefully. I was sure this was all foreign to Franki, since she talked to her mother every day.

"Well, have you tried calling her?"

"Yep." I nodded. "I called her the first day we moved in, a couple of days after that, and then again last night," I explained.

"Damn," Franki muttered.

Feeling my emotions start to get the best of me, I threw my things back in the bag and stood up from the couch. "I'm tired. I think I'm just gonna go lie down."

"All right. We still eating dinner in the I tonight?" Franki asked.

I shrugged. "If I feel up to it."

I trudged to my bedroom and immediately collapsed on the bed. I could feel my eyes beginning to water, but I refused to cry. My mother and I had never really been close, but her being so distant at this point in my life was truly breaking me. A part of me felt like she had just thrown me to the wolves. Then there was this other voice in my head that was wondering if something bad had happened to her. Now that she was my only parent, I found myself constantly worrying about her well-being. I didn't know what I would do if I was in this world all alone.

If she would just pick up the damn phone.

Chapter 8

Asha

Meeting Jaxon Brown

It had been a whole month since the start of school, and I still hadn't laid my eyes on Jaxon Brown. After doing a bit of research, I discovered that all the school's athletes frequented the Corbett Sports Center every day. Not that I was into working, because I wasn't, but I ended up getting me a part-time job in the head coach's office over there. Today was my first day on the job, and although it paid only minimum wage, I was excited. I decided to wear my heather-gray sheath dress, which fit snug around my ass and hips. On my feet were the gray Jimmy Choos that Mark had bought for me a few weeks ago. I had even spent the better part of yesterday getting a fresh sew-in that was styled in long, wavy-like curls. My makeup was on point, and *shit*, I was feeling good. In my mind, Jaxon would take one look at me and fall head over heels.

My job was on the third floor, so as I rode the elevator up, I practiced what I might say to him.

"Who, me?" I asked, placing my hand on my chest flirtatiously as I looked at my reflection. "I'm Asha Montgomery. Oh, my eyes? Yes, they're real," I said, batting my eyelashes.

Suddenly, the elevator chimed, and the mirrored doors slid open. I stepped off and found office 338 on my right. As I made my way inside, I spotted an older black lady with short gray hair sitting behind a desk. She was staring at her computer screen, so she didn't even notice me come in.

"Excuse me," I said to get her attention.

She looked up and smiled. "Yes? How may I help you, young lady?"

"My name is Asha Montgomery, and I'm supposed to be starting my work-study job here today."

"Oh, yes," she said, hopping up from her seat. "Don't you look lovely? I'm Miss Shirley, and you'll be reporting to me." She walked out from around her desk and extended her hand. "Come, let me show you to your desk."

She walked me over to a small desk in a back corner of the room. I turned my nose up because in my mind, I needed my own office. At least my desk was by the window, though, so I had a little view. After I set my purse down, Miss Shirley showed me around. We went to all the coaches' offices in the suite, and then she showed me where the fax machine and the printer were.

"You'll have to take the mail down every day, so let me show you where you'll need to go," she said.

I followed her to the elevator, and we rode it down to the first floor. Once we got off, she took me along a long, narrow hall that had workout rooms with large windows on either side. As we walked, I kept looking in the workout rooms to see if I could find Jaxon. I'd studied his picture so many times that I knew I could easily spot him in a crowd.

Room after room, my eyes scanned over so many fine young black men. They were all lifting weights, sweat dripping from their bare chests and abs. However, I did my best not to get distracted. I wanted only Jaxon. He was the star, *the money-maker*.

"And so here is where you'll drop off our mail each day and where you'll pick it up," Miss Shirley explained when we reached the mail room. "Now, I know that you'll be passing by all these young men every day on your way down here, but promise me that you won't get too preoccupied," she said knowingly, winking her eye.

"Oh, no, ma'am, I'm not thinking about these boys," I told her. When she turned her back to walk out of the mail room, I rolled my eyes.

After going back upstairs, Ms. Shirley instructed me on how to answer the phone properly. Then she gave me a few small tasks to complete before the end of my four-hour shift. The day went by fast, and although I didn't see Jaxon, I was actually proud of myself. For once, I felt like a real working girl.

At exactly five o'clock that evening, I headed back downstairs to leave for the day. As soon as the elevator doors opened, I was taken aback. Jaxon was standing there in the lobby. I swear, the nigga was finer than any picture I'd ever seen of him before. He was six feet, four inches tall and had milk chocolate skin. And since he was a basketball player, his body was naturally fit. I was so caught up in staring at him that the elevator doors closed on me before I even had a chance to step off. After quickly smoothing my hair down with my hands, I opened the doors back up and walked out.

I knew that you didn't chase guys like Jaxon. The idea was for them always to chase you. So, as I sauntered past him, I decided to put on a little show. Man, I swished my hips so hard, I was surprised them bitches didn't break. My heart was racing inside my chest because that was just how badly I wanted him. But if I didn't know anything else, I knew that I looked good. From my round ass and tiny waist to the light brown color of my eyes, I kept men in a trance. At the end of the day, Jaxon was merely a man.

"Hey, um. Excuse me," I heard him say behind my back.

Bingo!

I stopped, closed my eyes, and took a deep breath before turning around. He was standing there with a Nike duffel bag hanging off his shoulder and some Beats headphones clasped around his neck. "Are you talking to me?" I asked, trying to sound sophisticated.

Licking his lips, he continued touring my body with his eyes. "Yeah, I'm talking to you. Where you headed?" he said.

"I'm on my way home."

Looking me over once more, he rubbed the hairs on his chin, then tilted his head to the side. "So, are you a student? Or do you work here?"

I guess my dress and heels made me look older than I was. "Both," I said with a confident smile.

"Oh, yeah? You stay on campus?"

I nodded. "Holland Hall. You?"

"Oh, I stay in Cooper. So what's your name?"

"I'm Asha. And who are you?" I said, pretending not to know who he was.

He cracked a cocky smile. "My name is Jaxon. Jaxon Brown."

"Well, it's nice meeting you, Jaxon Brown."

Before I could spin back around completely to exit through the door, he said, "Hey, can I call you some time?"

Gotcha!

I was smiling so hard on the inside, but on the outside, my game face remained intact. "Sure," I said.

After we exchanged numbers, I walked outside, in search of Mark's Range. He was parked a little ways down from the door and was waiting on me.

"What the fuck took you so long?" he barked as soon as I opened the car door. The smell of weed filled my nostrils as I sank down into the seat.

"Nigga, I was working," I snapped right back.

"Well, don't tell me to pick you up at five if yo' ass ain't gon' walk out until five fifteen. You already fucking know I don't do that waiting shit!"

As Mark pulled off, I quietly sat back in the passenger seat. He was known to blow up over the smallest things, and I just didn't feel like dealing with all of that.

"So, who was that nigga you was in there talking to?" he asked, catching me by surprise. Although the building's front doors were made of glass, I didn't think he had seen me.

"What nigga?" I replied, feigning innocence.

"Yeah, a'ight. Keep playing dumb here, and I'ma fuck you up."

When I sucked my teeth, Mark reached back like he was going to slap me. He'd hit me many times before in the past, so naturally, I flinched.

"He was just some guy asking me where the coach's office was," I lied.

"And what the fuck was he asking you for?"

I looked at him like he was stupid. "Because I work there. Damn," I mumbled beneath my breath.

Although we weren't officially together, in Mark's mind, I was his. The first time we had sex, he told me that my body belonged strictly to him. In fact, there were several occasions where he even told me that he'd kill me before he'd let me go. His jealousy went so far that it was nothing for him to go through my phone or check my panties when I'd walk through the door. I honestly couldn't stand it, but Mark had lots of money, and he didn't mind spending it on me.

Mark ran with my selfish-ass brother and his crew. They were all a part of a gang who would sometimes sell prescription drugs to local professionals and college students around the way. The reason my brother and I didn't get along was that unlike Mark, he was stingy with his money. He would tell me that I needed to go to school and get a regular job rather than depend on his drug money.

Another big issue my brother had with me was the fact that I would sometimes sleep with men for money. I couldn't even count on two hands the number of times I'd been called a whore. And now that I was dealing with his boy Mark, he was really burning up inside. He didn't think that Mark was good enough for his little sister. Not only was Mark involved in some of the same criminal activity that he was, but he was twenty-five years old and a known ho throughout the city. In my eyes, it was the pot calling the kettle black. My brother wasn't a saint by far, so at this point, his opinion really didn't matter.

"Where are we going?" I asked, noticing that we were getting on the freeway.

"Mane, just sit the fuck back and ride," he said, placing a blunt between his lips.

After a twenty-minute ride, we pulled up to Proximity Hotel. While Mark parked the car, I glanced over at him, wearing a confused look on my face. "Mark, what are we doing here? You know I've got school in the morning."

"You already know I'ma take you back. Why you tripping?"

Before I could even respond, Mark hopped out of the car. I honestly just wanted to go back to my room and wait on Jaxon's call, but apparently, Mark had other plans. After he retrieved a few shopping bags out of his trunk, the two of us made our way inside. Although I've stayed in better, it was a really nice hotel. Once we checked in, we headed up to the sixth floor, where he had gotten us a suite.

"Here," Mark said, offering me the shopping bags in his hands.

"For me?" I asked, taking them from him.

I put the bags down on the bed, sat down beside them, and starting digging through them one by one. The first bag was from Victoria's Secret. Mark was a lingerie man, so I wasn't surprised. He'd bought me a new lace teddy and a silk baby doll nightgown. The next bag I grabbed was from Chanel. I pulled out a new pair of shades and a black leather belt.

"Thank you, baby," I squealed, jumping up to give him a hug.

He wrapped his arms around me, then kissed me on the lips. "There's one more," he said, tipping his head toward the bed.

I looked back and saw that there was a small blue bag from Tiffany. "Baby, you spoil me," I cooed. I picked up the bag and retrieved a little blue box that had a white ribbon tied around it. After unwrapping it, I discovered a pair of platinum diamond earrings sparkling back at me. "Oh my," I gasped.

"You like 'em?"

"Like them? Baby, I love them," I exclaimed.

After hugging Mark's neck once more, I lifted myself up on the balls of my feet and planted a kiss on his lips. I could feel his hands slowly begin to stray down to my ass. "Mmm," he moaned. "You gon' show me how much you love 'em?"

I knew what the deal was from the moment we pulled up to the hotel, so there wasn't any need for me to front now. With my lips still connected to his, I nodded and began unbuckling his pants. When I reached inside, his dick was already swollen and erect. As I began to stroke his shaft, he moaned into my mouth.

"Damn, Mama. Whatchu gon' do?" he murmured.

I knew exactly what he wanted, so I sank down to my knees and brought his pants right along with me. I wasted no time taking his entire length into my mouth and began to slurp. Mark's hands eased to the crown of my head, and together we worked into a steady rhythm.

"Shit, girl," he hissed, slowly thrusting his hips.

As I snaked my wet tongue up and down his shaft, I began to hum. It was something that Mark had specifically taught me to do. Glancing up, I took in the pleasure that was written all over his face. His eyes were closed, and he was biting down on his lower lip.

"Gah damn, girl. Whatchu doing to me?" he asked breathily.

At this point, Mark was pretty much gone, but I knew exactly what would send him over the edge. I wrapped my hand around the base of his dick and began fisting him. After bobbing my head back and forth a few more times, I slowly started to feel his muscle twitch. The pace of his hips quickened all at once, and he moaned out like a little bitch.

"Oh, shit! Oh. shit!" he yelled, his hot cream spurting out.

Later that night, after two more rounds of sex, Mark was sleeping like a baby. I, on the other hand, was lying there in the dark, staring up at the ceiling. Now, don't get me wrong. I had a pretty good time with Mark. I got me an orgasm and even a hot meal out of the deal, but there was always something about the way I felt afterward. *Cheap and unworthy.*

Suddenly, I heard my cell phone vibrating next to me on the nightstand. I glanced over at Mark first and saw that he was still asleep before I picked it up. There was a text from Jaxon Brown.

JB: Hey, beautiful. I know it's kinda late, but I wanted to say good night. Hope to see you again soon.

Like a little schoolgirl, I blushed and held the phone up to my chest. Maybe Jaxon really was the one for me. Instead of responding to his text, I closed my eyes and forced myself to dream of the wonderful future the two of us would eventually have together. I wanted to be Mrs. Jaxon Brown by the time I turned twenty-five. This would be shortly after he'd been drafted by the league. I'd already envisioned us having three children, all of us living in a large mansion, and owning several vacation properties around the globe. And, boy, would Jaxon spoil us rotten, providing us with the very best that money could buy. Yeah, I could already picture it. The only thing left to do was to put my plan in motion.

Chapter 9

Franki

Blindly Pegged

I honestly didn't want to be known as the ho around campus, so I hoped that Davion could be my cuddy buddy, at least for freshman year. However, he turned out to be too damn clingy. I swear, it felt like I couldn't even take a shit without Davion ringing my phone off the hook. Then, on top of that, he was extremely insecure. He would question my whereabouts and ask who I was with, like I was his girlfriend. No matter how many times I told him that we were not in a relationship, he insisted on spending time with me outside the bedroom. "Let's go out to eat," or "Let's go check out a movie," he would say. I'd be like, "Nigga, I don't do dates."

So after just two weeks, I broke things off with Davion for good. I was now kicking it with this guy named Jamel, whom I'd recently met out in the yard. Like me, he enjoyed smoking trees and was just real laid back. He was also from New York, which I think only added to his appeal. He looked and sounded like the guys I was used to dealing with, and somehow that gave me an extra level of comfort.

"Come on," he said, leading me down the narrow hall to his room.

This was his first time inviting me back to his place, and secretly, I was hoping that he'd bless me with some dick. To keep it short and sweet, Jamel was tall, dark, and rough. There was nothing pretty about him, and he was exactly my type. When we reached his dorm room, he stuck the key in the lock, turned it, and pushed open the door.

"Damn, my nigga. I thought yo' ass was gone," he said as he walked in.

I peeked my head inside and saw none other than Josh sitting on the floor, playing PlayStation.

"Come on, shorty. What you standing out there for?" Jamel asked.

For some reason, seeing Josh totally paralyzed me. I hadn't seen him since that first night when we went out to the club, and now here he was, staring right at me. Clearing my throat, I managed to peel my eyes away from his. "Um, I didn't know you had company," I said, still standing out in the hallway.

"Oh, nah, this my roommate, Josh," Jamel explained.

I thought that Josh would mention the fact that we'd previously met, but instead, he turned and focused on his game again.

"Aye, man, let me holler at you a minute," Jamel said to get Josh's attention. "Franki, you can come in and sit down."

With a partial roll of his eyes, Josh released a deep sigh. It was like all of a sudden, I could sense that he was bothered. After tossing the controller onto the bed, he stood up from the floor and walked over to Jamel. As I sat on the edge of what I assumed was Jamel's bed, I listened to them whisper.

"Man, you mind lending me the room for a few hours? I was tryna chill with shorty for a little bit," Jamel said.

Josh clenched his jaw and cut his eyes over at me. "It's whatever," he said through gritted teeth.

Josh went back over and aggressively snatched his jacket off the bed. Then, without uttering another word, he stormed out the door. I didn't know why my chest tightened at the sight of that.

"Yo, that nigga's bugging. That game shit can wait," Jamel said. He walked over and cut the game system off, then cut on the TV. "Take off your shoes, ma. Get comfortable," he said as he looked back at me.

After removing my shoes, I leaned back against his pillow. I watched as Jamel took off his shirt, revealing his bare chest. He wasn't a very muscular guy, but that didn't bother me in the least. In my experience, the skinniest guys were always the ones working with the biggest poles.

"You good," he asked, dipping down onto the mattress.

I simply nodded my head.

We took the next few seconds to get comfortable together on his twin-size bed. Unfortunately, they didn't live in a suite like I did. It was just one bedroom with two simple mattresses and a couple of dresser drawers.

Before long, I found myself snuggled beneath his arm, with my head lying against his chest. We were watching TV, and honestly, I was just waiting for him to the make the first move.

"You know I've been enjoying kicking it with you, right?" he asked as he looked down at me.

"Yeah. I've been having fun with you too." I wanted to tell him just to skip the damn small talk and get to it, but I didn't want to come off too strong.

Shifting his body toward mine, Jamel slipped his arm around my waist. "You know you pretty as hell, don't you?" he whispered, looking down at my lips. He didn't have those nice, pretty pink, kissable lips that Josh had. Instead, his were almost black from smoking weed every day. But either way, it didn't matter, because my body was in need. I leaned up and crashed my lips against his before he even had a chance to take the lead. He parted my lips with his tongue and allowed his hand to slither beneath my shirt.

"Um," I moaned, feeling his fingers suddenly tease my hardened nipples.

Just when I was getting into it, his bedroom door came flying open.

"Aye, man, I forgot my—"

Jamel and I jumped up and saw Josh standing there with a grimace on his face. Considering the dirty look he gave me, you would've thought that I was *his* woman and that I'd been caught red-handed cheating with another man.

Josh shook his head, then let out a little snort of annoyance. "I'ma be out y'all way. I just forgot my cell phone," he said.

After he went and grabbed his cell phone off the dresser, he left back out and allowed the heavy door to slam behind him.

Jamel looked at me, wearing a perplexed expression on his face. "Fuck is that nigga's problem?"

"Come on, Paris. You're gonna have to move faster than that," I snapped at Paris.

It was the very next day, and we were both running late to class. Since I had biology and Paris had geology, our classes were in neighboring buildings. Sometimes we'd walk together, but most days we didn't, because she was forever running behind.

It was mid-October, and although it was still fairly warm outside, the leaves were slowly beginning to change color. As we walked through the yard, I immediately spotted Josh's pretty ass standing with a few of his frat brothers. They all had on their black windbreakers and were laughing among themselves.

"Oh, there goes Josh," Paris said excitedly. As if we weren't already late for class, she skipped over to him and looped her arm around his.

"What's up, Ma? You headed to class?" he asked, looking down at her from his tall frame.

She smiled and flipped her long hair off her shoulders. "Yeah. Are you ready?"

My eyebrow instantly shot up when I heard her ask him that. I didn't even know they knew each other that well. Hell, other than the night he dropped us off from the club, I hadn't seen him at all. Well, other than last night, of course.

"A'ight, yo, I'ma catch y'all later," he said, dapping up a few of his boys. Then, to my surprise, he started walking along with us.

"What's up, Franki?" he greeted with a chuck of his chin.

"Hey," I said dryly, then rolled my eyes. I didn't know why, but I was so irritated seeing Paris hang all on him like that. When he let out a snort of laughter at my response, that only seemed to annoy me more.

"So you got family coming into town this weekend for homecoming?" Josh asked Paris.

She sighed, then shook her head. "No. My daddy passed away last year, and I'm not real close with my mother," she explained. "What about you?"

"Yeah." He exhaled, running his hand over the top of his head. "My mother and father supposed to be coming down. The Reverend and his First Lady wouldn't dare miss a family weekend," he said mockingly.

"I should have known that you were a PK," Paris said.

"A PK?" I questioned, although I was more than familiar with the term.

"Yeah, he's a preacher's kid," Paris explained.

"Figures," I muttered.

He let out another snort, then shook his head. "Anyway, we're throwing a party at the frat house after the homecoming game. Y'all should swing through."

"I'm totally in. What about you, Franki?" Paris asked, cutting her eyes over at me.

I simply shrugged my shoulders.

After another couple of minutes, we reached Paris's building, which was on the right. "All right. I'll see you guys later," she said before walking toward her class. That left just me and Josh.

As we walked a bit farther, I let out a little yawn.

"Late night, huh?" Josh asked.

I knew that he was being funny, referring to the fact that I had been with Jamel last night. "Well, when you're grown, you can have late nights," I retorted.

Josh just shook his head. "If you say so," he muttered. Once again, I felt like he was looking down on me. "So how long you and Mel been kicking it?" he asked.

I shrugged my shoulders. "I don't know. About a week or two," I said.

He released a soft snort, then shook his head again. "Ain't you been kicking it with Dave?" he asked.

How the hell does he know that?

"Look, if you wanted to fuck, that's all you had to say from the jump," I snapped, attempting to pull his card.

His eyes immediately ballooned, like he was appalled. "Yo, I wouldn't mess with a broad like you if somebody paid me to," he spat.

I didn't know why, but I was offended by that. I stopped in my tracks and turned to face him. "A *broad* like me! What the fuck is that supposed to mean?"

He gave me a dismissive wave and sucked his teeth. "Man, I'm going to class," he said, then continued to stroll along.

"No! I want to know. What's a broad like me?" I snapped, following behind him.

He just ignored me and kept walking. For some reason, that only fueled my anger. I finally caught up to him and grabbed him by the shoulder. "Answer me! What? You too afraid to say the word *ho*?"

When he glanced back at me, I could see his nostrils flaring slightly with disgust. "Just remember, you said it, not me."

Now, this wasn't my first time being called a ho, but hearing *him* say it actually stung. Before any weak emotions could rise to the surface, I shoved him. "Say it! Go ahead. Call me a ho," I snarled.

Josh's jaw flexed as he shot me a cold glare. "You need to learn how to keep your hands to yourself, ma," he said.

I shoved him again. At this point, I knew that I was being childish, but somehow, I'd allowed his words to get the best of me. "Say it, church boy!" I yelled. "What? Just because I'm not some fucking square and I enjoy sex, I'm a ho?"

Josh shook his head. "Man, you bugging. I'm gone," he said, then attempted to walk away again.

I grabbed his arm and yanked him back. "No, tell me! Why wouldn't you mess with a chick like me?"

Completely frustrated, Josh pinched the bridge of his nose. "Look," he breathed, gazing directly into my eyes, "I'm not trying to hurt your little feelings, so I suggest you walk away."

"Hurt my feelings? Nigga, you got me fucked up—"

"I would never deal with a girl like you because you don't know your worth," he said, cutting me off. "Until a woman values herself, she won't value her time. And until you value your time, you won't do shit but waste it. A man like me don't have no patience for that, a'ight?" he added.

For some reason, I instantly felt humiliated. "You think you're better than—"

"Nah, you're the one putting up this big front, like you're the most confident chick to ever walk the face of the earth. But, shorty, check it. I see right through you," he said, pointing his finger in my face. "I see right through the tough talk and the little games you play. That's why you can't come out your mouth to ever call me by my name. Or why you can barely stand to look me in the eye. 'Cause you know, just like I do, that you're nothing but a scared little girl running from . . . whatever. Thinking that nobody can hurt you if you hurt them first." He shook his head and sucked his teeth. "That ain't no way to live, Ma."

"First off, you don't know a damn thing about me. And second, I ain't running from shit. I'm just not gonna let no nigga walk all over me and get the last laugh. So, yeah, I fuck because I like sex, and if niggas can't deal with it, then fuck them," I spat, making him cringe. "That's what kills me about you niggas. When we do the same shit as y'all, it's a damn problem."

"Look, if you think the way you living is getting you somewhere, then continue to do you, ma." He shrugged. "Anyway, I'm late for class."

With that, Josh walked off and left me standing there all alone.

Chapter 10

Hope

Sleepover in Pride Hall

Since that first day of school, it seemed as if Meeko and I had actually become good friends. I'd learned that he was a sophomore and was attending A&T on a football scholarship. Since he'd redshirted his first year, he had plans to play ball for the next three years. His mother was named Kelsey, and his three sisters were named Kimberlyn, Keisha, and Kadia. He even had two nieces and a nephew back home. Although Meeko had big dreams of entering the league one day, he was majoring in business. He said that he would rather go into business for himself than work for some white man.

Although I had originally thought he was just another rude jock, Meeko had proven otherwise.

Occasionally, he would walk me to class, and he'd even send me random text messages throughout the day. Honestly, he was quite sweet.

Today would make the second time I'd ever been to his room. When he first called and asked if I wanted to "chill," I was a little hesitant. But after realizing that both Paris and Franki were gone, I said, "Why not?" I changed from one khaki skirt into another and opted for a long- sleeved red blouse. Instead of the canvas sneakers I usually wore, I chose a pair of brown leather boots that completely covered my calves. After re-pinning the bun in my hair, I combed my Chinese-cut bangs down over my forehead and gave myself the once-over in the mirror. No, I wasn't a knockout like Franki or the typical pretty, light-skinned girl like Paris, but as I looked at my reflection, I could honestly say that I liked what I saw staring back at me.

As I walked through campus, dusk was just beginning to settle in, painting the sky purple. Never before had I walked this far by myself at night. It was just one more item to add to the list of things my father had told me never to do. For some reason, the closer I got to Pride Hall, the more nervous I became. My stomach was twisting into knots. I honestly didn't know why I was feeling that way, because Meeko had never shown any romantic interest in me. I guess it was because I finally had to admit to myself that I was developing real feelings for him.

After entering the building, I went straight up to his room from memory. I didn't think I'd ever forget room 409. Before I could even knock, I heard a loud commotion on the other side of the door. Booming rap music, garish laughter, and even the scent of what I had recently learned was marijuana were seeping out of his room. I became slightly disappointed because I was hoping that we would be spending time alone. I took a deep breath and finally banged my fist on the door.

Meeko appeared before me, wearing only gray sweatpants and white socks on his feet, his chest bare.

"Ah, you made it," he said. Smiling, he leaned in to give me a *brotherly* hug.

As I wrapped my arms around Meeko's waist, I naturally closed my eyes and briefly allowed my cheek to hit the soft skin of his chest. All sorts of lustful thoughts rushed through me as he pulled me into the room by the hand. As expected, he had a couple of friends over. Sitting on the floor, in a couple of game chairs, were his friends Ty and the big guy, whose name I now knew was Big Mo. I was the only girl.

"What up?" Ty greeted, chucking up his chin, a joint dangling from his lips.

"Yo, you chilling with us tonight, Hope?" Big Mo asked. Grinning, he winked his eye at me. I didn't even realize he knew my name.

I just smiled and shrugged my shoulders. "I guess so."

"She wasn't doing shit else," Meeko said with a hint of laughter in his voice. Then he nodded his head toward his dresser, where I could see food, along with a few bottles of beer lined up. "I ordered some pizza and wings, if you're hungry," he offered.

"Maybe in a little while."

As Meeko took a seat on his bed, I awkwardly stood in the middle of the room. There were no more chairs for me to sit in, so I didn't know what to do.

"Shorty, why you standing there, looking all crazy? Come sit down," Meeko said, patting a spot next to him on the bed.

I took a seat and stared at the television screen, where the guys were playing *NBA Live* on the PlayStation 4.

"Aye, man, what's going on with you and Bree? Shawty called, looking for you last night," Big Mo said to Ty.

Passing the small joint over to Big Mo, Ty sucked his teeth. "Man, I done told shorty to just fall back for a minute. Shit between us ain't been right for a good li'l minute, but because we got so much history together, she still tryna hold on."

"Yeah, you and Bree do got a lot of history together. I mean, y'all got a baby together, so in her mind, y'all gon' be together for life," Meeko commented.

"Wait, you have a baby?" I asked, surprised.

Ty nodded his head. "I mean, she ain't no baby no more, but yeah, I got a four-year-old daughter. Her name is Brielle."

"Wow," I blurted. "How old are you?"

"Twenty," he said as his eyes remained focused on the television screen.

"Just 'cause y'all got a baby together don't mean y'all gotta be in a relationship, though. As long as you're handling your business," Big Mo said.

"Shit, that ain't the way Bree see it. Shorty see all this college pussy being thrown in my nigga's face and is about to lose her fucking mind," Meeko said, then held his fist up to his mouth for a chuckle. "Aye, y'all remember last year, when ole girl from Ragsdale Hall answered your phone?"

Ty sucked his teeth. "Man, don't tell that story."

Meeko was all smiles as he tapped me on the arm and continued. "So, look, right? His girl, Bree, was up in Baltimore, trying to get in touch with him one night. I think Brielle was sick or some shit—"

"She had a fever," Ty said, cutting him off.

"So it's about . . ." Meeko hesitated, narrowing his eyes as he put his hand up to his chin. "It's about three in the morning. I'm sleep in my bed, and across from me is Ty and ole girl all cuddled up in his bed. All of a sudden, his cell goes off on the nightstand. I wake up," he said. He patted his chest, eyes widening dramatically. "Heart racing. Whole room glowing up and shit. Then I see ole girl reaching over to get the phone. Ty's straight knocked." Meeko lay back on the bed and closed his eyes to demonstrate.

Ty, Big Mo, and I all fell out laughing.

"Ole dramatic-ass nigga," Big Mo muttered with a laugh.

"Well, shorty must've thought that it was her phone, because all of a sudden, I see her slide her finger across the screen and put it up to her ear," Meeko continued, putting this hand up to his ear. "Hello," he said, mimicking her girlish voice. Then he shook his head. "Yo, Bree laid that girl the fuck out. I could hear her cursing and screaming through the phone. 'Who the fuck is you, answering my nigga phone!'" As he mimicked Bree, he rolled his eyes and snaked his neck like a woman.

I was laughing so hard, tears leaked from my eyes.

"Didn't Bree take the train down here the next day to pop up on a nigga?" Big Mo asked, recalling what happened.

"Damn sure did," Meeko confirmed.

Ty shook his head. "Yeah, and I cussed her ass out too. How you gon' leave my daughter at home, sick, just to come all the way down here?"

"So what was wrong with her? Your daughter?" I asked after I caught my breath.

"She had a double ear infection, and Bree couldn't get her fever to break," Ty said.

"Oh," I said lowly.

"Nigga stay doing my girl Bree all wrong," Big Mo said.

Meeko nodded his head in agreement. "Bree cool, though. She just gotta let you do you right now," he said.

"Speaking of which, Hope, when you gon' hook me up with your roommate?" Ty asked as he continued playing the game.

"Which one?" I asked with a little cough. The smoke was starting to get to me.

"I'on know her name, but the thick, light-skinned one with the long hair."

"Oh, you're talking about either Asha or Paris."

"He ain't talking about Asha's run-through ass," Meeko muttered.

"What do you have against Asha?" I replied. "I mean, I know that she can have a bad attitude at times, but . . ."

"We met Asha last year, when we were freshmen on campus and she was still a senior in high school. Long story short, shawty let us run a train on her one night. She was supposed to be staying over-night in the dorms with us, but the next morning, we woke up and found that the bitch was already gone," Big Mo explained, crushing the remainder of his joint in an ashtray on the floor. "Not only had she snuck out without telling us, but shawty also took all our money and even stole a few pieces of jewelry we had laying around."

"Oh my," I gasped. "What's a train?"

After a few seconds of silence, Meeko, Big Mo, and Ty all burst out in laughter.

"What's so funny?" I asked, confused.

"Shorty, you serious?" Meeko asked, narrowing his eyes. I guess he got his answer by the humor-less expression on my face. "Well, a train is when a girl lets multiple men have sex with her, one after the other," he explained.

My mouth practically hit the floor. Never in all my eighteen years of living had I heard of such a degrading act. "An-and, the three of you . . ." I struggled just to get out the words as I pointed.

"Yeah, we hit," Big Mo said nonchalantly, shrug-ging his shoulders.

"But I thought you had a girlfriend?" I asked Ty, still in a state of shock.

"Sometimes shit just happens, nah mean?" he said, brushing his hand over the top of his head. Then, all of a sudden, it was like a switch went off inside his head. "And shit, I wasn't the only one with a girl at the time. Mister Sweet and Innocent back there was riding tough with Jazz last year."

I looked over at Meeko. "Jazz? You mean the *homie*?" I asked, making air quotes with my hands.

"Ahhh," Big Mo and Ty both laughed.

"You ain't call Jazz the homie, did you, big bruh?" Big Mo teased.

"That *is* the homie. Sometimes we just kick it like friends, and sometimes we get down like lovers. That's the homie," Meeko answer, clarifying matters.

"But you been knocking Jazz down since the beginning of last year. When you gon' finally commit?" Ty asked with a hint of laughter in his voice.

"Shit, I ain't. Jazz knows what's up." Meeko then shifted his body toward me. "And how you not gon' know what a train is? They don't do those down in Alto?" he joked, jabbing me in the side with his finger.

I jumped a little from the tickling sensation, then said, "I don't know what they do."

"So you a virgin, Hope?" Ty asked bluntly as he continued playing the game.

Not quite ready to reveal my truth, I released a deep sigh.

"Ain't no shame in being a virgin. Shit, we were all there at one point in time," Big Mo said.

"Yeah, when we was, like, thirteen," Ty joked.

"So what you waiting on? Marriage?" Meeko asked.

I swallowed hard and nodded. "Yes. I would like to be married first." Truthfully, I didn't even believe that myself, but it was what I had been taught my entire life.

"Well, shit, good luck to you and that lame-ass nigga you end up with," Ty said with a chuckle.

As the night went on, I listened to the guys as they sat around talking about football, girls, and sex. They were all comical in their own right, cracking jokes and even gossiping like a group of old women. Needless to say, I was thoroughly entertained. Never in all my life had I just hung out with a group of boys like that before. I could almost hear Deddy's voice in my head. *You shouldn't be alone in the room with them. Anything could happened to you, girl.* And although that would be the best advice for any father to give, I decided to throw caution to the wind. That was just how much I trusted Meeko. Seeing Ty and Big Mo sitting there when I first entered the room had made me want to run the other way, especially given their previous childish behavior. But as the night went on, I ultimately decided that they, too, were pretty decent guys.

"A'ight, homeboy," Big Mo said, getting up from the game chair on the floor. He clapped hands with Meeko, then reached down to clap hands with Ty. "I'ma fuck with y'all later, man."

"Yeah, I'm getting ready to leave too," Ty said.

Meeko stood up and stretched his arms out wide. "A'ight. See y'all fools tomorrow," he said with a little yawn.

I glanced over at Meeko's alarm clock on his nightstand and saw it was going on three in the morning. By this time, my shoes were completely off, and my feet were tucked beneath me as I rested back on Meeko's bed.

"So you coming to the homecoming game tomorrow night, right?" Ty asked as he looked at me.

"Yeah, me, Franki, and Paris are going," I said with a smile.

"A'ight, Dimples, don't forget to put in a good word for me."

I let out a light laugh. "Okay, I won't forget."

After Ty and Big Mo left out, I scooted over to the edge of the bed and began putting my boots back on.

"Where you going?" Meeko asked.

"Home. I didn't even realize how late it was," I said.

"Look, it's too dark for you to be walking across campus at this time of night, and I would walk with you, but I'm tired myself." He paused like he was thinking. "Why don't you just stay here tonight?"

My eyes widened. "Stay here?" I gulped.

"Yeah, shorty. I ain't gon' bite."

"B-but where would I sleep?"

"You take one side of the bed, and I'll take the other. I won't touch you." After a long, pregnant pause, Meeko must have sensed my hesitation, because he said, "Or I can just walk you home." He reached over and grabbed a sweatshirt that was hanging on the back of his closet door.

"No. I'll stay," I said lowly.

"You sure?"

I nodded my head.

After going into the bathroom and changing into one of Meeko's T-shirts and a pair of his basketball shorts, I stepped back out into his room. He was lying above the covers, staring up at the ceiling. Usually, I slept with my hair in a silk bonnet, but since I wasn't at home, I knew I'd just have to make do. I stepped over to his dresser and began removing the bobby pins from my bun one by one. I could feel my hair slowly unraveling down my back. Once I removed my eyeglasses and sat them on the dresser, I turned back around to face the bed.

"Damn," Meeko muttered, his eyes bucking. His gaze instantly softened and swept over me.

"What? What's wrong?" I asked, brushing my bangs out of my eyes.

He licked his lips, then shook his head. "N-nothing."

"So I guess I have to sleep against the wall?" I asked, noticing that he was on the side of the bed with the nightstand.

"I mean, I would sleep on the floor, but, um . . ." His voice trailed off as his eyes fell upon the hard linoleum floor. "I really ain't got enough blankets to be comfortable."

"It's fine. You stay on your side, and I'll stay on mine, right?"

"No doubt," he said. He got up from the bed and pulled back the covers, allowing me to slide right on in. "Can I get under the covers?" he asked.

"That's fine," I said, scooting closer to the wall.

With my back facing him, Meeko joined me under the sheets and cut off the lights. As we lay there in silence, I could feel the warmth emitting from his body, and, *God*, did he smell good. Like a heavenly mix of soap and sage. I was so nervous, yet I was surprisingly aroused. I mean, there I was, lying next to the boy who had been cast in the lead role of my most recent dreams.

"Hope?" Meeko said, taking me out of my thoughts.

"Huh?"

"You asleep?"

"Not yet. Why?"

"Just asking." He paused. "You know . . . you look really pretty with your hair down."

A surge of butterflies circled within my stomach. "Thank you," I whispered.

Chapter 11

Paris

Just One Kiss

It was a little after ten o'clock on a Saturday morning when I found myself sitting in the front lobby of Serenity Nails and Spa. It was nothing but a little hole-in-the-wall nail shop that had the nerve to include the word *Spa* in its name. See, I was accustomed to The Spa on Rodeo in Beverly Hills, where I had got my hair and nails done at least once a week. Hell, even once a month I would just pop in to get a facial and a massage. That was how much I had pampered myself on a regular basis. Now here I was, desperate, with split ends and cuticles as thick as a nickel.

I could've killed Asha for recommending this dump to me. Unlike Franki and Hope, she habitually kept up with her appearance, and since she was a "local," I figured she'd know the best place to go. However, when I pulled up at the little urban shopping center, my mouth practically hit the floor. Seeing the homeless man standing out on the corner with his grocery cart and all the impoverished people walking up and down the lot, I was almost too afraid to step out of the car when the Uber driver stopped. But after not having a facial or my nails done for almost two months, I decided to just go with it.

"Paris," a petite Asian lady called.

I stood up from the chair where I was squeezed in between two other young women and their children. As I made my way over to the glass counter, I nearly held my breath. All I could smell were the toxic fumes of acrylic nails and fingernail polish floating around.

"You want mani, pedi, facial, and eyebrow, right?" she asked with an obvious Asian accent.

"Yes, please." I nodded.

"Okay, you follow me."

She led me to a black leather pedicure chair that already had hot water bubbling at its feet. I took a seat. Immediately, I felt the chair roll up and vibrate down my back, almost creating a massage-like effect. By no means did it compare to the chairs at The Spa on Rodeo, but today I would just have to make do. I took off my socks and shoes, then allowed my feet to sink into the water.

"You pick color?" she asked.

I shook my head. "No, I just wanted a French tip. Is that okay?"

"Yes, yes. We do French," she said with a smile. "Now, you stay right here and relax. Okay?"

I simply nodded, then watched as she walked to the back. Before I could close my eyes and unwind, the front door chimed. Naturally, I looked up, and I saw some girl strolling in with a guy following behind her. Instead of waiting up front like everyone else, they immediately made their way to the back.

"Ming, where you want me at?" the pretty brown-skinned girl shouted. She stuck the pointed tip of one of her long red fingernails between her teeth as she shifted her weight onto one hip.

Up until this point, I hadn't even noticed that the guy she was standing with was the thug from the mall. He was wearing another pair of sagging slim jeans, which revealed a hint of his boxers. He had on a gray hoodie, and gold chains glistened around his tatted neck. And on his feet were a pair of gray Balenciaga high-top sneakers. *Hmm, the 2018 Speed collection.*

By the time my eyes reached his face, he was staring right back at me. An easy smile spread across his lips, exposing that gold and diamond grill in the lower half of his mouth. I had to look away.

"'Sup, Paris?" he said.

My eyes immediately widened at the sound of his voice. I couldn't believe that he actually remembered my name. "H-hi," I stammered.

"You remember me?" he asked, licking his lips.

The pretty brown-skinned girl flipped her long braids to the side and stared at him like he had two heads.

"You remember me?" he asked again, obviously ignoring her behavior.

"Yes," I said lowly.

"So, how you been? That nigga been treating you right?"

My eyebrows momentarily dipped, as I forgot all about the lie I'd previously told. Then it dawned on me. "Oh right!" I said, my eyes suddenly enlarged. "My boyfriend. We're doing fantastic."

He must have caught on, because he released a small chuckle through his nose. "Still spending that nigga's money, I see."

"Ha, ha, ha . . . very funny," I said, rolling my eyes.

All of a sudden, the pretty brown-skinned girl tapped him on the arm before pointing at me. "Malachi, who is that?" she asked just above a whisper.

Malachi sucked his teeth. "Mane, Reesie, get the fuck on somewhere," he snapped. "Here." He reached down into his jeans pocket and pulled out a thick knot of money. After licking the tip of his

finger, he peeled off four crisp one-hundred-dollar
bills, then handed them over to her as if she were
a child.

She placed the money down in her bosom, then
looked at me and smiled. "Thanks, bae," she said,
as if I actually gave a rip. In that moment I couldn't
help but roll my eyes.

As she made her way to the back of the shop,
where I'd seen the little Asian lady disappear,
Malachi moved in closer to me. His honey-colored
eyes gazed down at my feet in the water.

"Damn, you got some pretty-ass toes. You know
that? Make a nigga wanna suck each and every one
of them muthafuckas," he said with a chuckle.

I swallowed hard, cringing at the thought.
"Thanks, but, um . . . I don't think your little Reese's
cup back there would appreciate you saying that,"
I said.

His lips shifted into a crooked smile as he shook
his head. "So, when you gon' stop playing and let
me take you out?"

My eyes unwillingly took him in. The sagging
pants, the rough set of hands, even the rugged
hair on his face. He wasn't even remotely my type.
"Never," I said lowly.

He placed his hand over his chest, as if he had
been wounded by my words. "Damn, shawty. Just
break a nigga's heart, why don't you," he teased.

I shrugged my shoulders and allowed my head to fall back against the seat. Just as I closed my eyes, I heard him let go of a small chuckle.

"All right, Miss Paris. I see what it is," he said.

I opened one eye just in time to see him swaggering out of the shop.

Almost three hours later, I walked up to the front of the salon, feeling like a brand-new woman. My nails were beautiful, my eyebrows were arched, and Miss Ming had even given me a little facial. I was going to be stepping to the homecoming game and the after party with an added dose of confidence.

I walked up to the little glass counter and pulled my wallet out of my purse. "How much do I owe you?" I asked Ming.

She shook her head. "Oh, no charge. Paid for already," she said.

"Already paid for? By who?" I asked, my eyes roaming around the shop.

"The nice gentleman that came in earlier. With the gold necklaces and the teeth," she explained, pointing to her own mouth. I nodded, knowing right then that she was referring to Malachi. "You want make appointment for two weeks?" she asked.

After mulling over the idea in my head, I said, "Sure." The nail shop actually wasn't all that bad.

Once I made my appointment, I ordered an Uber on my phone. As I walked out of the shop, the first person I saw was Malachi. He was leaned up against a big-body Benz with his cell phone resting in the crook of his neck. When his eyes landed on me, he licked his lips and winked.

"Nah, mane, meet me at the spot on Battleground around five," he said into his phone, allowing his eyes to stay fixed on me. "I'ma definitely hit you before then, though. Fa' sho."

Since it was a bit chilly out, I decided to step back inside and wait. When I opened the door, he said, "So, you not gon' say thank you."

I spun back around and smiled. "Thank you, Malachi."

"Ah, so you do remember my name," he said with a cocky smirk.

Shit, he'd caught that.

"I remember most things," I said.

"Well, shawty, looka here," he said, walking up to me. "I know you not gon' give me your number, but at least let me give you mine. Shit, you never know. You might just have a change of heart and call a nigga," he said with an arrogant grin.

Just as I was getting ready to respond, two girls walked up to enter the shop. "Girl, is that Malachi's fine ass right there?" one whispered to the other.

"Shh," the other giggled.

As they went inside, I cleared my throat. "Dude, I really don't wanna waste your time. As I hinted around once before, you're no way near my type."

"So tell me, Miss Paris, exactly what is your type?"

I looked Malachi over once more, trying to disguise the repulsion on my face. "More, um . . . I don't know," I said, not wanting to hurt this poor guy's feelings.

"More what? Tell me," he urged.

"More clean cut, I guess."

"So you be dating them white boys, huh, Miss Paris?" He cracked a knowing smile.

"I've dated outside my race before, if that's what you're asking," I said, not really wanting to divulge the fact that all I'd ever dated were white boys.

"Well, let me take you out and show you something new, then. I mean, if it don't work out, then shit, it just don't work out. Besides, what you got to lose?"

"What about little miss Reese's cup in there?" I pointed my thumb back toward the nail shop. "She isn't going to mind you taking me out and showing me 'something new'?" I asked, bouncing my eyebrows up and down for effect.

He let out a little snort of laughter. "You just let me worry about that."

Just as I plugged his number into my cell, Reese came waltzing out. She looked me up and down before strutting over to his car. I was surprised by the fact that, like a gentleman, he actually opened her car door. I didn't even like this guy, but I'd be lying if I didn't admit to the smidge of jealousy I felt as I watched him care for her.

Ten minutes later, the Uber driver arrived and took me back to campus. As soon as I entered our suite, I saw Asha sitting on the couch with her cell phone up to her ear. "Oh, hey, girl. How was the *spa*?" she asked with a fake smile.

"They really did an awesome job, Ash," I told her, watching her wince at the mere sound of the little nickname I'd given her. "Thanks so much for the recommendation. Look," I said, wiggling my fingers back and forth to show off my pretty nails. Just as I knew it would, her jaw fell open from shock. "And I've already booked my next appointment. You should totally come with," I added, goading her.

She rolled her eyes and started speaking into the phone. "Now, what was you saying, Kiki?"

Bitch.

"That game was hella crazy, right?" I asked as I looked over at Franki. We were all walking back to the dorm so that we could get ready for the party tonight.

"Yeah, we did our thing out there today," she said, referring to our big homecoming win over Florida A&M.

"Oh my God, and that band. Amaze-balls!" I shrilled.

It was my first time actually hearing a live marching band like that. Everyone in the stadium was up on their feet, dancing to songs like "That's What I Like" by Bruno Mars and "In My Feelings" by Drake. And the Golden Delight squad—they were so pretty in their sequin leotards, whipping their long hair perfectly to every beat. I was sure whatever show Berkeley put on at homecoming didn't even compare.

"Yeah, you should join the dance team," she teased.

"Shut up." I pushed her in the shoulder, making her laugh. "You know I can't dance worth shit." It was no secret that I danced like a rhythmless white girl.

"Yeah, it is pretty bad," Hope chimed in with a giggle.

"Well, at least I dance and don't just stand near the wall all night, little miss 'I don't think God would want me to twerk,'" I mocked, pressing my hands together as if I were praying.

Hope rolled her eyes.

Franki doubled over in laughter. "Yo, you going straight to hell, ma," she said.

"And I saw you over there cheering for your little friend today too," I said to Hope. "What's his name? Taylor? Number eighty-three?"

Despite Hope's dark complexion, I witnessed a sudden flush of her cheeks. "Meeko's just a friend," she said.

"Bullshit," Franki mumbled beneath her breath, then coughed.

I let out a little laugh. "So, what are you guys wearing tonight?" I asked.

"We already know what Hope's wearing, so I don't know why you even asked," Franki said with a little laugh.

Hope threw her arms up, then let them fall down at her sides. "What is this? Pick on Hope day?" she whined.

"I'm just fucking with you, Hope." Franki laughed. "Let's play rock-paper-scissors. If I win, I get to dress you up tonight. If you win, I won't pick on you for the rest of the semester. Deal?"

Hope sighed, then finally said, "Deal."

"Rock, paper, scissors," they both said in unison with their fists pumping out in the air.

"Oh. My. God," I shrieked before I burst out laughing. While Franki's fingers appeared to be in the shape of scissors, Hope's hand was laid out flat like a sheet of paper. "She's so got you, Hope. Let the makeover begin," I said, giving Franki a high five in the air.

As we walked up to Holland Hall, we saw Asha stepping out of a white Range Rover. Her swollen face was red, and she was visibly upset. Once she got out, she slammed the passenger door so hard that I flinched. Not even a full two seconds later, a tall, dark-skinned man with a thick gold chain around his neck hopped out of the driver's side.

"Bitch, don't slam my fucking door! I'll fuck you up!" he barked, rounding the car.

Franki, Hope, and I stopped dead in our tracks. We quickly took notice of the fact that Asha's sweater was torn and was halfway hanging off her shoulder. Her hair seemed disheveled. She looked as if she'd just been in a fight.

"Get the fuck off me, Mark!" Asha yelled, attempting to yank herself free from the grip he now had on her arm.

"Don't you pull away from me! Get your black ass back here so we can finish talking." He looked around. "Got all these dumb muthafuckas out here in our business," he spat, glaring at students across the lawn.

"Let me go, Mark! I ain't got shit else to say to you," she yelled, still trying to fight her way out of his hold. When he snatched her back toward his car, she let out a loud, piercing scream. "Ahhh!"

Before any of us realized what was happening, Mark reached back and slapped Asha hard across the face. The force alone nearly knocked her down to the ground. As if I could feel the burning sting of her flesh, I unintentionally reached up and placed my hand against my cheek. Never in all my life had

I witnessed anything like that before. Instantly, I felt sick and scared.

"Nah, fuck that," Franki grumbled beneath her breath. As Hope and I stood frozen in place, Franki charged over to where they were. "Get your fucking hands off of her, son!" she snarled, pushing Mark hard in the chest.

From out of nowhere, I suddenly discovered some courage of my own. With trembling hands, I reached down into my purse and pulled out my cell.

"What are you doing?" Hope asked.

"I'm calling the police," I told her. I just couldn't believe that all of this was going down practically fifty feet from our dorm and no one had yet to call for help. With my phone in hand, I ran over to where Mark was now trying to pull Asha up off the ground by her hair. She was kicking and clawing beneath him, while Franki tried her best to attack him from behind.

"I'm calling the police!" I yelled out frantically.

That must've gotten Mark's attention, because he suddenly let go of Asha and slung Franki off his back. "I see how it is. You out here showing yo' ass, and now they wanna call the laws on me." He pointed to his heaving chest. "This ain't over, bitch," he seethed. And then he turned, made his way back to his car, and got behind the wheel.

As he sped off into the night, Franki and I helped Asha up off the ground. She sobbed as we brushed the leaves and dirt from her expensive clothes. As the four of us finally made our way into the building, onlookers stared at Asha in disbelief. Her face was badly bruised, and her weave was barely hanging on by a thread. Her limp body was so shaky that Hope and I had to literally hold her up by the arms.

Our resident assistant, Nina, walked up to us and asked, "Is everything okay? Do we need to call the police?"

Franki sucked her teeth and pursed her lips to the side. "Oh, now you wanna ask. Y'all didn't see that girl outside getting her ass beat!" Franki spat.

"I'm so sorry. Let me call the police . . ." Nina's eyes traveled down Asha's battered frame before she shook her head in dismay. "And an ambulance," she let out softly.

"No! Don't call nobody for me. I'm fine," Asha said adamantly.

"Are you sure? It's proper protocol—"

Asha waved her hand, cutting Nina off. "I don't care 'bout none of that. I'm fine. Don't call nobody."

"Asha, you've gotta let her call the police," I whispered in her ear.

"I'm fine," she insisted. She pulled away from me and Hope, then trudged over to the elevators by herself.

As she went on upstairs, the resident assistant let us know that she was totally breaking the rules by not calling the police.

"Look, if she says she's fine, then she's fine. It was just a small scuffle. Ain't no need to call nobody," Franki said, trying to be persuasive. When Nina didn't look convinced, Franki added, "Well, how 'bout this? If anything else happens, we'll let you know. Get you and the police involved right away, a'ight?"

I couldn't believe what I was hearing. This was a clear case of domestic violence, yet the police weren't here writing up a report. If this had been back home, Mark's ass would've already been shackled in handcuffs.

"You let me know immediately! I could lose my job and my scholarship over this," Nina said.

"Well, we wouldn't want that, now, would we?" I muttered sarcastically.

After the three of us went up to our suite, we peeked in Asha's room and saw her sitting on the edge of her bed. She was texting fast, with tears streaming down her face. In that moment, I couldn't tell if she was hurt or just plain old mad.

"You okay, girly?" I asked.

"Oh, I'm fine," she said. I could hear the cynicism in her voice. "I should kill that muthafucka."

"Who is he?" Hope asked.

"Some nigga that I've been talking to off and on for about a year and a half."

"Is this his first time putting his hands on you like that?" Franki asked.

Asha shook her head. "It ain't the first time we done got down," she offered.

Whatever the hell that means, I thought.

"Damn," Franki muttered, shaking her head.

Suddenly a hard knock sounded at our door. "I swear, that better not be Nina's bitch ass," Franki said.

"No, it's probably just my brother," Asha said.

"Well, I'll get it," I offered.

Leaving Franki and Hope standing in Asha's bedroom doorway, I made my way to the front door. Without even looking through the peephole, I quickly opened the door to find Malachi standing on the other side. My eyes instantly jumped at the sight of him. "Wh-what are you doing here?" I asked.

His neck jerked back as he narrowed his hazel-colored eyes in confusion. "Paris?" he replied with his head cocked to the side.

"How do you even know where I live?" I whispered, looking over my shoulder to make sure none of the girls had walked up on me.

Malachi sucked his teeth. "Mane, I'm here to see 'bout my little sister."

"Your little sister?" I was utterly confused.

"Yeah, Asha."

I felt so stupid that I was sure my face instantly took on a bright shade of red. Here I was thinking that the man was stalking me, when in actuality, he was just here to check on his little sister. Without another thought, I stepped aside, allowing him to enter our suite. As he walked ahead of me, my eyes brushed over his physique. Right away I noticed the showy gold and black Versace tracksuit he had on with the sneakers to match. He definitely had that urban rapper vibe down to a tee.

When he approached Asha's doorway, his tall frame allowed him to peek in over Hope's and Franki's head. "The fuck!" he spat.

At the booming sound of Malachi's threatening voice, both Franki and Hope scurried out of his way, permitting him full access to the room. Once he was inside, I stepped closer to Asha's doorway, looked in her room, and saw him grab Asha roughly by the chin.

"Now look what this nigga's done to yo' fucking face!" he roared. Asha's face had already begun converting to various hues of black and blue. Since she was only a shade or two darker than me, her injuries were very much evident. "I done told you to stop fucking with this nigga, but nah, you hard-headed," he scolded, jabbing his index finger into her forehead. "And now I gotta fuck my money up just to go beat this nigga's ass."

Any other day Asha was a total bitch. She'd have some smart-alecky remark or give a hard roll of her eyes, but today, with Malachi, she was very much a helpless little girl. I stood and watched Asha cry, as if she were being reprimanded by her very own father. "Don't go do nothing, Malachi. Please, just leave it alone," she begged, tears slipping from her eyes.

"Mane, what the fuck is you talking about, 'just leave it alone'? I left that shit alone the last time he put his hands on you. Nah." He shook his head. "I'm finna get at the nigga," Malachi spat, crashing his fist into the palm of his other hand.

"The school already got the police involved," Asha lied. "Just leave it alone."

Malachi's temper suddenly quieted, as if he were mulling something over in his head. "A'ight," he finally announced. He nodded as he licked his lips. "Bet. I'm gon' back off for now, but you need to stop dealing with him," he said, unexpectedly using a softer tone.

Asha sniffed and wiped the wetness from her face. "I am. I'm gonna leave him alone this time," she promised.

"You need me to take you to the hospital?" he asked.

"No. Just don't tell Mama and Daddy."

I could tell he had mixed feelings about that, because he clenched his jaw, making it flex.

"Y'all still going out tonight?" Franki asked. She was standing beside me in Asha's bedroom doorway now.

"No. How can we just leave her at a time like this?" I said.

"Y'all go out and have fun," Asha insisted. "My girl Kiki is on the way over here anyway. She's probably gonna stay the night."

Malachi looked down at his sister, then gently rubbed the top of her head with care. "So you gon' be a'ight? You need anything?" he asked, admittedly being rather sweet.

"Nah, y'all just go. I'm about to jump in the shower," she replied.

With that, we all left Asha's room. For some reason, I was thinking that Malachi would flirt or say something to me before he left, but he didn't. He just stormed out the front door and allowed it to slam behind him.

As Franki was walking back to her room, she looked back at me. "So, what are you wearing again?"

I shook my head. "I just don't feel right about going out tonight," I admitted.

"Okay. Well, Hope, you come with me," Franki said. Hope followed behind her, and together they went inside her bedroom.

The day had been so overwhelming for me, comprised of so many highs and lows. Between the nail shop, the football game, and Asha being attacked, I didn't know what to make of it all. Without a second thought, I left back out of our suite for some fresh air. As I rode the elevator back downstairs, I was still very much shaken. Again, I'd never seen firsthand such a display of violence as that.

Once I pushed open the front door of Holland Hall, I took in a deep breath of air. The unmistakable smell of weed instantly invaded my nose. As I looked to my right, I saw Malachi standing on the side of the building with a lit joint suspended from his hand. His frustration was obvious as he used his other hand to wipe down the front of his face.

"Hey," I said, getting his attention. I walked over to where he stood. "You know you could get in trouble for smoking that out here, right?"

Instead of answering me, he put the joint up to his lips for a pull. The orange tip crackled and glowed in the darkness.

"You mind if I take a hit?" I asked.

Malachi's eyebrows instantly knit together as he gave me a puzzled expression. "You smoke?" he asked.

I simply nodded my head in response, because it was true. I was no stranger to weed. Hell, Heather and I had turned into complete potheads our senior year of high school. The only difference was, we preferred to smoke ours out of a bong. While

I think weed helped me cope with the loss of my father, it allowed her to be that much freer.

"Shawty, this ain't that watered-down legal shit y'all be buying out there in Cali," he warned.

"Well, thanks for your concern, but I can assure you that I'm a big girl," I told him, batting my eyes.

He let out a light snort of laughter. "A'ight, Mama, suit yourself," he said with a lazy grin.

When he passed over the joint, I quickly placed it between my lips and took a few small puffs. Although I'd never admit it to him, he definitely was smoking something potent. As soon as the smoke filled my lungs, I could feel myself getting baked. I closed my eyes and just tried to relax. After taking just a few more tokes, I heard people talking loudly in front of the building.

"We have to smoke somewhere else," I said, feeling paranoid.

"We?" he questioned with one of his eyebrows raised. "You speaking French now?"

I let out a giggle. "Well, I mean . . . you are going to share, aren't you?" I asked. Poking out my bottom lip, I gave him my most convincing set of puppy dog eyes.

He shook his head. "You something else, you know that? Come on. My car is right over there," he said, then pointed down the small alleyway on the side of the building.

I followed him to his car. Like a true gentleman, Malachi opened the car door and allowed me to slip inside. When he got in, he removed a pistol from his waist, then tucked it under his seat. I swallowed a big gulp of nerves. Never in my life had I seen a real live gun before, but I tried to play it cool. Slowly, he leaned his seat back and cranked up the engine before turning the radio on. My ears immediately recognized the sound of "It Ain't Me" by Selena Gomez. When he went to change the station, I reached out and lightly slapped his hand.

"The fuck?" he muttered, whipping his head in my direction to glare at me.

"Sorry," I said with an innocent shrug. "This is my song."

"This?" He pointed to the radio.

I nodded my head and began to sing the lyrics. "Who's gonna walk you through the dark side of the morning? Who's gonna rock you when the sun won't let you sleep? Who's waking up to drive you home when you're drunk and all alone?" I belted out passionately with my eyes closed.

"Damn, shawty, you sound horrible," he said, causing my eyes to pop open.

"Oh, shut up," I said, playfully hitting him in the arm.

He let out a little chuckle. "Sound just like Mary J. Blige without the auto tune," he joked.

I wagged my head. "Oh, no. Don't even go there about Mary."

His head quickly whipped back. "And what you know about Mary, witcho white ass?"

"First of all, I'm not white. 'Kay? Secondly, why would I not know MJB? She a living legend, for Christ's sake."

"Yeah, a living legend who *can't* really sing."

"What-evs," I told him, giving him the hand. "Besides, before my daddy got appointed, he used to represent her ex-husband, Kendu," I revealed.

He let out a sarcastic snort and shook his head. "Should've known," he muttered.

After we passed the joint back and forth a few more times, I saw Franki and Hope walk out of the building and stand at the top of the alleyway. More than likely, they were waiting on an Uber.

"Hey, would you mind giving my girls a ride to a party just a few blocks away?" I asked, glancing over at Malachi. "It looks like Hope's about to fall and break her ankle in those heels."

"Hmm . . . maybe," he said.

"Maybe? What do you mean? Either you will or you won't."

"Well, what am I gonna get out of it?" he asked with a sly grin on his face.

"Uh, how about being a Good Samaritan? Maybe I'll even call you a friend."

"I'll take them if you give me a kiss."

My eyes ballooned. "A kiss?" I shook my head.

"Damn. It's like that?"

"I don't know you, Malachi. And . . . and you're not my type. I've told you this."

"So, what that mean? I asked you for a kiss, not your hand in marriage, shawty."

I rolled the window down and stuck my head out of the car. I saw both Hope and Franki standing there shivering in their skimpy little outfits. *Poor Hope.* "You guys need a ride?" I hollered out.

Franki's head dipped forward in our direction as she narrowed her eyes. "Paris?"

"Yeah, it's me." I nodded vigorously. "Do you guys need a lift?" I asked again.

"Yeah!" she yelled back. Before I could say another word, she grabbed Hope's hand and shuffled toward the car.

I shifted in my seat until I was facing Malachi on the driver's side. "Just *one* kiss," I told him firmly, holding up my index finger for emphasis.

"One kiss, shawty. You got it," he confirmed, lifting both of his hands up in submission.

As the girls approached the car, I recognized the matching two-piece set of Franki's, which I was sure she had pressured Hope to wear. It was a rust-colored ensemble that included both leggings and a long-sleeved crop top that exposed her midriff. On her feet were a pair of brown high-heeled pumps. Although it wouldn't have been my first choice, given the cheap material, I had to admit that Hope did look a million times better than before. Her long hair cascaded down her back, and I could even see a hint of makeup on her face. *I guess the little outfit does give her more curves*, I thought. Hope's butt looked huge.

"You look so hot," I told her as she slipped into the back seat.

"This is so embarrassing. I'm practically naked, and my feet are hurting already," she whined.

"A bet's a bet, ma. Now, suck it up," Franki said, shutting the door. "And stop playing with your eyes," she fussed.

"You act like I wear contacts every day. They're irritating," Hope complained.

Malachi turned around and reached his hand through the seats. "I don't think we formally met back there. I'm Malachi," he said, shaking Franki's and then Hope's hands.

Once introductions were made, Franki told Malachi exactly where to go. We rode for about five minutes toward the other side of campus before pulling up to what appeared to be a frat house. Loud music poured from the two-story brick home, and people were out dancing and drinking on the lawn. Even the front porch was crowded with partygoers.

"You guys have fun," I told the girls as they exited the car. Malachi stayed put until they were finally out of view.

"Why didn't you go with them?" he asked, finally accelerating down the road.

I shrugged. "I don't know. I was going to, but after seeing everything with Asha today"—I swallowed hard and shook my head—"I just didn't feel up to it, you know?"

"Yeah, I feel you. That shit killed my plans too. Fucked up a nigga's *whole* vibe," he admitted.

"So, how did your sister even end up with a scumbag like him? Like, I just don't get it."

Malachi took a deep breath, then ran his hand down the waves of his hair. "We ain't grow up with no silver spoons in our mouths like you did, but we come from a good family. To this day, my mama still works for the Guildford County school system as a teacher, and my pops, he works for UPS. So as a family, we ain't never really struggled for shit."

I nodded, slipping my foot beneath me as I shifted toward him in my seat. For some reason, I wanted to get comfortable and give him my undivided attention.

"But then my senior year of high school, I fucked around and got caught up with the wrong shit. I joined a gang," he said, pointing to a black tattoo on his neck that boldly displayed the number 859. He looked over at me with furrowed brows, one hand on the wheel. "I can trust you, right?"

"Yes, you can trust me." I smiled.

"So, like I said, I started running with them niggas. Gangbanging, slanging rock, whatever was needed—I did that shit. And once I started getting money, I stopped trying to hide the shit from my parents. I moved out, got my own crib, my own car. Shid, eight fifty-nine—that was my family," he said.

"Wait, how old are you?" I asked.

"Twenty-three."

"Wow," I uttered in a low voice. "So what does this have to do with Asha?"

"Hold tight, mama. I'm finna tell you," he responded. "See, Asha saw me getting paper and wanted that shit for herself. Given that she was my baby sister, I would spoil her here and there, but when she started to hang with the crew, I said nah." He adamantly shook his head. "Fuck all that. My li'l sister too good for this shit, ya feel me? I wanted her to finish high school. Go to college and settle down. Maybe end up marrying some square-ass nigga. I don't know."

He shrugged and licked his lips. "But Asha's ass is hardheaded. Whatever I wouldn't buy her, she would get one of my partners to buy. Now, I ain't stupid by far. I know she got niggas out here tricking off on her ass, but what she fail to realize is that these cats she dealing with are on a whole 'nother level. She fuck around with the wrong nigga and get her ass got!"

My eyes widened in horror at his words.

"Now she done got caught up with Mark's punk ass. I can't believe she let them call the law . . ." His voice trailed off as he finally put the car in park. Just that fast, we were back in front of Holland Hall.

"Well, actually . . ." I hesitated. "No one called the police."

Malachi clenched his teeth, once again making the angle of his jaw flex. "She just didn't want me to get at the nigga, huh? I see what it is," he muttered, nodding his head.

"Don't be so hard on her. At least not today. She's really been through a lot."

He said nothing in response. When he cupped both of his hands around his nose and mouth, I sensed that he was really frustrated.

"You okay?" I asked, placing my hand on his shoulder.

He peered over at me and let out a deep sigh. "I'm a'ight. Thank you."

"For what?"

"For being there for my sister today. For kicking it with me tonight. All that," he said.

Taking in the vulnerable tone of his voice and the sudden softness in his eyes, I smiled. "Anytime, Malachi," I said.

Just as I turned to open the car door, Malachi gently grabbed me by the arm. Without even thinking, I turned back to face him but was immediately seized by the softness of his lips, which had crashed into mine. Malachi eased his hand to the base of my neck and parted my lips with his tongue. He kissed me so deeply that I think I literally stopped breathing. The only things I felt were the prickly goose bumps rising to the surface of my skin, my heart pounding relentlessly in my chest, and the smooth skin of Malachi's cheek, which was now resting beneath my palm.

When he pulled back, his bright hazel eyes were still focused on my lips. "You have a good night, Miss Paris," he said before taking his bottom lip between his teeth.

With one hand over my heaving chest and the other covering my lips, I tried to restore the air in my lungs. "You too," I barely whispered. As fast as I could, I jumped out of his car and headed to the front door of the dorm.

Chapter 12

Hope

Rock, Paper, Scissors

"Franki, I don't wanna go in there like this," I whined, wrapping my arms around my bare stomach in shame.

We were standing on the front porch of the frat house, ready to go inside, when I stopped in my tracks. Over and over, I kept envisioning the disappointed look on my father's face if he were to see me like this. Then there was Pastor Reeves and the members of my church. *What would they all have to say*? I kept asking myself.

"Come on." She reached for my hand and nudged me toward the door. "We aren't going to stay that long," she said.

I let out a deep sigh, because I knew that she was lying. Franki didn't leave parties until they shut down. That was just how she was. With as much fun as she'd been having these past couple of months, it was a wonder that she still managed to ace every single one of her tests. I guess she was just smart like that. Nonetheless, I allowed her to lead me inside.

We could barely walk over the threshold, because the place was so jam-packed. The music was blaring, and as we made our way through the crowd, we seemed to bump into bodies left and right. "Damn, li'l mama," some guy muttered, gawking at me like I was his next meal. I instantly hugged my body in hopes of shielding myself from his eyes.

"Come on. Let's go see if we can find some drinks," Franki said, pointing toward the back of the house.

We eventually ended up in the kitchen, where liquor bottles were lined up on every counter. There were a few people in there, but it wasn't as crammed or as loud as the front room. Franki immediately went to pour herself a drink.

"You're not going to mix it with anything?" I asked, watching her fill the red Solo cup to the brim.

She shrugged her shoulders. "What for? It's peach," she answered, referring to the peach Cîroc. Placing the cup up to her lips, Franki took a big swig and hummed as it went down. "Um, now, that's good. You want some?" she said as she looked at me.

"No, thank you." I scrunched up my nose.

"*Please*," she begged. "Just one eensy, weensy, teensy little shot?"

I shook my head. "Franki, you know I don't drink."

Her left eyebrow hiked up as a devilish grin suddenly spread across her face. "Rock, paper, scissors?"

I mulled it over for a second, wanting to redeem myself after the last time. "Fine," I sighed. "But if I win, we have to leave in the next hour."

"The next hour!" she complained.

"Yep. Deal?"

"Fuck it," she said, balling her hand into a fist.

"Rock, paper, scissors, shoot!" we chorused.

My mouth instantly dropped when I saw that she had paper this time, while I had made a stupid rock. "You've got to be kidding me," I groaned.

"Yo," Franki uttered before putting her fist up to her mouth to hold in a laugh. "We 'bout to get it in tonight, ma. Just me and my girl Hope, yo," she said, practically cheering.

"You said a *little* shot. That's all I'm drinking."

Franki was all smiles as she grabbed a clean cup and filled it a third of the way with vodka. "What you waiting on? Drink up," she urged, holding it out to me.

I took the cup from her hand and inhaled a deep breath. Just as I put the cup up to my lips, I heard Meeko's voice coming from behind me.

"Hope?" he called out.

As soon as I turned around, I could see his wide eyes moving down my frame. It was clear that he was marveling at me. "Wh-what you got on?" he asked.

Instantly, I froze in place. Although my mouth opened to respond, absolutely nothing came out.

"Dimples said she came to get her *drank* on tonight," Ty clowned with a chuckle. He, too, was eyeing my body as he stood next to Meeko.

Meeko cocked his head to the side and delivered a look of confusion. "So, you drinking now?" he asked, undoubtedly perplexed.

"I—I," I stuttered, my shoulders hiked, the cup of vodka unsteady in my hand.

Suddenly, a group of guys entered the kitchen and walked behind me to get through. "Damn, li'l mama thick with it too," I heard one of them say. I glanced over my shoulder to see that they were all staring at my butt. Immediately, I tried tucking it under my hips, in hopes of making it disappear.

"Yeah, your ass does look fat in those pants," Franki agreed with an approving nod and smile.

Ugh! I was now regretting that I had let her talk me into wearing these pants. To me, they looked more like workout tights than anything else. Definitely not something someone should be wearing to a party. Other than the tiny cross that hung from my necklace, I didn't even feel like myself.

"It damn sho do," Big Mo chimed in as he stepped into the kitchen. While he and Ty clapped hands together, sharing a hearty laugh at my expense, Meeko's face went cold.

"Hey, I see Jamel over there," Franki said, pointing at someone who was standing in the next room. "I'ma be right back, okay?"

I nodded my head, then went over to place the cup back on the counter. Suddenly, I felt someone's presence close behind me. I didn't even have to look back to know that it was Meeko. I had already committed the scent of his cologne to memory. As he planted his arms around me and placed his hands on the counter, I felt him rest his chin on my shoulder.

"I'm not used to you looking like this," he whispered. "And you drinking too? What happened to my li'l sweet, innocent Hope?" he asked.

I spun around to face him, my body slightly pressing into his. "I lost a stupid bet. Well, two, actually," I said, rolling my eyes.

"Hmm." He gently stroked his hand down my hair, then rolled the ends between his fingers. "I do like your hair like this, though," he admitted.

I smiled. "Why are you always talking about my hair?"

He shrugged. "I'on know. Where I'm from, most girls don't have long hair that's real like this. And if they do, they stuck up," he explained.

"Hmm," I said in response. "Oh, I forgot to congratulate you guys on the big win today. You looked great out there."

As I stared into Meeko's warm brown eyes, I could feel myself cheesing from ear to ear. He stuck the tip of his finger inside the crater I must've made in my cheek. "Thanks," he said.

"Meeko!" I heard someone suddenly call out. We both looked over to see the tall, light-skinned girl with the green eyes. She had her arms folded across her breasts, and the expression she wore could only be called pissed. "What are you doing?" she asked with an attitude.

Meeko stepped back from me and frowned. "What the fuck it look like? I'm talking," he told her.

"Oh, shit," I heard Big Mo mutter.

"Well, you not about to sit here and disrespect me, I know that. I don't care what li'l game you *think* you playing." Suddenly, her gaze shifted over to me, and I could see her slowly taking in my appearance. Given the unexpected flare of her nostrils, I knew that she wasn't too impressed. "Don't let this li'l girl get you embarrassed," she snarled.

Meeko charged over and yanked her up by the collar. "Lemme holla at you for a minute," he said, then practically dragged her into the other room.

I looked over at Ty, who just shrugged, while Big Mo simply shook his head and laughed.

"Is that his girlfriend?" I asked. "Because he specifically told me that he didn't have a girlfriend."

"Man," Big Mo drawled with a sigh. "I don't know what that girl's problem is. Come on in here with us while he handles his business," he said.

Reluctantly, I followed behind Big Mo and Ty as they entered a den area at the back of the house. There were a lot of people in there smoking and playing cards, but I was somehow able to find a seat. After I plopped down on one of the sofas, Ty squeezed right in next to me. Big Mo was pulled away by some girl, who was now shaking her butt all over him in the corner.

"I'm just ready to go," I complained.

"Ah." Ty chuckled. "What? You let Jazz get under your skin?" he asked knowingly.

"Jazz," I muttered.

Ty tapped me on the thigh. "Look, man, just relax and have a good time. Let him worry about shorty, a'ight?"

"But why did he lie to me?" I was so confused.

"I have no idea, Hope." He shrugged. "But, aye, did you talk to your girl for me yet?" he asked, referring to Paris.

Wearing a deep frown, I simply shook my head.

"Look, come on." He stood up and reached down for my hand. After he pulled me to my feet, he began dancing in front of me.

I stood in place, feeling extremely awkward. Then finally, I leaned in and whispered in his ear, "I don't dance, Ty."

He nodded and flashed me a smile. "I know. I'm just trying to loosen you up a little bit," he said.

Without warning, he grabbed me by the waist and began twisting me from side to side. At first, it was embarrassing, but as he playfully sang the lyrics to the song, dancing up and down my body with his tongue hanging out of his mouth, I couldn't help but laugh.

"Watchin' me whip up, still be real and famous. Dance with my dogs in the nighttime. Yeah, woo, woo, woo, roof. In the kitchen, wrist twistin' like a stir fry. Whip it," he sang, dramatically twisting his wrists. Then he pulled me in close and put his lips up to my ear. "What you know about Migos, Hope?" he asked.

Just as I shook my head to let him know that I'd never heard of them before, I felt someone grab me by the hand. I looked back and saw that it was Meeko. "What y'all got going on over here?" he asked, looking exclusively at Ty.

Ty let out a low snort of laughter. "It ain't like that, homeboy, so just chill out. 'Cause I can already see you flexing for nothing."

Looking back and forth between the two of them, I felt even more confused than I had before.

"Whatever, yo," Meeko grumbled before placing a beer bottle to his lips for a quick swig. Then he grabbed me by the waist and pulled me down with him on the couch. All of a sudden, I was sitting in his lap openly.

With a smirk on his face, Ty shook his head and walked off. I watched as he grabbed some girl from across the room and began to dance again.

"I don't think this is appropriate. Since you have a girlfriend and all," I said, trying to get up from his lap. However, Meeko held me in place.

"I already done told you, that ain't my girlfriend. She's just a friend," he said with certainty.

Narrowing my eyes at him, I looked for the truth in his gaze. "Well, why is she acting like that, Meek?"

A big, beautiful smile crested upon his face.

"What? This is no laughing matter," I told him.

"I know. It's just . . . you called me Meek."

"Oh," I said lowly, not even realizing that I had given him a nickname. "Sorry, I just . . ."

Meeko grabbed me gently by the chin and peered into my eyes. All words momentarily escaped me.

My pulse was racing, and suddenly I felt tingles in places that had never tingled before. Without warning, he placed his face next to mine and whispered in my ear. Naturally, I closed my eyes.

"You staying with me tonight?" Meeko asked.

As his thumb grazed down my cheek, my eyes fluttered open. I didn't know what to say, so I simply tucked my lips inward and remained quiet.

"What up, Meeko?" said some guy who had walked up out of nowhere. "You did your thing out there today."

"Thanks, yo," Meeko told him with a chuck of his chin.

"Well, I ain't gon' hold you. I see you with your girl and all," the guy said.

Girl?

As the guy strolled on, Meeko slid me off his lap. "I'll be right back. I'm going to the bathroom," he said.

I waited for about five or so minutes before I finally got up to find Franki. If I was going to spend the night with Meeko, I at least wanted to let her know. This would be my second time staying with him, and I was feeling a mix of emotions. Of course, I was excited, because Meeko was every girl's dream: tall, dark, and handsome. Although he was one of the most popular guys on campus, he could be so sweet at times. But I was also feeling very nervous. I kept asking myself over and over if he would now expect more from me. Especially since it felt like things had somehow shifted between us now. Then there was this part of me that felt constant guilt and shame. I knew I'd have to repent morning, noon, and night just for the carnal thoughts that were running rampant through my brain. I hadn't even had my first kiss yet, but each time Meeko spoke, I'd carefully watched his lips, hoping that they'd one day devour mine.

As I squeezed my way through the crowd, my ears pounded inside from the loud music. I looked high and low for Franki, but she was nowhere to be found. Finally, my eyes landed on Josh. He was standing by the front door, talking and laughing with a pretty girl at his side. When he noticed me watching him, he raised his chin and smiled.

"Hey, Josh," I practically yelled. I slid in between a few more people and made my way over to him. "You seen Franki?" I asked.

Josh sucked his teeth and frowned at the mere mention of her name. Honestly, that surprised me, because I thought he might have a crush on her. "She went upstairs with Jamel somewhere," he said nonchalantly, shrugging one of his shoulders.

I thanked him and turned back around to make my way upstairs. Before I could reach the staircase, I felt someone bump into me. I looked up to see Jazz's green eyes glaring back at me.

"Oh, excuse me," I said, attempting to walk around her.

I was caught completely off guard when she pushed me back. "So, what? You thought I was gon' just let shit slide?" she asked and cocked her head.

I looked over my shoulder because I was certain that she wasn't talking to me.

"Yeah, I'm talking to you, bitch! So you thought I was just gonna let you come in here and take my man?"

Shaking my head, I put both hands up in surrender.

"Ugly dark bitch!" she seethed.

"Look, I don't want any trouble," I told her.

Her eyes were burning with anger. "Nah, you looking for trouble, all right. Seeing as how you were in there"—she pointed to the back of the house—"all hugged up on my man." She curled her hands into fists at her sides. "Y'all fucking?" she asked point-blank.

"I—"

That was all I got out before I was hit with a hard blow to the face. I immediately covered myself with both hands for protection, but eventually, there were multiple fists striking my body at every angle. In less than sixty seconds, I was on the floor, curled up in the fetal position, suffering spiked heels and hard boots kicking at my back and skull. My long hair felt like it was practically being ripped from my scalp. All the while I just lay there, hands covering my face while I screamed out Franki's name. The sound of my cries seemed to be overpowered by the blaring sounds of the music and the hyped crowd that had quickly formed around us. My vision unexpectedly went black, and slowly, I could feel myself starting to fade away.

Chapter 13

Franki

Even through the Pain

"Yo, what are you doing?" I giggled.

Exactly eight minutes ago, Jamel had led me up the stairs and into one of the vacant bedrooms of the fraternity house. I was now above the covers in some stranger's bed, with him kissing all over my neck. The room was completely dark, and all I could hear was the thumping of the music down below us.

As his fingers slithered up my bare thighs and beneath the dress I wore, I became lightheaded. All of a sudden, the room was spinning, and my words were coming out slurred. "Jamel. Hold up," I tried to say.

However, Jamel didn't let up. He hiked my dress farther above my hips and pried his fingers into the waistband of my panties. My heart was now beating erratically. Clearly, something wasn't right. My mind traveled back to the last drink I'd had. It was a cup of PJ that Jamel had gone and got for me.

"Wait!" I think I said, but honestly, I don't know if the word even came out right.

"Stop fighting, baby, and let me take care of you," he whispered against my skin.

When I heard the bedroom door creak open, a flash of light peered through the darkness. I attempted to put my palms up against his hard chest, but I was just too weak. My limbs felt totally lifeless.

"Stop," I said softly, but again, he didn't. He was now sliding my panties down over my thighs.

Suddenly, the shadows of two men entered the room before I heard the door close and then lock. I could hear their footsteps coming closer to the bed as the stench of alcohol conquered the room. Although my mind was telling me to get up and fight, I could hardly move. My eyes were closing against my will, and again, my heart was pounding out of tune.

"Hope. Help me," I whispered in a desperate plea.

The clicking sound of the lamp next to me got my attention. With the light now on, I could clearly see Levar and Twan. Levar was one of Josh's frat brothers. He was this short little guy with big, bulging muscles, ordinary brown skin, and a dark pair of bug eyes. He kept a low haircut and had a chipped tooth in the front. Twan, on the other hand, wasn't a part of their fraternity. He and Jamel would just hang from time to time. He was tall and lanky like a Russian basketball player, his arms practically hanging down to his knees. His pimply face and skin was the color of butterscotch, and his hair was always in an unkempt 'fro.

"The more the merrier, right, baby?" Jamel said into my ear before swirling his tongue inside it.

As Jamel lay on top of me with his thick body wedged between my thighs, I could feel tears slowly trickling down my face. I screamed out for God's help, but only a low murmur escaped me. Before I knew what was happening, Jamel lowered his pants and reached down between us to pull out his dick.

"I know you love this nasty shit," he groaned, wrapping his hand around my neck before sliding his hard muscle inside me. He was hurting me, but at this point, I couldn't even speak. Although Jamel and I had been having sex pretty regularly for the past few weeks, nothing about this felt right. I was no longer in control, and I had never felt so low in all my life.

My eyes fluttered open, and I saw that his friends were now starting to undress as well. It was at that very moment that I knew that they were going to rape me.

Over and over, Jamel drilled into my limp body until he finally released. No condom served as a barrier between us. As his heavy body rested on top of me, I looked over to see Twan and Levar now completely naked. Both were holding their hard-ons in their hands. When Jamel finally lifted himself up, out of breath, he kissed my forehead. I just wanted to throw up. He climbed out of the bed, and I watched him take a white hand towel off the nightstand to dab the beads of sweat from his brow before wiping his privates.

Then came Twan. When he climbed on top of me, he smelled like he had drunk an entire gallon of vodka by himself. Just as he lifted my wilting thighs, the sound of sirens blared outside the house. Blue and red lights flashed through the windows as a hard knock sounded on the bedroom door.

"Who the fuck is that?" Twan asked in a hushed tone.

Jamel shrugged his shoulders and proceeded to zip his jeans back up.

"Yo, is Franki in there?" I heard Josh ask from the other side of the door.

Help me. Please.

"Nah," Jamel answered.

As Twan covered my mouth with his sweaty hands, more tears slipped from eyes.

"Well, if you see her, tell her that they're taking her girl to the hospital," Josh said through the closed door. *Hope?* "The police are shutting the whole party down and asking everyone to evacuate."

I looked up and was somehow able to lock gazes with Twan. Pleading only with my eyes, I silently asked for him to release me. He bit down on the corner of his lip, then said, "Fuck! We gotta get out of here." He unpinned my legs and got up from the bed. I could see his long piece of meat dangling between his legs.

"Damn, I didn't even get to get my dick sucked," Levar complained.

"Next time, man. She loves this type of shit," Jamel told him.

Once they were all dressed, they walked out of the room and left the door wide open. Not one of them had had the decency to cover me up. The lower half of my body was naked and completely exposed. I was still unable to move, and I felt like all I wanted to do was go to sleep.

As time went on, I eventually drifted off, but at some point, I was awakened by someone shaking my shoulder. My eyes opened partially due to the bright sun that was now pouring into the room. The first face I saw was Josh's pretty self. He was sitting next me on the bed, wearing an unreadable expression. When I thought back to the horrific events of the night before, I inadvertently looked down at my body. I now had a blanket covering me.

"What time is it?" I croaked. My mouth was extremely dry.

"It's almost noon," he said.

I tried to sit up but immediately had to lie back down because my head was throbbing.

"Oh *God*," I said, grabbing my forehead.

"Here. Take this." He handed me two small pills and a glass of water.

You would think that after everything I'd experienced the night before, I would've questioned what Josh was giving me, but I didn't. I just popped the pills in my mouth and swallowed them down. For some reason, I trusted him. Perhaps it was the whole church boy thing. I didn't quite know.

Suddenly, a thought occurred to me. "Oh, shit. Where's Hope?" I asked in a panic.

"They took her to the hospital in the ambulance last night."

"Hospital?"

"Yeah." He sighed before swiping his hand over his face. "She got banked. Meeko's girl, Jazz, and a few of her friends caught her while she was looking around for you," he said. Again, there was that flicker of disapproval in his eyes.

"Damn," I muttered, all of a sudden feeling guilty. "I gotta get over there. Can you take me up to the hospital?" I tried to sit up in the bed for a second time, and this time I succeeded, ignoring the pain in my head.

"Yeah, come on. My truck's outside," he said. As he stood up and walked toward the door, my eyes absorbed his tall frame. I could see the lean muscles of his back beneath the white T-shirt he wore. He had on slim blue jeans and Timberland boots, their tongues flapping as he walked.

I eased to the edge of the bed, feeling slightly sore from last night. I managed to stand, and as I pulled my dress down over my hips, my eyes fell to the floor. Instantly, I spotted my red panties. I glanced up only to find that Josh's eyes were on them as well.

He let out a little snort. "Wild night, huh?" he asked.

"It wasn't like that," I told him.

I shot across the room and immediately snatched my panties off the floor. When I stood upright, I noticed a long mirror in front of me. I glanced at myself in the mirror and saw that I was standing there in the shortest dress I owned. Curly hair all over my head, with black mascara stains around my eyes. I looked like a hooker straight out of a horror movie.

"Ain't none of my business, ma," Josh mumbled. "I'ma be outside."

When he walked out of the room, I wanted to scream out, "*I was raped!*" but I didn't. I slipped on yesterday's panties in silence before sinking my feet into my heels. As I walked down the stairs of the frat house, I was half expecting to see Jamel or one of the other guys, but the house appeared to be empty. Only the remnants of last night's party could be seen.

I made a quick stop in the half bath at the bottom of the stairs. After washing my face and rinsing my mouth out, I ran my fingers through my hair. Once I was somewhat satisfied with my reflection, I went looking for my leather jacket. I ended up finding it in the kitchen, where I'd last seen Hope. I could only *pray* that she was all right.

As I headed out the front door, I saw Josh waiting in his truck for me. I trekked across the leaf-covered lawn, listening to the constant crunch beneath my feet.

"Do you know which hospital she's at?" I asked after I pulled open the passenger door. Greensboro was all new to me, so I really didn't know one hospital from the other.

"Cone, I think," he said.

When I hopped in, he motioned for me to put my seat belt on, and then we took off. For a while, we just drove in silence. I was thinking about the bits and pieces of last night that I could actually remember, while he just kept his eyes on the road ahead. As we pulled up to a red light about fifteen minutes later, I saw a blue hospital sign out the window.

"We must be getting close," I said.

"Yeah, just a few more lights down." After a pregnant pause, he looked over at me and said, "Can I ask you something?"

"I guess," I said, shrugging my shoulders.

"What do girls get out of having trains run on them?"

My neck jerked back, and I could feel my eyes stretch wide. "How the fuck should I know!" I snapped.

Judging by the embarrassed look on his face, I immediately knew he didn't mean any harm. My reaction had caught him completely off guard. In all fairness, it wasn't even two weeks ago when I'd told him much how I liked to fuck and how I didn't care about being called a ho. It was all total bullshit.

"My bad, ma," he said. "I just thought . . . you know. Last night . . ."

My throat began to constrict, and I could feel the water welling in my eyes. "I was raped, Josh," I finally confessed through a whisper.

He was stunned to complete silence. In fact, the light had turned green many seconds ago, yet he still had his foot planted on the brake pedal. When horns started honking behind us, he let out a deep sigh and took off down the road. For the remainder of the ride, we didn't even speak, and I was regretting the fact that I'd even told him at all.

When we pulled up to the hospital, he quickly found a parking spot up close. As soon as he killed the engine, I grabbed the door handle to let myself out.

"Why didn't you tell me this when you first woke up this morning?" Josh asked out of nowhere.

I looked over at him and hunched my shoulders. "I don't know," I said lowly.

"Franki, you need to tell the police. This probably happens all the time, and don't nobody ever say nothing." He was quiet for a bit, like he was thinking of something. "Was it all three of them?" he asked nervously.

Taking a deep inhale, I mentally recalled the events of last night. "I think Jamel put something in my drink, because I could barely move or even talk. I thought we were going upstairs to, you know . . ." I cleared my throat, suddenly feeling embarrassed. "Make out or whatever," I said sheepishly. "Well, not long after my head hit the pillow, I started feeling dizzy. I kept telling him to stop, but he wouldn't listen. Then Twan and Levar entered the room." Taking a hard swallow, I shook my head. My hands were now trembling and, *fuck*, I could now feel tears.

Josh leaned over the console and swiped his thumb beneath my eye. "Stop crying, ma. You gon' make me cry," he said as soft as his voice would allow.

For some reason, envisioning his gay ass crying made me laugh a little, even in the midst of my pain.

"What? That's funny to you?" he asked, trying to lighten the mood.

"Yeah, I always figured you to be a crier," I clowned, sniffing back tears.

"You got jokes, huh?" he said with only a half smile, removing a wispy curl from my face. Then his eyes turned intense again as he gazed at me. "So then what happened?"

I clamped my eyes shut and shook my head, not even wanting to remember what had taken place.

"Tell me," he urged.

"Jamel raped me, and if you . . ." I was so choked up at that point that I could barely let go of the words. I sucked in a deep breath, and when I finally opened my eyes, a lone tear slid down my cheek. "If you hadn't knocked on the door and told us that the police were downstairs, Levar and Twan would've raped me too."

I could see Josh grit his teeth in anger. "Damn, ma," he muttered. Leaning over the console again, he slipped his arms around me and allowed me to bury my face in his chest. His body was warm, and his scent was comforting. "When we leave here, I'm taking you to file the report," he said.

I shook my head. "No! I'm not filing a report. I don't want to get the police involved."

He pulled back and looked at me like I was crazy. "Yo, ma, don't do this. Fa' real," he said. "What if they do this to other girls? You gon' be able to live with yourself after that?"

"I just want to forget it ever happened," I told him. "Please, yo, just let it go. Forget I ever told you, a'ight?"

Josh's eyes burned with fury, and I could see that he was clearly pissed by my response. As I opened the truck door to get out, I heard him say behind my back, "So whoever knows the right thing to do and fails to do it, for him it is sin."

I glanced back at him over my shoulder. "No need to throw scriptures at me, Josh. I already know I'm a sinner."

With that, I got out and walked up to the hospital's entrance without him. I knew that Josh would judge me and my decision, so now I was angry at myself for even confiding in him in the first place. It was just that I was feeling so vulnerable, and I needed to let it all out. Not only that, but I felt like Josh had practically saved me from getting gang-raped. What I experienced with Jamel was bad enough, but who knows what kind of damage would've been done if Josh hadn't knocked on that door.

When I reached the nurses' station, I grabbed a Kleenex out of the box on the counter and asked for Hope's room. One of the nurses told me that she was in room 226, so I rushed over to the elevator and headed on up. As I traveled down the hall, I tried eliminating my own burdens from my mind. I wanted to be there for Hope. Once I reached her door, I noticed that it was already open.

From out in the hallway, I could see an older man sitting at the foot of her bed. As I stepped into the room, my eyes immediately flew over to Hope. "Oh *God*," I gasped, covering my mouth with both hands.

I could barely recognize the person lying back in the bed in front of me. The only reason I knew it was her was that I saw Paris curled up in the lone chair in the corner. Both of Hope's eyes were swollen shut. She had a bloodstained bandage around her head, as well as a cast on her left arm. Her lips were doubled in size, and her pretty dark brown complexion was now all black and blue.

"Franki," she croaked out.

Paris sat up in the chair and looked at me. "Franki, where have you been?"

"I—I." I was paralyzed.

"Franki, I screamed for you," Hope whispered.

I screamed for you too, I thought.

"Franki!" Paris yelled again.

"I—I'm sorry. I'm so sorry that I couldn't get to you, Hope. Had I known . . ."

"I'm Hope's father," the older man finally said as he rose to his feet. "So you're the one she went to the party with?"

"Yes, sir." I dropped my head in shame.

He shook his head like he, too, was disappointed in me. "Look, my daughter is all I have left. She doesn't need to be out here partying and getting caught up with the likes of you. I sent her out here for an education. That's it." Then he turned to Hope. "You're coming back home."

"Deddy, no!" Hope cried. I could see water forming in the creases of her puffy eyes.

"For Christ's sake, Hope, look at you! Sitting in a hospital bed because you were out there fighting over a boy, and God only knows what else you've been up to. Not once have you gone to church since you've been out here. You never call home anymore, and look what you're out here wearing!" He raised a clear bag containing the outfit I'd let her borrow the night before. "Your mother is probably rolling over in her grave."

At the mere mention of her mother, Hope wept out uncontrollably.

"I will not allow you to succumb to the devil and give in to his worldly ways," her father continued. "You're coming back home, and that's not up for debate!" With that, Hope's father stormed past me and exited the room.

My eyes cut over to Hope, whose shoulders shook from crying so hard.

"Franki, I can't believe you just left her like that. What happened to us having each other's back?" Paris asked as she put her arms around Hope in an attempt to console her.

Before I could respond, I felt a sudden presence behind me. I figured that Hope's father had come back in the room, but when I glanced over my shoulder, I saw Josh.

He said, "Look, I know y'all not trying to hear this, but it's really not Franki's fault. I was there. I was one of the guys trying to break up the fight—"

"It wasn't a fucking fight, Josh! Look at her face," Paris interrupted and pointed to Hope. "She was fucking attacked."

"So, let me ask you this. What's Meeko got to say, huh? Where he at?" Josh quizzed, fuming.

"He called me when it all happened, and he was up here with her all night. But as soon as her father got here, he kicked him out," Paris explained.

Josh shook his head. "Regardless, shorty was fighting Hope over him. He gotta have something to say for that."

"He said that he would handle her, but I really don't even know what that means," Hope uttered.

Suddenly, Hope's father reentered the room with a nurse behind him. "Everybody needs to get out. My daughter needs her rest," he said.

I walked over to Hope's bedside and gently grabbed her by the hand. "I'm sorry this happened to you. But don't you worry. I'm gon' see that bitch again," I promised.

She shook her head. "It's okay, Franki. I'll be all right." She gave me a crooked smile and lightly squeezed my hand.

Josh, Paris, and I headed back downstairs and hopped into his truck. Of course, Paris rode in the front, while I sat in the back. By the time we made it back to campus, the sky was already turning gray. I hadn't had a thing to eat all day, but I wasn't even hungry, I just wanted to get in bed.

"Thanks for the ride, Josh," Paris said before letting herself out of the truck.

Just as I reached for the door handle to get out as well, Josh called my name. "Aye, Franki."

I looked back and saw that his hand was extended through the seats. He was holding an old receipt that had his number scribbled on the back. "If you ever need to talk, ma." He dipped his head down toward the paper. "I'm only a phone call away."

I gave him a closed-lip smile as I took the small slip of paper from between his fingers. "Thanks, Josh. I'll keep that in mind."

Chapter 14

Paris

Birthday Probability

As I lay in bed, my eyes shifted over to the clock on my nightstand. Today was my birthday, and as of 12:43 p.m. I had yet to receive one single birthday wish. I hadn't heard from my mother, which didn't surprise me, because I hadn't heard from her in months. Even when I was in high school, she had never made a big deal out of my birthday. She'd just send me off with friends to do some shopping with her Black Card, but I never spent any real time with her.

Then there was Franki, who for the past few weeks had been extremely distant. Every day she would go straight to class, then come right back and lock herself in her room. She rarely spoke to me these days, and I could only assume it was

because of the guilt she felt over Hope's attack.
Speaking of Hope, she hadn't been back to the
dorm since she was discharged from the hospital.
Every blue moon I would catch her on campus,
which was how I had found out that she was now
living with her aunt Marlene, at least until the
end of the semester. After the whole incident with
Mark, it seemed as if Asha kept right on going with
her life. It was as if it never even happened. She
went right back to not speaking or acknowledging
any of us, and whenever she did, there was always
that lingering chip on her shoulder.

Suddenly, my cell phone vibrated beside me on
the bed. I picked it up and saw my and Heather's
face flashing across the screen. I rushed to answer
her call. "Bestie," I said cheerfully.

"Happy birthday, bitch!" she screamed into my
ear.

My lips instantly spread from east to west.
"Thank you, babe. What are you doing?"

"What am *I* doing?" she stressed. "I should be
asking you that. It's your birthday."

I quickly thought about lying and telling her
about a bunch of made-up plans I had for the day,
but then I just sighed. "I'm not doing anything.
Just laying here in my bed, actually."

"Aw," she cooed. "You sound totally bummed,
Par."

"I'll be all right. I've got some studying to do anyways."

"And Franki's still down in the dumps?" she asked. Heather and I talked almost every day, so she was fully aware of everything that had occurred on homecoming weekend.

"I guess. I haven't seen her today," I said and sighed again.

"And I guess Cruella de Vil didn't call either, huh?" she asked, referring to my mother.

I let out a tired little laugh. "Nope. Haven't heard from her."

"Well, what about that thug guy? The one you kissed. Have you talked to him?" she asked.

Malachi.

"Nope," I said again.

"And just why the hell not? You said that kiss was everything. Do I need to remind you?" she demanded. "He had you *so* horny, remember?" She giggled and then started moaning all crazy into the phone like a childish middle schooler. This was exactly why I should've never told her.

I simply rolled my eyes. "Okay, enough," I said, trying to put an end to her silliness. "I just don't want to be the one to call. I don't want to seem . . . thirsty."

She laughed. "Dude, you need to get over it and just call the man. He doesn't even have your phone number, remember?"

I pursed my lips. "Well, he knows how to find me . . . if he really wanted to."

"I swear, you're so high maintenance. For once, just let your hair down and do something out of the ordinary. You turn eighteen only once," she told me.

For a split second, I considered her words. It was true that every night for the past seventeen days, I had gone to sleep with that kiss on my mind. I could still smell his scent, and I don't think I'd ever be able to forget the sweet taste of his lips. Malachi was every bit of a thug from the way he walked and talked, even down to the way he wore his clothes. And never in my life had I been attracted to excessive tattoos, gold teeth, and gaudy jewelry on a man, but . . . there was something about Malachi that I couldn't quite put my finger on.

"Fine," I blurted. "I'll call him."

"Oh my God!" Heather squealed. Just hearing the excitement bubble over in her voice, I could only imagine the stupid little dance she was probably doing in her seat. "Call me as soon as you hang up with him, 'kay? Don't forget. Bye," she said, rushing her words, and then she hung up the phone.

I sat there for five whole minutes, just trying to gather up enough courage to call him. Finally, I scrolled through my contacts, where I found his number stored under the name My Malachi. I hadn't notice it when he plugged his number in at the nail shop. *Cute.* I tapped the screen and held my breath as the phone rang.

One ring turned into two and then quickly turned into three. But just as I started to hang up, I heard his voice come through the phone.

"Yuh," he answered.

I cleared my throat. "Malachi?"

"Who dis?"

"Um. It's me . . . Paris." My leg nervously bounced up and down as I waited for him to respond.

"Ah, Miss Paris," he said in his smooth but raspy tone. "So, what's up, Mama? How you been?"

"I've been okay. Just trying to find something to get into today." I was still undecided as to whether I should tell him that today was my birthday. I was sure he'd think I was a real loser if I was calling *him* to spend my special day with me.

"Shit, me too," he said with a hint of a smile in his voice. "You gon' come fuck wit' a nigga today?"

"Excuse me?" I had no earthly idea what he was asking me.

"Can I take you out today, Miss Paris?" he asked in the most proper way he could.

"Oh, yes." I let out a little laugh. "Yes, you can take me out."

"A'ight. Well, I'm gon' swing through around six. Is that cool?"

I really didn't want to wait all the way until six o'clock to finally do something on my birthday, but instead of putting up a fuss, I simply said, "Six o'clock sounds good."

It was now a quarter past seven, and I still hadn't heard from Malachi. Here I was, standing in a sexy red dress from Chanel, with five-inch Manolos on my feet. I'd spent more than an hour curling my hair and trying to apply my makeup just right. I couldn't believe that Malachi had stood me up, and on my birthday, no less. Other than the phone call earlier from Heather, not one other person had acknowledged the day I was born. At this point, I was just over the whole damn day.

As I kicked off my shoes, I reached up and took my left earring out of my ear. Just as soon as my hands went around to take out the other, I heard a text chiming through. I reached down and grabbed my phone off the dresser.

My Malachi: I'm outside.

"He's got some fucking nerve," I muttered, rolling my eyes.

I slid my feet back into my heels and put my earring back on before going downstairs to meet him. At the moment, I no longer had a desire to go out with him. My day had been completely ruined, and I was allocating him half the blame. When I walked out into the cold, I saw his Benz parked directly out front. I wobbled across the lawn, feeling my heels sink into the ground along the way.

When I finally reached the car, I just stood there fuming, with my arms folded across my chest. It took him only a few seconds to realize that I wasn't getting in. He rolled down the window, allowing a cloud of smoke to escape, before leaning over the passenger seat.

"What's up, shawty? You ain't getting in?" he asked, demeanor cool as a fucking fan cap.

Unbelievable.

"So, let me get this right. You come here over an hour late. No phone call, no text, nothing. Then instead of you coming up to get me, you send me some thoughtless text saying, 'I'm outside,'" I said, fussing, making air quotes with my hand. "Like, *dude*. Who the fuck do you think you're dealing with?" I ranted, dramatically raising my arms up in the air. "And now you're sitting here asking me if I'm going to get in your car? Get the fuck outta here!" I spat, mimicking Franki to a tee.

Malachi got out of his car and calmly walked around. My eyes swept over him, and I was unable to deny just how good he looked, from the lambskin leather jacket he wore, which I knew cost a few grand, to the Prada jeans and the matching boots. Haircut lined to perfection as diamonds glistened from both his teeth and his neck. He looked just like a rich, famous rapper. The entire time I checked him out, I could see this stupid little smirk on his face. I swear, I just wanted to slap it off.

When he got in front of me, he cockily leaned back against his car and rubbed his chin. "So, what you want, Miss Paris? An apology?" He was too calm.

"You're damn right!" I shouted. He continued to smirk, making me even more pissed. "And what's so goddamn funny?" I asked.

He shook his head and let out a little chuckle. "Ain't nothing funny, shawty. It's just . . . you look beautiful as fuck when you're mad."

I couldn't care less about the sudden moisture in my panties; he was not about to charm me. "I look beautiful even when I'm *not* mad, so save that line for someone else," I returned.

"Look." He held his hands up in surrender, then placed one hand over his heart. "I apologize. I got caught up with work, but I should've called."

Even though I could hear the sincerity in his voice, I just stood there giving him a blank look. That was just how riled up he had me.

"So, what, you ain't got nothing to say?" he asked, leaning away from the car before stepping into me.

"Fine. Apology accepted," I said lowly with a shake of my head.

When I turned around to go back inside the dorm, he said, "So you not gon' roll out with me, Miss Paris? You just gon' waste that sexy-ass dress?"

Shit, he was right. It was my birthday, and I did look good.

"Fine," I responded.

I walked back to his car and quickly opened the passenger door. In my mind, he had blown all chances of being classified as a gentleman, so when I slid in, I swiftly shut the door behind me. I didn't even grant him the opportunity to let me in. All thoughts of this evening turning out to be romantic had been completely destroyed. My only hope at this point was to maybe get a meal out of the deal. That was my last birthday wish, a full belly.

When he got in on the driver's side, he just looked at me.

"What?" I asked with an attitude.

He let out a little snort and shook his head. "Look, if you gon' be a brat all night, then just get the fuck on. I done already apologized, which is some shit I *don't* do. So, if you wanna leave, shawty, there go the fucking door." He pointed.

I was completely taken aback by how he had just spoken to me. And although I truly wanted to give him a piece of my mind, the crazed look in his eyes told me to just shut up and ride, which was exactly

what I did. For the next twenty minutes or so, the
two of us just rode in silence. Then, finally, we
pulled up to a restaurant named Dame's Chicken
and Waffles. From the looks of it outside, the place
appeared to be just a step up from a quick carryout
spot.

I was used to my dates taking me to restaurants
such as Spago or Maude on Beverly Drive, where
the valet would park your car, fine linens draped
every table, and the prices weren't even on the
menu. But for some odd reason, Malachi thought
it would be a good idea to take a girl like *me* to a
place like *this*. I just didn't understand it. He drove
a brand-new Mercedes-Benz, and every time I saw
him, he was draped in the most expensive clothes.
I knew he could afford to take me somewhere nice,
so what was the point of all of this?

"What's this?" I asked with an attitude.

"This little spot right here got some banging-ass
food. Come on," he told me before getting out of
the car.

When we stepped into the restaurant, I took a
good look around. The atmosphere was quaint.
Cheap tiled floor, booth seating, and the smell of
fried chicken floating in the air. Definitely nothing
to write home about, but I would make do. I was
starving.

Not even ten seconds had passed before a cute
little hostess appeared and smiled in Malachi's

direction. "Hey, Malachi. Table in the back?" she asked.

"Yuh," he answered. As the hostess led the way, Malachi put his arm around my waist and guided me to the back of the restaurant. For some reason, I didn't pull away.

When I slid into the booth, Malachi said, "Nah, ma. That's my seat."

"Why can't you just sit right there?" I asked, pointing to the seat across from me.

He just glared at me and waited.

"Fine," I huffed. I got up and moved over to the other side of the booth.

After we ordered our food, Malachi just sat there staring at me.

"What?" I asked.

"Why you so mean, Miss Paris?"

"I'm not mean. I just have standards," I told him.

"And I don't meet your standards?"

Although I wanted to tell him that, no, he didn't meet my standards, my kind nature wouldn't allow me to do so. Instead, I just shrugged my shoulders.

Malachi took a sip of the beer he'd ordered, then looked at me as if he were waiting on me to speak. When I didn't say anything, he asked, "So, what made you come all this way for school?"

"My mother made me," I told him straight out.

I was so glad when the food came, because I was ready to just eat and leave. This whole night had turned out to be a total waste of a good outfit. As I scarfed down my shrimp, which were cooked to absolute perfection, Malachi tried making small talk. I was determined to make his night just as miserable as mine, so I didn't respond very much. I just kept giving him one-word answers and hunching my shoulders every so often. I was being a total bitch, but I didn't care.

When we were all done eating, Malachi asked the waitress for the check.

"I'm going to use the restroom," I told him before I slipped out of the booth.

"A'ight. I'll meet you out at the car," he said.

I simply rolled my eyes and kept walking. The arrogant thug, the bastard, didn't even have the decency to wait for me at the table.

When I finally walked out to the car, I realized that I would have to open my own door. An abundance of smoke rolled out of the car as I slid inside. I glanced over at Malachi, who was leaning so far back in his seat, I was certain he couldn't even see over the wheel.

"So, what you 'bout to get into?" he asked. I had to do a double take just to make sure that he wasn't talking to me. That was when I noticed the phone up to his ear. "Shit, I just might be," he said lowly with a hint of seduction in his voice. It was obvious that he was talking to a girl on the phone.

"Really, Malachi!" I exclaimed, fuming.

He cut his eyes over at me for the first time since I'd gotten into the car. "Aye, let me hit you back," he told whomever, then turned to face me. "What's up?"

"What's *up*!" I repeated. "I don't know. You tell me. You couldn't wait for me to use the restroom, and now you're sitting out here talking to another girl on the phone."

"Man." He sucked his teeth. "You acted like you didn't even wanna be seen with a nigga. I tried carrying a conversation with yo' stuck-up ass, but you couldn't even open your fucking mouth to do that right. Now you wanna sit here and cry about who I'm talking to on the phone." He shook his head. "I ain't one of them lame-ass white boys you used to fucking with, ma. Shit like that just don't fly with me."

I flopped back in my seat and folded my arms across my breasts. "Whatever, Malachi. Just take me home," I said.

"Nah, I got a stop to make," he said coolly.

"Un-fucking-believable," I mumbled.

Thirty-two minutes later, we ended up on the opposite end of town, in a neighborhood that didn't look very safe. Small brick homes lined the streets with chain-link fences out front. It was almost ten at night, but people were walking up and down the sidewalk as if it were broad daylight.

When he came to a stop and put the car in park, I looked over at him and asked, "How long are you going to be?"

"Long enough. Now, come on," he demanded. He got out of the car and left me sitting there.

Not wanting to be left alone in the sketchy neighborhood, I got out and followed behind him. As he pulled at the crotch of his sagging slim jeans, he looked up and down the block before taking the stairs to a small home two at a time. The porch light flickered on and off as he knocked hard on the door. I could hear music playing and people laughing on the other side of it.

"Who is it?" someone with a deep voice finally answered.

"It's Chi, mane," Malachi said.

A tall, heavyset, dark-skinned guy with a bald head opened the door. "What up, fool?" he said, clapping hands with Malachi as he brought him in for a brotherly hug.

I stepped into the cramped house behind Malachi and noticed that there was a little gathering in full swing. There was music playing, and people seated in the front room were holding red cups. Here I was dressed in Chanel and high heels, while other girls were walking around in tights and Ugg boots. I wanted to kill Malachi. When the big, dark-skinned guy turned back and looked at me, I saw that same 859 tattoo displayed on his neck. I looped my arm through Malachi's.

"Who's that you got with ya?" the big guy asked.

Malachi cut his eyes at me. "Oh, this is my friend Paris. Miss Paris, this here is Bull."

I gave Bull a small smile and wave before turning my attention back to the little party. That was when I noticed that the eyes of everyone in the room were on the two of us. A lot of the guys were giving him head nods of respect, while the girls were either admiring him or shooting daggers at me. For some reason, I gripped his arm tighter.

"You all right?" he whispered in my ear.

I nodded. "I'm okay."

"Hey, man, everybody's in the back," Bull said.

I was confused by that, because if everyone was in the back, who were all these people up here? Either way, I didn't question it. I just walked with Malachi as we followed Bull to the back of the house. There was a separate little den area, which looked like it had been added on to the house over the years. Some people were sitting on the floor, several were playing cards on the coffee table, while others sat around on the couches, talking and drinking beer.

"What up, Chi?" said some short, light-skinned guy as he stood to greet Malachi. He, too, had tattoos covering his arms, his neck, and the border of his face. They clapped hands before others in the room stood up to do the same.

"Aye, y'all gon' have to get up," Bull told some guy who was sitting on the couch with a girl in his lap.

The couple hopped up immediately and headed out of the room. "Y'all can sit down, man," Bull went on to say.

Malachi sat down where the guy had previously been sitting, but there was no room for me, so I just stood in place. "Shawty, why you just standing there? Come sit," he commanded, patting his thigh.

Although I was still pissed at him, I knew how stupid I would look if I just continued to stand there, so I sat down on his lap. Malachi wasted no time possessively wrapping his arms around my waist. I wanted to tell him to get off me, but I knew he would cuss me out, and I didn't want to be embarrassed in front of a bunch of strangers.

As Bull moved about the room in his Nike slides and white socks, it was more than obvious that he was the owner of the home. "Y'all want something to drink?" he asked.

"Yuh. Nita got some wine in there?" Malachi asked.

"Let me go see," Bull said.

I looked back at Malachi with my eyebrow raised. "You drink wine?" I asked.

"Nah, that's for you, Mama," he said, placing his hand over my knee. From just that simple touch, a chill shot down my spine. Not exactly sure of what I was feeling, I took a deep swallow and tucked a feathery piece of hair behind my ear.

A few minutes later Bull returned with a red plastic cup full of wine. Instead of handing it to me, he passed it over to Malachi. Malachi took a swig from the cup and instantly nodded his head. "I think you can fuck with that," he said, as if he really knew me.

When Malachi placed the cup to my lips, I closed my eyes and took a small sip. He was right. The sweet Italian red wine agreed with my taste buds. I took the cup from his hands and guzzled down some more.

"You good, Mama?" Bull asked.

"Yes, thank you," I told him.

Bull's eyes then shifted over to Malachi. "And, uh, just wanted to give you a heads-up . . . Your baby mama just walked in."

Baby mama.

My head whipped back in Malachi's direction. "You got a kid?" I whispered.

He nodded. "Two."

I put the cup back up to my lips and tossed the rest of the wine down in one big gulp. Although I wanted my body to relax, it did just the opposite and went as stiff as board as I was waiting for this *baby mama* to appear. The whole time, Malachi acted unbothered.

As time went on, there seemed to be no traces of his babies' mama. I was now on my second cup of wine and was bobbing my head to the music.

"Pretty girl, Malachi," said one of the girls sitting on the floor. She had long cornrows in her hair and was shuffling a deck of cards in her hand.

"She a'ight. When she wanna be," was Malachi's response.

I playfully pushed him in the shoulder, causing him to smile.

"You play?" the girl asked me.

"Oh no, I . . ." I shook my head. The only card game I knew how to play was Go Fish.

Malachi leaned up and put his lips to my ear. "You want me to teach you?" he asked lowly.

"No, that's all right."

"Come on," he insisted.

He reached down and, one by one, removed the high-heeled shoes from my feet. "Mike, hand me that pillow, mane," he told some guy at the far end of the couch. Malachi took the pillow from Mike's hand and placed it down on the floor.

"Here. Sit down," he said, dipping his head. I did as he said and sat Indian-style across from the girl with the braids. I was surprised when Malachi got down there with me, which allowed me to nestle between his legs.

"This hand is just for teaching," Malachi told the three players. They all nodded their heads in agreement. "So look," he told me. "That's Nya." He pointed across to the girl with the braids. "That's Boo," he said, then pointed to the brown-skinned girl on my right, who wore a purple wig on her head. "And that right there, that's Tee Tee," he said, nodding toward the fair-skinned girl on the left. "Y'all, this here is Paris," he added, introducing me. I said hello, noticing that all three girls were branded with 859 either on their necks or wrists.

Then Malachi rested his chin on my shoulder from behind. "The big joker beats out any other card in the deck. Then the little joker, then the ace of spades, and then the deuce," he explained. I nodded, only halfway listening, because I was too caught up in how good he smelled.

As Nya passed the cards out around the table, Malachi told me to pick them up without showing anyone.

"How many you got?" Nya asked me once I had them all in my hand.

Not understanding what she was asking, I glanced back at Malachi.

"How many cards in your hand do you think will beat what's in theirs?" he said. When I pointed to the big joker in my hand, Malachi whispered in my ear, "Good girl." The warmth of his minty breath swept across my cheek, causing my eyes to close temporarily. "And what else?" he asked, getting my attention.

With Malachi's help, I ended up telling Nya that I had four books in all. We went on to eventually win that round. As we continued to play, Bull's girlfriend, Nita, filled my cup up two more times with red wine. I was now dancing in my seat to the music while getting to know the other girls. I learned that Nya was twenty-one years old and bisexual. Boo had just turned twenty-three last month and was a single mom of three. Then there was Tee Tee, who was eighteen, just like me. She had no children, and in her own words, she was "strictly dickly."

To my surprise, my birthday was actually turning out to be okay. Although things hadn't gone as planned, I was finally enjoying myself.

"I've got to use the ladies' room," I said just as we ended another hand.

"I'll show you where it's at," Nya offered.

"Nah, Ny, sit yo' friendly ass down somewhere. I got her," Malachi said.

When he stood up, he reached his hand down to help me to my feet. Cardi B's "Bodak Yellow" was blaring from the corner speakers. That was my and Heather's anthem. Since the wine had me feeling a little loose, I began to dance. I threw my arms up in the air and rocked my hips like I always did.

"Go, Paris. Go, Paris. Go, Paris!" Nya, Boo, and Tee Tee all cheered. I laughed and danced even harder.

Malachi sucked his teeth and shook his head. "Man, don't let them gas you up," he told me. Then he looked down at the girls and said, "Y'all tryna clown my friend."

I frowned.

"What? You really thought your ass could dance?" he asked with a little smirk.

I didn't answer him. Instead, I starting dancing on him. Grinding my backside into his crotch, caring little to none that I didn't have any rhythm. Everyone in the room had a field day with that, and they all laughed and cheered me on. Without warning, Malachi scooped me up off me feet and slung me over his shoulder. I squealed out in laughter, trying to pull my dress over my bottom.

"Non-dancing ass," he muttered as he carried me into the other room.

He took me down a narrow hallway and placed me back on my feet. "The bathroom's right here," he said, pointing to a door. He went to open it up, but it was locked. We then heard flushing from the other side, which told us that it was occupied.

As we stood out in the hallway, waiting, Malachi leaned up against the wall and pulled me into him by the waist. He naturally wrapped his arms around me so that his hands were resting on the small of my back. "You enjoying yourself, Miss Paris?" he asked, peering down into my eyes.

"Actually, I am," I answered and smiled. Standing on the tips of my toes, I planted my hands on his firm chest.

Suddenly the bathroom door flew open, and the girl Reese from the nail shop appeared.

"What's up, Reesie?" Malachi said.

Reese glared at me, then rolled her eyes. She never did acknowledge Malachi, just kept on walking toward the front room.

"That's my kids' mama," he admitted.

My eyes ballooned. In my tipsy state, I had temporarily forgotten that Malachi had not one but *two* children. And li'l miss Reese's cup was their mother.

"Hmm. I've got to pee," was all I could say. I removed his hands from around my waist, then went inside the bathroom.

When I came out minutes later, Malachi was standing by the door with his jacket on.

"We're leaving?" I asked.

"Yuh, let's roll," he said.

I didn't even get a chance to say goodbye to the girls, or even to Bull, for that matter, because Malachi led me straight to the front door. When we got out to the car, he opened my door for me this time. I thanked him and gave him a small smile. And as we pulled off, his hand somehow found its way back to my knee. I didn't know if it was the four cups of wine or what, but I didn't say anything. I just sat back and enjoyed his company.

On the way to campus, Malachi shared with me that he had a two-year-old son named Mekhai and a five-year-old little girl named Maevyn. At a red light, he scrolled through his phone to find their pictures. They both were the spitting image of him, down to their dark skin and bright hazel eyes.

"Oh, wow. They're beautiful."

"What you thought? A nigga like me would make some ugly kids?" he joked.

I shook my head and laughed.

When we pulled up to my dorm, he parked the car and got out. He ran around and opened my door for me again. He was really putting on the charm. "So, you're actually gonna walk me up to my room this time, huh?"

"Ah, you still on that?" He smirked.

I shrugged. He grabbed me by the hand and laced his fingers with mine before leading the way. As we rode the elevator up to the third floor, he kissed the back of my hand. I wanted his lips in other places, but I was no way near bold enough to tell him so. When the elevator stopped, we got off and headed down to my door. I momentarily appreciated the emptiness of the hallway because it gave us a bit of privacy.

When Malachi unexpectedly backed me up against the wall, my heart began to race. He didn't ask or even hint around about kissing me. He just went right in, full throttle, softly at first, then gradually intensifying the kiss, making my hands cling to the sides of his arms. As he sucked on my lips and allowed his tongue to dance with mine, I could feel tremors at the end of every nerve in my body. My leg lifted robotically and caught around his waist, while these embarrassing, crazy-like moans floated from my lips. Brad had never made me feel like this.

"Happy birthday, Miss Paris," he said when he pulled back. Brushing my hair back from my face with his hand, he pecked my lips once more.

Speechless, I felt my mouth fall open from shock. "H-how did you know?"

He pulled my cell phone out of his jacket pocket. "You left it on the table at the restaurant," he confessed. "Heather texted and asked if you'd gotten the big black dick for your birthday yet."

My hands shot up to cover my face, which was burning from embarrassment. "Oh my God," I sighed into my palms. "I've got to start locking that thing."

He pulled my hands down and cracked a glittery smile. "No need to be embarrassed, Mama," he said. Then he pressed his body against mine and put his lips up to my ear. "And just for the record, when you're ready for this big black dick, I'll be right here," he whispered.

I was rendered speechless as he planted a final kiss on my cheek, winked his hazel eye, and swaggered toward the elevators.

Chapter 15

Asha

Unofficially Mrs. Brown

Jaxon and I had been texting each other nonstop since the day we exchanged numbers. We'd been out on two dates: a nice dinner on one occasion and bowling on the other. A bitch was already starting to fall in love, and the only thing that could make me fall any deeper at this point was getting the dick. That was just how much I felt we connected. At first, I'd been on the whole "marrying a baller" mission, but to my surprise, Jaxon had turned out to be much more than that. He was extremely smart and kind, and he was even sexy when he wasn't trying to be.

"What are you over there smiling about?" Kiki asked. She had stopped by to pick me up for a lunch date at Chili's. We were sitting on the couch talking before we headed out when a text from Jaxon came through.

I held up my cell phone so that she could see. "Bae's texting," I told her, grinning from ear to ear.

She rolled her eyes. "That's all you talk about these days. Bae this and bae that," she joshed.

I quickly responded to Jaxon's "Thinking of U" text.

Me: Will I see you tonight?

Jaxon: Of course. I've got practice, but I'll see you after that.

Me: Text me when you're on your way.

"Have you talked to Mark?" Kiki asked.

I swung my long micro braids over my shoulder and shook my head. "Fuck no! I told you, I'm not dealing with that nigga no more," I snapped.

Kiki held her hands up in defense. "Well, you said that the last time, so I had to ask."

I could count on both hands the number of times Mark had hit me, so I guess she was right. But this time was different. The day of A&T's homecoming, Mark and I had been laid up in a hotel from the night before. From sunup to sundown, we'd been smoking and fucking like the shit was going out of style. When I finally got up from the bed to take a shower, Mark began snooping through my phone. That was where he found the text messages between me and Jaxon, along with a string of others from my previous li'l dips.

By the time I stepped out of the bathroom, Mark was calling me every bitch and whore in the book. He slapped me around the room until I could only cry and beg for mercy. That was all he wanted anyway—for me to beg.

Mark had always made it clear that I wasn't his bitch. There were never any titles shared between us. However, the money he spent and the gifts he gave, I guess, were supposed to keep my pussy on lock. Although he didn't belong to me, he truly believed I belonged to him, and that was where we always bumped heads.

"Girl, fuck Mark!" I spat.

Out of nowhere, Franki came shuffling through the living room in her pajamas and slippers. I was sick and tired of seeing her mope around. Every day she'd stay locked up in that room until it was time for her to eat. And even then, she'd come out only to get her food and then go right back. I'd heard about what went down at the frat party with Hope and wondered if that was why she was sulking. However, I honestly didn't care that much to ask.

Being that I was in a good mood, thanks to Jaxon, I did say, "Franki, you need to get out and stop staying cooped up in that room."

"I agree," I heard Paris say behind me. I turned around and saw her stepping out of her bedroom.

"I'm fine," Franki muttered.

"Why don't you guys go to lunch with us?" Kiki offered. My eyes shot over to her, and I gave her a look. She knew damn well I didn't like hanging with a bunch of bitches.

"I'm totally in," Paris said. "Franki, how about you?"

"Not today," Franki muttered. With a bottle of water in one hand and a bag of chips in the other, she began shuffling back to her room.

"Franki, come on. You need to get out," Paris pleaded.

"I don't feel good." That was her excuse.

"You never feel good anymore," Paris told her. "If it's about what happened to Hope, it's over. I just saw her on campus the other day, and she's perfectly fine. She doesn't blame you, Franki." When Franki didn't respond, Paris said, "Come on. Let's go get dressed." She softly nudged Franki into her bedroom and closed the door behind them.

I looked over at Kiki and pointed one of my long nails in her direction. "See what you done did now, bitch? I'm not trying to be depressed all damn day," I said, which caused Kiki to laugh.

About forty-five minutes later, the four of us were piled up in Kiki's Camry, on our way to Chili's. I could tell that Paris had tried her best to pull Franki's look together in that short amount of time, but she was a five at best. Her curly hair was thrown up into a messy bun, and she wore an old

Pink jogging suit from the 2016 collection. As a matter of fact, she didn't even have earrings in her ears, and not a single trace of makeup was on her face. If Jaxon didn't have me in such a good mood, I would have told her that she couldn't ride with me looking like that.

Paris, on the other hand, looked cute in a cream YSL sweater dress and brown riding boots. Her white-girl hair was fluffed out in curls, and her makeup was soft and natural. I envied the Chanel bag she carried in her hand. It was one I had had my eye on a couple of months ago, while shopping with Mark. Now that he was out of the picture, I knew I needed to find alternate means to get the things I desired.

I was smart enough to know that asking Jaxon for anything other than his time would rule out all possibility of him taking me seriously. So for now, I played things cool. Hell, I often found myself buying gifts for him: cologne, clothes, and even shoes. I needed him to know that he could count on me for anything. I was all in.

"Damn, it's crowded in here for it to be lunchtime," Kiki said as we entered the restaurant. It was almost two o'clock in the afternoon, and the place was completely packed.

"Y'all wanna go somewhere else?" I asked.

"Let's see how long the wait is," Paris suggested. She stepped up to the hostess's podium and got our names added to the list.

"How long?" Kiki asked when Paris returned.

"Just ten minutes."

We all took a seat in the waiting area by the door. Other than Paris whispering to Franki, none of us made much conversation. We were all engaged in our phones.

Suddenly, I felt a cool draft of air beside me as someone entered through the door. I looked up to see Mark walking in with a girl on his arm. He didn't notice me, but my eyes instantly followed the two of them. She was light skinned, about the same as my complexion, and had long bundles in her hair. Short, with a small waist and an outlandishly big ass, which bounced when she walked. I then took notice of their matching Armani bomber jackets and the identical Armani shades covering their eyes.

How fucking cute.

As they stood waiting in line for the hostess, the girl looped her arm through his.

Kiki abruptly tapped me on the shoulder. "Girl, ain't that Mark's trifling ass?" she leaned over and whispered.

Rather than responding, I clenched my jaw. *This motherfucker.* As if he could hear my inner thoughts, he glanced over his shoulder and locked his eyes with mine. A cocky smile suddenly spread across his lips. Then he took the girl by her hand and made his way toward us. I could tell by the expression on her face that she was confused.

Standing directly in front of me, he removed the shades from his eyes. "Meelah, baby," he said as he looked down at her, "this here is Chi's little sister, Asha." He gestured to me with his hand. My eyes drew into slits. I was making sure my face revealed my annoyance. "Asha, this is my *girlfriend*, Meelah," he announced with a smug grin.

"Oops," I heard Kiki utter.

Meelah stuck out her hand for me to shake it, but I continued staring at Mark. "Girlfriend, huh? How long?" I asked.

Meelah smiled cluelessly, then glanced up at him with adoration. "It'll be what? Two years next month, right, babe?" she asked.

Mark's eyes were fixed on me, and that arrogant little smirk remained on his lips. "Yeah, two years and counting, Mama," he told her.

"Paris, party of four," the hostess called out.

I rose to my feet without breaking my glare at Mark. "Come on, y'all," I told the girls.

"See you later, *sis*," he said. I could hear the sarcasm in his voice.

As if it had a mind of its own, my middle finger shot up without warning. Together, the girls and I strolled off behind the hostess. As we trekked deeper into the restaurant, I could hear Meelah ask, "What that was all about?" I was sure he told her some bullshit lie, but since I was now out of earshot, I couldn't confirm this.

"*Girl*, that nigga is crazy," Kiki said with a hint of laughter in her voice.

I rolled my eyes and slid into the booth. "That's fine. That's why Malachi cut his ass off," I told her.

"Malachi?" Paris uttered from across the table.

I cut my eyes over at her, then shook my head. "Yeah, my brother," I said. "Anyway, my brother said that since he can't kill him, he gon' make sure that nigga can't eat."

"What do you mean?" Paris asked. For some reason, the subject of Malachi piqued her interest.

"Let's just say that Mark has got to find a new job," Kiki tried to explain.

"Oh," Paris replied. She then looked over at Franki, who was sitting next to her, scrolling through her phone. "What are you getting?" she asked.

Franki shrugged her shoulders. "I'm not really hungry."

Paris let out a dramatic sigh and rolled her eyes. "What about you, Kiki?"

"Ribs probably. That's what me and Asha always get," Kiki said.

"Nuh-uh," I muttered. Holding up my hand, I wiggled my fingers. "Not today. I just got my nails done, and I'm not trying to get all that sauce in them."

Minutes later, the waitress came over and took our orders. I ended up getting the grilled chicken breast, while Kiki got the ribs. Paris took the lead and ordered a salad for both herself and Franki. As Kiki and I continued talking about Mark's hateful ass, Franki just stared out the window. Paris went back to texting on her phone. It was like we were in three different worlds.

"What are you over there smiling at?" I asked Paris, having noticed the light in her eyes as she tapped away at the screen.

"Nothing," she answered, beaming.

"Mm-hmm. Let me find out you got a man that you're not telling us about," Kiki teased.

Paris shook her head. "Just a friend. That's all," she said, although her blushing cheeks told a different story.

"So, Franki, how'd you do on your midterms?" I asked.

She hiked her shoulders. "I aced them all, I think," she said, still looking out the window.

"What about you, Paris?" I asked, but I didn't give her a chance to respond. "All I know is I passed," I bragged.

She glanced up from her phone to meet my eyes. "I passed. I got an A on all my exams except for one." She shook her head. "Dr. Montgomery's Western Civilization," she groaned.

"Yeah, I gotta take that class next semester," I said.

"Well, good luck," Paris said, shaking her head.

"I passed my midterms too," Kiki chimed in.

"Oh, what college do you go to?" Paris asked.

"I go to—"

"She don't go to no damn college," I said, cutting her off.

Kiki rolled her eyes and sighed. "Well, I was getting ready to say that I go to Empire Hair School."

"Oh, cool." Paris stretched her eyes excitedly. "Maybe I'll let you do my hair one day."

"Ooh, I would love to do your hair. It's *so* pretty," Kiki replied, swooning.

I rolled my eyes to the ceiling, mimicking Kiki's voice in my head. *It's* so *pretty*.

When our food arrived, the three of us dug right in, while Franki just sat there staring off into space. As it became quiet around the table, my mind went back to Mark and his little *girlfriend*. It really bothered me that although I was the one who had taken all his abuse, including the name-calling and the degradation, he hadn't even found me worthy enough to hold that title. I needed something, anything, to get my mind off him once and for all.

Right on cue, my cell phone vibrated against my thigh. I looked down and saw another text from Jaxon.

Jaxon: I'll pick you up at seven.

***

"What you wanna watch? *Girls Trip* or *Get Out*?" Jaxon asked, holding up two Redbox DVDs in his hand.

"It's whatever you wanna watch," I told him, curling my feet beneath me to get comfortable on his couch. He squatted down in front of the television and popped one in. "Rod's not gonna be here tonight, is he?" I asked, referring to his roommate.

Although it was recommended that all freshmen live on campus, Jaxon had somehow weaseled his way out of that rule and was now living in a nearby apartment with a teammate.

"Nah. It's just you and me tonight." He winked over his shoulder.

As he stood up and walked toward me, my eyes drank in the movement of his bare chest and arms. Beautiful maple syrup–brown skin swathed his entire being, and his hands were the size of a *real* man's. He was comfortable in his home, wearing a simple pair of gray sweatpants and white crew socks on his feet. When he sat down next to me, he pulled me in close. My body eagerly submitted, and I tucked myself beneath his arm.

"I heard this movie is funny," he said. Then he looked down at me. "You cold?"

I nodded. "A little bit."

He removed his arm from around me and got up from the couch. After making a quick trip down the hall to his bedroom, he returned with a gray throw blanket in his hand. He covered me, reclaimed his seat, and allowed me to nuzzle against his chest. "Better?" he asked.

"Yes, thank you." Whenever I was around Jaxon, I made sure to use my best manners. A man in this league deserved a classy woman on his arm. At least that was what I told myself. Around Mark and some of the other guys, I could be as ratchet as I wanted to be, but not with him. With Jaxon, I was Asha 2.0, always stepping everything up a notch.

Once the movie got rolling, I realized he'd put *Girls Trip* on. I had never seen it before, but like him, I'd heard it was funny as hell. In fact, we were both laughing uncontrollably within the first twenty minutes. The laughing gradually turned into playful touching and small conversation about the movie. Midway through, my head found a home on his lap, while his fingers played in my braids.

"You staying at home with your family for Thanksgiving?" he asked.

I shrugged. "Probably. Unless you want to take me with you," I said, looking up at him.

Although it came out as a joke, I was secretly hoping that he would take the bait. Having an invite to his family's home for Thanksgiving would be like an early Christmas present for me. However, instead of replying, Jaxon let out a light chuckle.

Suddenly, he lifted me from his lap and gazed into my eyes.

"Come 'ere," he whispered before biting down on his bottom lip.

A soft giggle escaped me. "I'm right here," I told him, because if I were any closer, I'd literally be on top of him.

After grabbing me by the waist, Jaxon pulled me over him so that I was straddling his lap. His strong hands brushed my long braids behind my shoulders before taking ahold of my face. As he cradled it in his palms and stared into my eyes, light flutters erupted in my belly.

"You're so pretty. You know that?" he said lowly.

I just smiled and then leaned in to kiss his lips. That one kiss encouraged him to pick me up and carry me down the hall to his bedroom. There in the dark, he laid me across the cool sheets of his bed and rooted himself between my thighs. My back arched from the mattress as he used my neck as a canvas, tenderly brushing his lips and tongue all over it. Bit by bit, my breathing grew erratic, and my pussy started to ache from its core.

"Mmm," I moaned. At eighteen years old, I admit to having traveled around the block a few times, but not once could I recall wanting a man as badly as I wanted Jaxon Brown.

"What we gonna do?" he murmured. The tip of his tongue slithered up to my chin, and his fingers inched beneath my shirt.

"I wanna feel you," I whispered, lifting my pelvis to meet the hardness of his abs.

When Jaxon hopped up to grab a condom out of his nightstand, I hurriedly pushed my tights down over my hips. I hadn't even gotten to my shirt when he reached for my ankles and pulled me to the edge of the bed. With urgency, he slid his pants midway down to his thighs, freeing himself. My eyes bucked at his impressive length, which showed itself in the partial light coming through the blinds.

Then he climbed back up to my lips, his throbbing muscle teasing me. As we engaged in a deep kiss, he reached down between us and grabbed ahold of his dick. His head slid up and down my soaking-wet center as he breathed in my ear. "Damn, baby."

I moaned. In one swift motion, Jaxon plunged into me, stealing the air from my lungs.

"Oh God," I cried out. I gripped his muscular shoulders as he filled me up, *inch by inch*.

"Shit," he hissed. The only thing I could imagine were his eyes squeezing shut from our bodies meeting for the very first time.

As he stroked in and out of me, I rocked my hips, attempting to match his rhythm. I knew I'd have to do whatever just to be considered Jaxon's very best lover. But tonight, as moan after moan fled from my lips, I just wanted him to take me. I wanted him to make love to me like I had seen in the movies and had read about in books. That one beautiful thing I'd never experienced.

Out of nowhere, my legs started to quake. "Jaxon," I moaned. He kept going, driving in and out of me until the sounds of our wet bodies filled the entire room. I bit down on his shoulder just so I wouldn't scream out loud.

"Fuck," he gasped, still working his hips. Over and over, Jaxon bucked into me, making the mattress squeak beneath us and the headboard knock against the wall.

All of a sudden, I could feel that all too familiar stirring in my groin, and again, my legs trembled. "Jaxonnn!" I wailed.

He placed his cheek next to mine and allowed his hips to pick up speed. "I'm cumming," he growled.

As I firmed my grip on his shoulders, a massive orgasm ripped through me. "Ahhh," I cried out, shuddering beneath him. When his weight collapsed on top of me, I could feel our hearts beating out of sync. And before I knew it, or even had a chance to rein them back in, the three most forbidden words floated from my lips. "I love you," I whispered.

Chapter 16

Hope

A Shameful Surrender

"Okay, guys, your drafts for the allegory analysis are due in class this Friday. Anyone needing extra credit before the end of the semester will need to stop by and see me during my office hours," Professor Shipley announced. Then she peered over her glasses and scanned the room for a final time. "All right. Class dismissed."

I gathered my things off the desk and slid them inside my book bag. As I slipped my coat on, I mentally prepared myself for the chilly November weather outside. I sighed just thinking about the hike I'd have to make to the bus stop. For the past three weeks, I'd been staying with my aunt Marlene, who lived across town. According to Deddy, unless I wanted to go back home to Alto, staying with her was my only option. And my only means of transportation would be the city bus.

When Deddy came to the hospital that morning after my attack, I swear I'd never seen him so infuriated in all my life. If only Pastor Reeves had heard the way he cursed that day, I think he would have been banned from the church. Then he kicked Meeko out of my hospital room like a madman and forbade me from ever seeing him again. I literally cried for three days straight after that.

The day the doctors finally discharged me, Deddy was determined to take me back to Alto, but I begged and pleaded until he finally caved in. Of course, Aunt Marlene reassuring him that she would keep a close eye on me was what really sealed the deal. Now here I was, face completely healed of all the bruises and trying to get back into the swing of things.

As I approached Bluford Circle, someone behind me abruptly shouted my name. I looked back to see Meeko jogging toward me, burgundy sweatpants and matching hoody, with a baseball cap turned to the back. Clean construction boots covered his feet, while a glimpse of that simple gold chain sparkled around his neck. Like always, he looked incredible. I, on the other hand, had on a simple navy-blue coat with a red Hanes turtleneck underneath. My long khaki skirt covered my lower half and skimmed the tops of my brown leather boots. My signature bun sat at the back of my head, and my glasses, of course, rested against my face.

Immediately, I turned back around and walked faster, hoping that he would catch the hint. However, after just a few paces more, I felt his hands grip the tops of my shoulders. "Damn, girl. Hol' up," he said, spinning me around.

As my fingertips swept the overgrown bangs from my eyes, I gave him a pretentious smile. "Oh, hey, Meeko," I said.

"*Hey, Meeko!*" he repeated with authority, narrowing his eyes. "That's all you got to say to me?"

I shrugged. "I don't know what else you want me to say."

"How about telling me how you've been for the past three weeks and why you haven't been returning my calls?"

I released a deep sigh, and then I closed my eyes for a moment. "Look, Meeko, after I got attacked . . ."

"About that. I'm so fucking sorry, Hope. Jazz and her girls had no right putting their hands on you like that. I've already checked that bi—"

"Well, I've already pressed charges, and the school is fully aware," I interrupted. "So . . ."

"So, if that's the case, then why did you cut *me* off?"

In a state of semi-disbelief, I gave a small, sarcastic snort. "Meeko, I have never in all my life been physically attacked like that before. Sure, I've been bullied. I've been in fights before, but this . . . I couldn't even see out of my left eye for five days straight." I pointed below my breasts. "My ribs, even at this very moment, are still sore. And even though I know you weren't the one who did it, I'm fully aware that you're the reason for it all."

Meeko dragged his hand down over his face and sighed. "Jazz ain't my girl, shorty. I can't control what she does."

"Oh, I know!" I said that with conviction. After rehearsing this conversation in my head over and over for the past two weeks, I was more than prepared. "She's just your homie-lover-friend, right?" I asked mockingly.

He cocked his head to the side and took in a deep breath. "So, what? We can't be friends no more?" he asked dejectedly.

"Sorry, but being friends with you comes with too high of a price. Plus, my deddy—"

"So, it's your pops?" he asked, cutting me off, one eyebrow raised.

Instead of giving him an answer, I simply looked away.

It was true that if Deddy hadn't been so adamant about me staying away from Meeko, I probably would've answered his calls. I mean, even as I stood there facing him, I couldn't deny that I missed him. The daily calls and texts, the walks to my class, and the way he would always make me laugh . . . I still yearned for it all. In just a few short months, Meeko had become more than my very first crush. He had truly become my friend.

"So, what? You not gon' say nothing?" Meeko said, pressing the matter.

My mouth parted, but I couldn't speak. As I cast my eyes down toward the concrete, I could only shake my head.

"So, you letting him make decisions for you, even though he's a million miles away?" he asked, exaggerating. "You in college now, Hope. You're not no little girl no more."

As I allowed his words to sink in, I became irritated. It was clear that Meeko was trying to manipulate me. "I will not disobey my father, Meeko. Not even for you."

"So, were you supposed to be calling and texting me on that cell?" he asked, pointing to the purse hanging from my arm. "Or how about kicking it with me in my dorm? Does your pops know about that?" he asked, jabbing back.

An abrupt and overwhelming feeling of guilt consumed me because Meeko was completely right. I had been disobeying my father from the start. It was just that after everything— the attack, my father's red-eye flight to Greensboro, and all the medical bills that were to come— how could I go back to being friends with this guy? The logical part of my brain was laying it all out in front of me, but then there was my heart.

"I can't," I whispered.

As soon as I turned to walk away, Meeko gently grabbed me by the hand. I hadn't felt his touch in so long that a warm shiver immediately eased down my spine. My eyes fluttered, then lifted slowly to meet his. That was when I noticed the desperation in his eyes. He was silently pleading with me, and I could no longer breathe. If that weren't enough, he took that full bottom lip of his between his teeth and silently waited.

Jesus.

"So, you not even gon' help me study for my finals like you said you would?" he asked in a low, pitiful voice.

Meeko knew exactly how to get to me. In fact, I believed he often played on my faith just to get the things that he wanted. Just like now, he knew I would keep my word.

I clenched the strap of my book bag, which was hanging on my arm, and tilted my head to the side. "I know what you're doing," I told him.

Suddenly, the right half of his lips curled into a devious smirk. "What?" he teased.

"I'll help you, Meeko, but that's it. No more hanging out."

Before I could say anything else, he squeezed me in a bear hug. Clearly, he was already violating my "no friends" rule, but I didn't possess the will-power to push him away. Instead, I closed my eyes and inhaled his familiar scent, which I had missed tremendously. When he released me, I craned my neck back to look toward the bus stop.

"All right, well . . . I'll talk to you later," I said.

Meeko's eyebrows immediately gathered in confusion. "Wait, where you going?"

"I live with my aunt Marlene now. The one I told you about."

"Damn," he uttered. "I didn't know that."

"Yep. Well, anyways, I gotta go catch the bus. I guess I'll see you around."

Just as I turned to walk away, Meeko said, "Well, let me give you a ride."

"No, I—"

"Come on," he said, taking me by the hand.

Although I should have refused, I allowed Meeko to lead me over to a nearby parking lot on campus. There in his car sat Big Mo in the front seat and Ty in the back. As soon as we approached the car, Big Mo stepped out, a rolling cloud of smoke drifting behind him. Meeko released my hand and went around to the driver's side.

"What up, Dimples?" Big Mo said, throwing the remains of his joint to the ground before giving me a one-armed hug. His clothes reeked of marijuana.

"Hey, Big Mo," I replied.

"So, you been doing a'ight?" he asked.

I smiled because I could hear the utmost sincerity in his voice. "Yeah, I've been doing all right."

As soon as Meeko closed the driver's-side door, I went to get in the back seat. "Nah. Big Mo, you hop in the back," Meeko said from inside the car.

With a frown on his face, Big Mo dipped his head down low to see Meeko through the open car door. "Nigga, I'm six feet five. Fuck I look like sitting in the back?"

"Look like a nigga that's not walking, if you ask me," Meeko shot back.

I felt bad because Big Mo was a rather large guy, and Meeko drove an old Honda Accord coupe, white, with two doors and minimal space inside. However, after sucking his teeth, Big Mo did as Meeko had asked and hopped in the back.

"What's going on, Hope?" Ty asked when I got in.

I twisted around in the front seat and waved. "Hey, Ty."

"So, where we going?" Meeko asked. Looking over at me, he reached out to cut the radio down.

"Do you know where Bellwood Village is? She lives off Peppervine Trail," I said.

Meeko shook his head. "Nah. I'on think I know where that's at."

"Yeah, you do, yo," Ty chimed in from the back. "Remember ole girl from this summer?"

Meeko narrowed his eyes and looked at him in the rearview mirror. "Who? Shanae?"

I heard Big Mo instantly scoff behind me. "Man, don't even mention that girl's name," he said.

Ty just chuckled. "Yeah. Shanae live over there in Bellwood Village."

"Who's that? Another one of your *girlfriends*?" I asked Meeko with a hint of cynicism in my tone.

"Nah, that was Big Mo's girl last summer," he explained, pressing on the gas to pull off.

Feeling an instant sense of comfort with this particular group of guys, I turned back around in my seat. "So, what happened? With you and Shanae?" I asked Big Mo.

For a while now, these guys had been my main source of entertainment, and over the past few weeks, I had been deprived of their wild and funny stories. I was more than eager to hear another one.

"She was just something I was doing for the summer, until she got all serious on me. Shorty went crazy on my ass." He shook his head.

"See, during the summer, while everyone else goes back home, we actually gotta stay out here for football camp," Meeko explained. "And sometimes when we get bored, we roll out to the community colleges, 'cause that's where all the locals be at. So one day after practice, we decided to swing through Guildford Tech. It's about twenty minutes away . . ."

"Wow. That's kinda far to be driving around, looking for girls," I teased.

The guys all laughed. Then Ty said, "Aye, shorty, desperate times . . ."

"So, anyway, it's hot as fuck outside, but we steady rolling through with the windows down, hollering at girls and shit. Big Mo riding shotgun, Ty in the back, and we just cruisin'." Meeko paused for effect. "Next thing I know, Big Mo starts shouting out the window, like, 'Ooh weee!'" he howled, cupping his hand around his mouth. "Yo, I slowed the car down, and Ty leaned up between the seats to see ole girl that Big Mo talking about. Of course, it's some skinny broad with a long flowery church dress on. That's his type."

Suddenly, I felt Big Mo lean forward and tap me on the arm. "See? You ain't know you was my type, did you, Hope?" he asked jokingly.

"Nigga, if you don't sit yo' ass back," Meeko chuckled. "So, anyway, Big Mo kept calling shorty out, but she wasn't really trying to hear him. She looked back at us and scrunched her face up."

"Yeah, matter of fact, shorty started speed walking and shit just to get away from our asses, remember that?" Ty asked with a laugh.

"She damn sure did. And what I do?" Meeko looked at the rearview mirror with a smile.

"Nigga started driving up beside her just so Big Mo could rap," Ty said.

"Big Mo was sounding all desperate, like, 'I can't have five minutes of your time, baby? You just gon' keep ignoring a nigga, huh?'" Meeko mocked as we all laughed.

As we sat at a red light, Meeko craned his neck around and asked, "And what was it you kept calling her, yo?"

I could hear Big Mo let out a chuckle behind me. "I called her Daisy."

"Daisy? Why?" I asked.

"The flowers on her dress. Plus, she looked like her name could've been Daisy," Big Mo explained.

"Man." Ty sucked his teeth. "Shanae's ghetto ass don't look like no damn Daisy."

I giggled at their banter.

"But anyway, Big Mo ended up having to hop out of the car just to get shorty's attention," Meeko went on to say. "Eventually, she gave him her number."

"So, what made her so crazy?" I asked.

"You talked to her for what?" Meeko asked Big Mo. "Like, a couple weeks?"

"Yeah, it was three weeks until she finally let me hit." I looked back to see him shaking his head. "And I swear, as soon as I came and pulled out the pussy, shorty gon' look at me and say, 'I'm a virgin,'" he scoffed, making me cringe at his vulgarity. "Had I known that shit from the jump, I would've never even looked her way."

"Why? What's wrong with virgins?" I asked out of curiosity. After repositioning myself in the seat,

I looked back and forth between the three guys. Meeko gave a hesitant smile as he scratched the side of his handsome face. "Tell me," I urged.

"Women get clingy as fuck, Hope. I mean to us, it's just sex, but to y'all, it's more than that. To an inexperienced girl, sex and love are damn near one and the same. I mean, let's be real. Most of the time when a woman loses her virginity, she's already thinking about marriage," Meeko explained. "Shit, I bet you anything in Shanae's mind, she was already picturing herself living in some big-ass house in the burbs, raising this nigga's badass kids." He laughed. "But to us, it's just the feeling of . . ."

"The feeling of what?" I desperately wanted to know.

"Of bustin' a nut," Ty cracked from the back. The three of them instantly erupted in laughter.

Although their words were brash and deplorable in a way, I was somehow able to appreciate their candor. It wasn't every day that a young black woman from Alto who was a virgin got her ears full of this kind of indirect advice like this. Sure, my father had told me similar things in the past, but hearing it from a group of my own peers was completely different.

After another ten minutes on the road, we were finally at the top of Aunt Marlene's street. She lived in a fairly new neighborhood, with modest-sized homes lining each side of the block. Even though it was a good ways away from campus, I was still thankful to be living in such a nice area.

"Hey, just drop me off right here," I told Meeko. There was no way I was going to have him pull up in front of the house. If Aunt Marlene saw or even suspected that I was back to communicating with Meeko, she would call Deddy in a heartbeat. And at this point, I wasn't willing to take the risk.

"You sure?" he asked and hiked his brow.

"Yeah, I'm sure."

As he pulled the car over and shifted the gear into park, I glanced in the back seat. "It was good seeing you guys," I told Big Mo and Ty.

"We gon' see you around. Now get out, so I can stretch my legs, Dimples," Big Mo said.

Laughing, I opened the car door. Meeko was already waiting in front of me when I got out. As soon as I stepped onto the sidewalk with my book bag already on my back, Big Mo let up the seat to hop in the front.

"You gon' answer when I call, right?" Meeko asked.

I pushed my glasses farther up on my nose and said, "I'm helping you study for finals, Meek. That's it."

A wide smile instantly crested upon lips.

"What?" I asked, curious as to why he was suddenly beaming from ear to ear.

"Nothing," he said, shaking his head. Although his smile partly diminished, it was still very much present as he bit down on his bottom lip.

Gripping the right strap of my book bag a little tighter, I looked down the street, toward Aunt Marlene's house. Even from a distance, I could make out her car sitting in the driveway. "Well . . . I guess I'll see you around," I said.

"Yeah," he let out lowly.

When I turned around and began to walk away, Meeko reached out and gently grabbed me by the hand. Instantly, he laced his fingers with mine, causing the tiny hairs on my arms to rise. With a parted mouth, I glanced back and noticed a weird look in his eyes, one that I had never seen before. It was suspended somewhere between desire and desperation, and perhaps there was even a hint of nervousness in it, which completely threw me for a loop.

"Don't play with me, Hope," he said firmly. "Answer that phone when I call."

With a deep swallow, I nodded almost submissively. "When you're ready to study, just let me know."

When he released his hold on me, I continued on my way to Aunt Marlene's place. Seconds later, I heard the engine of his car roar and the volume of his radio increase. I didn't look back until I finally reached the front porch of her house. That was when I noticed his car still sitting there at the end of the street. It was as if he was waiting for me to get safely inside. After letting myself in, I couldn't help but press my back against the closed door and smile.

"What you smiling for, girl?" Aunt Marlene's voice caught me by surprise. I looked over to see her sitting on the living-room sofa.

"Nothing," I said. "I just had a really good day."

Chapter 17

Franki

Praying for Courage

As I sat on the edge of my bed, reading over my biology notes for a second time, I heard a text chime through on my cell. I glanced down at the screen and immediately saw that it was Josh.

Josh: You almost ready?

Feeling hesitant, I bit down on the corner of my lower lip and typed back a reply.

Me: I guess.

Josh: It'll be fun. You'll see.

Me: Church? Fun? Are you sure you're using the right adjective?

Josh: LOL. Yes, it'll be FUN. Be outside in ten.

I released a deep sigh before sending back a simple okay.

Ever since the morning after that party, Josh and I had talked every day, oftentimes over the phone or by text. And on rare occasions, he had actually stopped by to check in on me. At first, I'd interpreted his kindness as being somewhat weird. I mean, let's face it, I'd given him such a hard time from the beginning, yet he still found it in his heart to befriend me. Where I came from, people didn't often give you the opportunity to shit on them twice, but it was obvious that Josh was cut from a different cloth. I was now able to see clearly that both his heart and his mind were something out of the ordinary.

After tossing my biology book to the side, I stood up and stared at my reflection in the mirror. I had a bare face, with the exception of a sheer coat of pink lip gloss on my lips. My black curls were swept up into a bright African-print scarf, exposing my elf-like ears. I wore a long black sweater dress that tied around the waist, and on my feet were a pair of classic black booties.

As I reached to grab a bottle of perfume from my dresser, gold bangles jingled from my wrist. "Here goes nothing," I sighed, spraying lightly behind my ears.

I threw on my leather moto jacket and grabbed my purse before heading for the door.

"You look pretty. Where ya going?" Paris asked from where she stood in the small kitchen.

I groaned before saying, "To church."

"Oh, wow. You should have told me. I would have come with. I haven't been to church in years," she said.

"Me either," I muttered. "But maybe next time." After tossing a half smile in her direction, I walked out the front door.

Moments later, I found myself walking down the redbrick steps of Holland Hall. Beneath the glow of the streetlights, I was able to spot Josh's black Yukon sitting alongside the curb. We were going to an evening service, so as I hiked across the lawn, I could already see darkness overpowering the sky. When I approached the truck, Josh leaned over and pushed the door open from inside.

After sliding into the passenger seat, I placed my purse on my lap before closing the door.

"Seat belt, ma," he said.

I wasn't sure if I had heard him correctly, so I said, "Huh?"

"I said put your seat belt on. You never wear your seat belt."

"Oh, my bad," I said, reaching back to pull the strap over my chest. "Back home I rarely ride in cars. My muva don't even own one, so . . ."

"Yeah, I feel you," he said, finally pulling off.

My eyes automatically floated in his direction, which caused a natural smile to form on my face. I instantly noticed the black tie peeking out from beneath the neck of his jacket. *Such a church boy*, I thought. Now, I know I teased Josh a lot, but don't get me wrong. He was definitely fine—curly coal-black hair, tapered dark eyes with eyelashes that curled to the heavens. His smooth skin was the color of butter pecan ice cream, and he had this thin goatee that perfectly traced the angles of his jaw. He was the absolute definition of *pretty*, but he just wasn't *my* type.

"You look nice, by the way," he said. He let his eyes momentarily rake over my thighs before his gaze moved up toward my face and hair as we stopped at a red light.

I took a deep swallow, unconsciously reaching up to pat the side of my hair. "Thanks," I said.

As we rode in silence, without the sounds of the radio or our voices to fill the confined space, I began to gaze out the window, reflecting on the fact that tonight would be my first time attending church in almost four years. My faith in God had dwindled so much by the time I reached the age of fourteen that it was then that my mother decided she would no longer force me to go. It was *then* that I began to totally lose my way, allowing the voids in my life to fill with rebellion and promiscuity.

"You still having those dreams?" Josh asked, taking me out of my thoughts.

"You mean nightmares," I said, correcting him with a roll of my eyes. "Yes, unfortunately."

"Damn," he muttered beneath his breath. "Maybe you should go to counseling or . . ."

"I just want to let it go," I told him. "The sooner I forget, the better."

Being in such a vulnerable state had ultimately led me to confide in Josh. I'd ended up telling him all about the nightmares and how I often woke up in a cold sweat. Of course, I'd left out the part where I would wet myself in the bed. I'd been too embarrassed to tell him all of that, even though he would never judge me. He would just listen.

Not giving too much detail, I'd basically told him that Jamel and his friends were the ones haunting me in my dreams. The physical rape persistently replayed in my subconscious and somehow was able to rerun at night.

"So, have you seen your roommate?" I asked, referring to Jamel.

"Nah," he said, thumbing the side of his nose. "He knows not to come back to that room." Although Josh's eyes remained steady on the road ahead, I could hear a calm fury in his voice. "Have you seen him?" he asked.

"Nope. Not even once since that night." The memories of that horrible night and the days that followed briefly entered my mind. Josh had truly been there for me. The day after the rape, he had taken me to the store to get Plan B, and then a week or so later, he'd even driven me to the doctor to get screened for STDs. Thank *God*, I was all right. Josh had truly been my rock every step of the way.

Minutes later, we were pulling into the graveled lot of New Hope Baptist Church. For some reason, I felt anxious. In fact, when Josh cut the engine off and got out of the truck, I continued sitting there, frozen in place. That was, until Josh came around and knocked on the window.

"You coming?" he asked through the glass.

I nodded and opened the car door. Side by side, we walked through the rocky parking lot until we reached the large double doors of the church. As we crossed the threshold, the familiar sounds of drums and tambourines immediately filled my ears. Even the closed-in smell of the place brought back so many memories of when I used to attend church as a child. My heart instantly began to race, because I knew that this night would finally bring my reunion with God.

Before we could step any farther, we got stopped by an elderly woman passing out programs.

"How you doing tonight, Brother Joshua?" she asked, taking Josh by the hand.

"I'm blessed, Sister Patrice. Definitely blessed." He paused for a moment. "Oh, and I brought a visitor with me tonight," he said, cutting his eyes over at me. "Franki, this is Sister Patrice. Sister Patrice, this is my good friend Franki."

"Wonderful. And how are you doing tonight, sweetheart?" she asked.

I felt an uneasy smile spread across my face before I said, "I'm doing fine. How are you?"

Her eyes narrowed, like she knew something was off about me. Then she said, "I'm well, dear. Thank you for joining us tonight. I'm sure you'll enjoy Pastor Marks's service. He's always got something special up his sleeve."

Josh gave a slight nod of his head and then began leading the way down the center aisle. As I followed behind him, my eyes wandered around the sanctuary. Right away, I noticed the stained-glass windows and the red tweed carpet beneath my feet. On each side of the church were rows and rows of carved wooden pews, the backs of which held Bibles. My gaze wandered to center stage, and I looked beyond the pulpit, where I was able to make out an already assembled choir dressed in burgundy-colored robes. A set of drums was being played in one corner, while a vacant organ sat in the other. And hanging on the wall in the background was the image of Jesus Christ etched on a wooden cross. Everything about this church was traditional and seemed so familiar.

"You all right?" Josh asked as he looked back at me.

"Yeah, but, um . . . do we have to sit up front?"

He smiled. "I gotta get up on that stage a little later, so it's better if we sit up front," he said.

I shot him a pointed look. "Yo, you better not get up there and call me out as no visitor, or I swear to God, I will fu—"

"Shhh." He chuckled. Glancing over his shoulder, he placed his finger over my lips. "Watch ya' mouth in here, girl."

"Josh, don't play with me," I warned.

He continued to laugh and shook his head. "Nah, I wouldn't do you like that. Just wait and see," he told me.

After we finally took our seats, *in the front pew*, it wasn't long before the church started to fill up. People both young and old, black and brown, took their seats. Then a little old lady with a big lavender hat walked up on the stage. She gave a small welcome speech before saying a quick prayer. When she stepped back from the microphone, the church instantly quieted and the drums completely ceased. That was when I heard the organ begin to play. I glanced over to find that it was one of Josh's frat brothers teasing the keys.

I tapped Josh on the arm. "Is that Mike?" I whispered in his ear.

Josh responded with a simple nod of his head.

As the music flowed melodically through the air, I watched someone who I assumed was the pastor take the stage. He was a tall, dark-skinned man with low-cut silver hair. A burgundy robe, a bit more elaborate than those of the choir, sat about his broad shoulders and burly chest. He laid his Bible down on the pulpit's podium and adjusted the microphone before he finally spoke.

"Good evening, brothers and sisters. Thank you for joining me on this glorious evening," he said, his deep tenor instantly commanding attention. "How are y'all feeling tonight?" he asked.

People all around me shouted, "Fine, Pastor" or "Just fine" or "Blessed." I, on the other hand, remained quiet.

"You know, most Christians are routine liars," the pastor said, instantly shocking the crowd. Then he nodded. "It's true. Of course, we don't call it lying. In fact, to most of us, it doesn't even register as lying. It's just something we do. We've become so accustomed to speaking untruths that we don't even take a moment to reflect on what we're actually saying. Let me take a moment to explain, Amen?"

"Tell it!" I heard someone shout out from behind me.

"You see, every day we encounter friends or associates and engage in small talk. We ask, 'How are you doing?' or 'How's the family?' or 'How are things coming along at work?' And typically, without giving it any thought, we respond positively. 'I'm fine.' 'Work is fine.' 'The family's fine.'

'Everything's just fine.'" He paused. "Isn't that what we say?" he asked the congregation.

"Well," he went on, placing the tip of his finger to his chin, "that's up until those divorce papers get filed or until the doctor reveals that the blood in your stool is because of cancer. But *no*, everything's fine, right? Even though you're worried about losing your job, because they're laying folks off three and four at a time. Everything's fine, even though you're struggling with anxiety and feelings of low self-esteem. Burying secrets from your past." He was silent for a moment.

"There may be a few people who know what you're really dealing with, but on a typical day here at church, we put on a good show for each other. At church, you tell everyone, 'Everything's fine. We're working it out. The Lord will bring us through.' Isn't that what we say? Then you both smile and nod, content with the little falsehood you've shared, both knowing full well that you're not really telling the truth, but neither of you wanting to take the risk of bringing it out into the open."

I don't know why, but suddenly, I felt like everyone's eyes were on me. You know when you go to church and the pastor's sermon seems to be based on the very pages of your diary? Well, that same eerie feeling was beginning to wash over me. Even the tiny hairs on my arms and neck were starting to rise. The words *I'm fine* might as well have been my personal hashtag these days. It was all I ever said.

"Now, you may say, 'Hey, that isn't lying. It's just common courtesy. People don't go around asking questions like that to get honest answers. They don't really want to know the truth,'" he said, scratching his head. "Well, I say you're wrong." He pointed at the crowd. "At least when it comes to your brothers and sisters in Christ. You *can*, if you're willing, choose to be honest. In fact, you should, because it's highly needed. God describes the church as the 'body of Christ,' because our lives are supposed to merge together as *one*, where not only our joys can be shared but our sorrows too. Amen?"

"Amen," the church agreed.

"Being open and honest with not only yourself but also with others who walk with Christ allows you to help carry each other's burdens, by doing things like listening, being supportive and encouraging. But if you hold back your truths by saying things are fine, well, then, that keeps you that much further from God. God does not expect perfection. In fact, the one prerequisite for entering the kingdom of heaven is an admission of failure, some acknowledgment of your sins. And so, we have no grounds to look down on anyone else. We are loved and accepted wholeheartedly by God because of Christ. Our worth comes from Him.

"And so, we don't need to pretend to be better than we are. We don't need to put on a mask. What freedom, right? To have nothing to prove! Not to worry about impressing anyone with our holiness, not even God, but to be able to admit openly who we are, flaws and all. Even through our darkest hours, we must still speak our truth!" he rasped, causing the entire church to erupt. "Amen?"

"Amen!"

As hot tears sprang from my eyes, I felt the sudden warmth of Josh's hand connect with mine.

"Folks, I'm not lying to you. Read the book of John. It tells you right there in the seventeenth chapter. 'Sanctify them by the truth. Your word is truth,'" he said, stabbing his finger into the Bible that lay before him. "Or how about Psalms one-forty-five, verse eighteen?" He licked the tip of his index finger, then quickly flipped the pages. "It says, 'The Lord is near to all who call on Him, to all who call on Him in truth.'"

"Tell it, Pastor!" someone yelled from the crowd.

"You must not be ashamed to open your mouth and tell someone your story. You must not be ashamed to confess what you did or why you ended up where you're at. You must not!" he yelled, making his voice echo throughout the sanctuary. "Be not ashamed to let your brothers and sisters in, so that they can help you. Open up your hearts, people . . . ," he bellowed, his voice so melodious that it sounded almost like he was singing a song. With his right hand waving in the air, he said, "Open up your hearts."

When the organ started to play, those who had remained seated rose to their feet and waved their arms in the air. But I just couldn't move. With my arms wrapped tightly around my body, I rocked from side to side. More tears spilled from my eyes as the pastor asked us to bow our heads to pray. And for the first time in years, I did just that.

As the pastor led the congregation in prayer, I silently gave my own supplication to God. I specifically asked for courage. Courage to let someone know that *I*, the badass Francesca Wright, had been raped as a result of my own promiscuity. Although it didn't justify what those fuck boys had done to me, I'd be lying if I said that the words they spoke that night hadn't replayed in my mind. "I know you love this nasty shit," I could still hear Jamel say. Or how about when he told his friends, "She loves this type of shit." Those were the kind of words that stuck out the most. Simply because I was an openly sexual person, I had been perceived as mere trash, something that could be used and abused before tossing it to the wayside. That part was breaking me.

And then there was the story of my father and how he'd left me behind all those many years ago. I hadn't told a soul; not even my own mother knew

that it was my fault he had to go to prison in the
first place. At this very moment, I needed all the
courage God was willing to give. I needed it all,
and so I prayed. I prayed for so long, with my eyes
closed, that the only thing able to break me from
my trance was the sound of Josh's angelic voice.

"You did not create me to worry. You did not
create me to fear. But you created me to worship
daily. So I'ma leave it all right here," he sang.

I opened my eyes and saw Josh standing on
the platform, with a microphone in his hand,
singing the lyrics to Anthony Brown's "Trust in
You." Goose pimples covered my entire being, and
a peculiar shiver coursed throughout my frame.
And when he sang, "My hands are raised because
I surrender," I stood up and lifted my hands in
the air. I closed my eyes again, which only caused
more tears to flow.

As soon as the choir joined in with, "I will trust
in you, Lord," I couldn't help but sing right along
with them. The spirit was definitely moving in that
church, and it was evident by the many cries that
could be heard from the crowd. By the time Josh's
performance came to a close, the church was on
fire, with people dancing and hollering all around
me, speaking in distinctive languages I hadn't
heard in forever.

After Josh shook the pastor's hand and gave
him a half hug, he jogged down the steps of the

stage. When he reached my side and his eyes connected with mine, which were still very wet and full of emotion, he opened his arms and wrapped them around me. Pressing his lips to my brow, he whispered, "You a'ight, ma? You gon' be okay?"

I nodded before fully laying my head on his chest. For the rest of the service, Josh kept me near, his arms around me. It was crazy, because I didn't even like niggas touching me like that, yet Josh was quickly able to put me at ease. He gave me such a level of comfort and protection, which I hadn't felt since I was a little girl.

When he later pulled up in front of my dorm to drop me off, I glanced over at him in the driver's seat. I didn't want him to leave.

"Can you come upstairs with me? Hang out or whateva?" I asked, trying my best not to sound needy.

His eyes shifted to the digital clock on his dash, which read 9:46 p.m. "A'ight."

As we entered my suite, I noticed that every-thing was dark and quiet. I flipped on the lights and began leading the way to my bedroom. When I passed by the room that Hope used to occupy, an instant feeling of guilt and sadness engulfed me. It was the exact same way I felt whenever I would think of her and that fucked-up night.

As soon as we entered my room, Josh went over to the TV and picked up the remote. "What you wanna watch?" he asked, holding the remote in his hand.

I shrugged my shoulders. "Whatever. Don't matter to me," I told him, leaning down to take off my shoes.

Once I removed my jewelry and the scarf that was tied around my hair, I told Josh that I was going to go change. By then, he had removed his jacket and was sitting on the foot of my bed, trying to find something to watch. He didn't pay me much attention, simply nodded his head.

After a quick shower, I threw on an oversized T-shirt and a pair of boy shorts. When I reentered my room, I noticed that Josh was still seated in the same spot, legs cocked open wide as he leaned over, engrossed in the final minutes of a basketball game. I grabbed my bottle of lotion from the dresser and sat beside him to moisturize my legs.

As my hands slid up and down my calves, Josh peered at me. "You want me to step out?" he asked.

I shook my head. "Nah. Why? I'm just putting my lotion on."

He didn't respond. Instead, he stood up from the bed and went over to lean his back against the closed door. "So, did you have a good time tonight?" he asked, watching me.

I smiled, thinking about the entire service, and then I shrugged. "It was cool, I guess. A lot of surprises."

"Surprises? Like what?"

"*Like what*?" I repeated. "Like the fact that you can sing. I mean, a nigga's pretty *and* can sing. Shid, I know you gay now," I teased. Laughing, I moved my hands over to the other thigh.

When I shot a quick glance up to catch his reaction, a smirk appeared on his face. "You wild, ma. I'm definitely not gay," he said, shaking his head.

"Mm-hmm," I muttered. "That's what they all say."

"Man," he drawled with a hint of laughter in his voice. "I'm not."

Completely finished with the lotion, I sat up straight and looked into his eyes. "You ain't gotta lie to kick it with me, Josh. It's cool."

He didn't say anything, just sucked his teeth.

I don't know why, but I enjoyed pushing his buttons. Slowly, I stood up from the bed and tiptoed toward him. When I planted myself precisely in front of him with my breasts no more than an inch away from his abs, he chucked up his chin. Judging by his lips, which were twisted to the side, and his eyes, which had shifted up toward the ceiling, it was obvious that he was uncomfortable.

Hell, maybe he is gay, I thought.

"Well, what would you do if I told you that I wanted to kiss you?" I asked, challenging him.

He sucked in a deep breath and looked down into my eyes. "I'd tell you that I've wanted to kiss you since the very first time I saw you on Sutter Avenue," he said in an even tone. No longer was there a smirk or a hint of a smile on his face, just thoughtful eyes gazing into mine.

My neck lurched back. "Sutter Avenue?" I asked in disbelief.

He licked his lips and nodded. "Yeah. Back home, in Brooklyn."

"But I was so rude—"

"You were beautiful," he said, cutting me off.

In that moment, every last bit of air seemed to escape my lungs. My heartbeat had doubled in speed, and I was now rendered speechless. Somehow Josh had been able to turn the tables on me. Instead of me pressing him into a corner, he had quickly gotten the upper hand.

"What? You ain't got nothing to say? No 'church boy' comment? No 'You's a gay-ass nigga' remark?" he mocked, slowly backing me up toward my bed.

As he continued to stalk toward me, making me take a few steps back, I almost tripped over my own feet. Finally, when the backs of my thighs hit the edge of the bed, I fell back, with him towering over me. I gazed up and took in his commanding presence. It was something I hadn't recognized in him before now. My body instantly grew hot all over, and a rhythmic pulse quickened between my thighs.

Damn.

"Cat got your tongue?" he asked. Licking his pretty dark pink lips, he cocked his head to the side.

"Um, I—I . . . ," I stuttered breathily.

"Yeah, that's what I thought. Now, scoot over so I can finish watching this game."

Chapter 18

Paris

Friends?

"Yo, you sure you don't wanna just come back home with me?" Franki asked, tossing her clothes into a duffel bag.

"No, I'll be fine. I promise," I told her.

Here it was the Monday before Thanksgiving, and I was standing in the doorway of Franki's bedroom, watching her pack to go home. I, on the other hand, would be spending the break on campus. My mother still hadn't reached out, and at this point, I refused to be the only one who called. With my father being gone, my mother was now all I had, and she knew this. That was what hurt the most. Sure, I was eighteen, technically a full-fledged adult, but I still felt abandoned.

"So what are you going to do, then?" she asked.

"I'll probably just hang around here and study. I think they're having turkey and dressing in the café on Thursday, so . . ." I shrugged.

Franki looked at me with concern in her eyes. "You sure?" she asked again.

"Yes, stop worrying. You'll be back on Sunday, right?"

"Yeah," she sighed. "My muva would have a damn fit if she knew I left you here alone, especially on a holiday. For Christmas, you're definitely coming back home with me," she said.

"We'll see. Besides, I wouldn't want to be a third wheel with you and your *man*," I teased, bouncing my eyebrows, a smirk on my face.

Franki scrunched up her nose. "Josh is *not* my man. We're just friends."

"What-evs," I told her, then twisted my lips in doubt.

When my eyes shifted over to the clock on her nightstand, I saw that it was almost six. Unintentionally, I bounced on the balls of my feet, trying to contain my excitement. I was expecting a call from Malachi, and the mere thought of him made me giddy all over. It was not like I talked with him every day, but on the rare occasions I did, I was thrilled.

"All right, babes. Give me a hug," I told her, extending my arms.

She rolled her eyes but hugged me anyway. "A'ight, I'ma call and check on you. Be safe."

My eyes stretched. "No, you be safe. You're the one that's going to Brooklyn."

She released a snort of laughter and shook her head. "Brooklyn *is* safe. One of the best, if not *the* best city on this earth. Stop believing everything you see on the TV."

As soon as she finally left the suite, I waltzed over to my room and flopped down on the bed. Like a total dweeb, I stared at my cell phone for almost five minutes, until it rang.

"Hello," I answered mid-ring.

"Miss Paris," Malachi said smoothly.

My cheeks warmed at the mere sound of his voice. "This is she. Who am I speaking with?" I asked. Phone pressed to my ear, I propped my chin up in my hands.

"Shawty, why you acting like you weren't sitting by the phone, waiting for a nigga to call?" He laughed. "So, what's good wit' you? You ready for me to come scoop you or what?"

"Come get me?"

"Yuh. Come hang wit' ya' boy. Ain't like you got shit else to do tonight," he said.

"Um . . . I don't know," I said, although I knew for a fact that I was going.

He let out a guffaw of laughter. "I'm pulling up in fifteen. Pack an overnight bag," he said.

At the sound of unexpected silence in my ear, I looked down at the screen. I couldn't believe he'd actually hung up on me. For that, I made a mental note in advance to give him a piece of my mind.

After placing a few outfits and some toiletries in a gym bag, I headed out the door. When I got down to the lobby of our dorm, I noticed quite a few girls huddled by the exit, each with her face pressed up against the cold glass of the windows. One, surprisingly, was our RA, Nina. "Girl, ain't that Malachi?" I could hear them ask each other in a whisper as they peered out at the front lawn. I was not exactly sure why, but Malachi was well known, not only around the city, but on campus as well.

"Hey, Paris. Heading home for the holiday?" Nina asked.

"No, just going to go stay with a friend," I told her.

After squeezing my way through the small crowd that had gathered by the door, I made my way outside. Instantly, my eyes honed in on Asha, who was leaning down in the window of Malachi's Benz. Although I couldn't see her face, I instantly recognized the long braids down her back and the gold rings that were sprinkled throughout the tips.

Shit.

Other than Heather, I hadn't told a soul that I'd been spending time with Malachi. Each time he would call, I'd make sure there was no one around.

And during the few occasions when we'd actually hung out, I'd been able to slip out of the dorm with ease. Franki had been caged up in her room, while Asha had been constantly out and about. This thing between Malachi and me, whatever it was, hadn't been hard to keep under wraps. But now, with Asha standing just a few feet away, I realized there would be no more hiding.

When she stood up straight, she must have felt my presence behind her, because she glanced over her shoulder. "Oh, hey, girl," she said, lifting her eyes in surprise. "What you waiting on? An Uber?"

I forced myself to swallow the lump in my throat before shaking my head. That was when I heard Malachi getting out of the car. Her eyes immediately followed mine as they traveled over to her brother and somehow lit up at the sight of him.

As he swaggered around, pulling the hood of his gray sweatshirt over his head, he sent a wad of spit into the grass. Clearly, he was unbothered by Asha's presence, but for me, things were a bit awkward. Asha looked back and forth between the two of us but ultimately allowed her eyes to land on me. I could tell by her expression that she was confused.

"You ready?" he asked, looking at me.

Unable to respond, I tucked a piece of wispy hair behind my ear and gulped.

"Oh, so, what?" She turned to Malachi. "You tricking off on my friends now?"

Friends? Since when does Asha consider us to be friends? I thought to myself.

"Aye, man, mind ya' business," he told her in an even tone.

She rolled her light brown eyes and stomped off toward the dorm. As she passed by, she made sure to bump shoulders with me. "Wit' your ole sneaky ass," she mumbled beneath her breath. I could only sigh.

Malachi opened the passenger door, then looked back at me before dipping his head toward the car. "Come on," he commanded.

After getting inside, I slid my gym bag over the center console and tossed it on the back seat. Seconds later, Malachi hopped in as well and immediately swept those sparkling hazel eyes over me before placing a single wet kiss to my cheek. "You miss me?" he asked arrogantly.

"No. I didn't," I lied. "And I don't appreciate you hanging up on me," I told him, folding my arms across my chest.

"So, what? You gon' be a brat all night?" he asked, then smirked with his bottom lip pulled between his teeth.

"No, but I needed to get that off my chest."

He let out a little snort and nodded his head. "I feel you, Miss Paris. I feel ya," he said.

As we pulled off into the night, I didn't bother to ask where we were going. I just sat back and relished the ride, inhaling the sweet scents of vanilla and expensive leather, which always seemed to perfume his car. My head fell back against the seat as I listened to the profound lyrics of Tupac that resounded from his speakers. I took note of the quick flashes of light from the streetlamps that flew by out the window. Malachi and I didn't speak a word. We didn't need to, because we simply vibed.

While he rapped along to the music, guiding the steering wheel with a single hand, he made sure to hold mine with the other. Occasionally at a red light, he would pull my hand up to his lips, subtly kiss the back of it. Although many would never know it from the violent tattoos covering his body, the gold teeth in his mouth, and the arrogant bop in his stride, Malachi was sweet like that. Always gentle and tender, handling me like a princess.

Well, besides hanging up in my face earlier.

Fifteen minutes later, we were pulling into a subdivision where townhomes with alternating brick and vinyl siding stood on every street. When we rolled up a driveway and parked in front of a one-car garage, I looked up to see every light on inside the house. "Whose house is this?" I asked.

"It's mine. Come on," he told me.

After unlatching the seat belt, I got out, gym bag in hand, and made my way over to his wiggling fingers, which were summoning me to hold his hand. Together, we walked up to the front door, where he pulled out a key and let us inside. I had anticipated a bunch of noise and people partying in his place, but neither was present. Other than the alarm system going off when we entered, his house was as quiet as a barbershop on a Monday.

"Why are all the lights on if no one's here?" I asked.

"People don't need to know when I'm here and when I'm not," he answered. Then he looked down at my feet. "Take your shoes off."

After removing my shoes, I followed Malachi farther into the house, wearing just my socks. As I trailed behind him, slipping on the polished oak that stretched across the floor, I looked all around. The first room we entered was his den, which had one glass coffee table surrounded by a few brown leather chairs. No art hung from the tan-painted walls; nor were there any curtains covering the windows. Just one flat-screen television with wires dangling from the back. My mother would be appalled.

"So, you really live here?" I asked.

"Yuh. You want something to drink?" Malachi didn't wait for an answer. He simply continued on a path toward the kitchen.

As he opened the fridge, I rested my elbows on the slab of granite covering the top of his bar. "It looks like no one lives here, Malachi. You have kids," I stated, wondering how anyone could live in a place that felt so cold.

"They got a bunch of stuff in their rooms," he said defensively. "Their mama decorated it."

Little miss Reese's cup. I sighed. "And where exactly does she live?" I was curious to know.

"She got her own spot across town. Why? Why you asking about her?" he questioned, passing me a bottle of water.

I quickly spun the cap and took a small sip. "Just making sure there's no drama with me being over here, is all," I said, flipping back my hair.

"Ain't no drama with me, baby," he boasted, pulling me into him by the waist. "You hungry, Miss Paris? You wanna order some food?" he asked, looking down at me.

"Um . . . sure," I replied.

Gently, his fingertips pushed the untamed strands of hair away from my face. His golden irises drew me in as he peered down into my eyes.

For some reason, being this close to Malachi, pelvis to pelvis and chest to chest, made my belly quiver. Sure, we'd kissed and often held hands, but not once had we crossed the line to sex. He was a grown man who had already conceived two children, and although he had never pressed me for anything more, I sometimes felt guilty for making him indulge in child's play.

At first sight, I was completely turned off by Malachi. His rough, thuggish appearance did absolutely nothing for me, because for as long as I could remember, I had been attracted only to guys who looked like Nick Jonas from the Jonas Brothers or Robert Pattinson from *Twilight*. One would think that I'd be naturally drawn to black men since my father was one, but it had never been the case. In the places I frequented, from the private schools to the luxury malls, black guys were a rare sight. For me, men like Malachi were really seen only on social media and on the television screen.

But the more time I spent with him, the more those piercing hazel eyes and his formidable presence won me over. It also didn't hurt that our conversations were always so easy. When I explained to him how my father had died and how I now had a strained relationship with my mother, he just listened. He would always say, "I got your back, Miss Paris," or "Shawty, don't worry. You gon' be all right." And on the days when I felt most alone, it was he who would make me feel just the opposite—comforted, safe, and secure. I was starting to like him. *A lot.*

Then there was the part of me that was strictly drawn to him by ego. I had quickly come to realize that out of all the women roaming around this college town, Malachi could just about have his pick. Every woman at the nail shop, young and old, seemed to swoon over him. And at the restaurants we ate at, the waitresses would all flirt with him, going above and beyond just to cater to his needs. Even the girls on campus would all gawk and stare whenever he pulled up to the yard. He was admired and desired by so many, yet he was chasing after me.

"Look in that drawer to your right and get the menus," he said, releasing his hold around my waist.

After stepping over to my right, I pulled out the kitchen drawer. There in the cramped space appeared to be menus from just about every restaurant in town. Pizza, Chinese, Thai—you name it, he had it all. Underneath the menus were mini packets of ketchup and soy sauce, which I could tell had accumulated over time. From just this one drawer, I concluded that Malachi was a single man, living alone off carryout food.

"You like Thai?" I asked, looking up from the menu.

"I eat whatever," he said. "Just order what you want so we can go upstairs."

After I ordered our food, he grabbed my gym bag, which was by the front door, and guided me upstairs. As I climbed each step, sliding my hand up the wooden rail, curiosity consumed me. I became eager when we finally reached the top landing and he flipped on the lights. Every bedroom door was wide open except for the one down at the end of the hall.

The first room to my right had to be his little girl's, because even through the darkness inside, I was able to make out the soft hues of purple and pink. Next door was a toddler's room. Its small bed was pushed up against the wall, and above it were wooden letters that carefully spelled out the name Mekhai.

"Your kid's room?" I asked.

Midstride, he glanced back over his shoulder and let his eyes trail over to his son's room. "Yeah," he said, cracking a little smile.

Finally, when we reached the end of the hall, he opened the double doors. Before me appeared a king-size bed with four mahogany pillars that stretched up to the ceiling from each corner. Black tufted leather covered the massive headboard, while a thick golden comforter lay neatly on top of the bed. There were matching mahogany night-stands on either side of the bed, and thick golden drapes hung from the large bay window overlooking the front yard.

"Wow," I murmured in surprise. His bedroom was a clear contrast to what I had seen downstairs.

Then my eyes traveled up to the black-and-white portrait hanging over the bed. The image was from another time and of a man I didn't recognize. It was obvious that whoever he was, he was a boxer, evident by the boxing gloves he wore and his traditional fighting stance. Malachi must have noticed me staring at the portrait, because out of the blue, he said, "Henry Armstrong."

"Huh?"

He pointed his finger up toward the picture. "The boxer," he said.

"Oh. You like boxing?" I asked, thinking how odd it was for him to have a random picture of some old-school boxer hanging on his wall.

He nodded. "Yeah. I studied as a little kid down at my father's gym up until I was in high school," he admitted. Then he dipped his forehead toward the picture. "But Henry Armstrong, that's someone my great-grandfather used to train back in the late nineteen thirties. He was a world boxing champion. Nigga was legit," he said.

"Wow," I said again. My eyes danced around his room a bit more, and I took in all his unique trinkets and treasures that I'd somehow missed the first time around. Mindlessly, I wandered over to the long cheval mirror he had angled toward the wall. Dangling from the top right corner was a pair of ancient boxing gloves that seemed to have cracked over time. I looked to my left, where I saw a black leather chair in the corner. Above it were more black-and-white action shots hanging on the wall. In the ring, pound for pound, blow for blow, each picture told a different story.

This was his thing.

"What made you get into boxing?" I asked, eyes still glued to the photos on the wall.

"My pops was a boxer, and so was his pops," he answered.

"And you don't box anymore?"

"Nah, not for sport."

I turned around to face him, pouting my lips over the fact that he had broken with tradition. "And I bet you were really good."

"Still am," he bragged.

I walked over and grabbed the remote control from his nightstand. Just as I was about to cut on the TV and jump on his bed, he stopped me. "Nah, you ain't showered yet," he said.

"Excuse me?"

"Go wash up before you get in the bed, shawty. I don't touch my sheets when I'm dirty." He was serious.

"But I was just gonna sit—"

"There's soap and towels already in there," he said, cutting me off as he nodded toward his bathroom door.

Rolling my eyes, I grabbed my gym bag from the floor and headed inside the master bath. After closing the door behind me, I quickly noticed just how neat and clean everything was. No toothpaste stains speckled his mirror, and there were no traces of soap scum lying in the dish. Even his toilet seat was down, and the faintest scent of bleach could be smelled in the air.

I turned back and noticed the floating mahogany shelves on the wall. On them were precisely stacked bars of Dove soap, along with folded white bath towels and washcloths. *Hmm, neat freak*, I thought.

I pulled out one of each of the towels before my eyes finally connected with the large soaking tub in the corner. Inwardly, I shrilled, because I hadn't had a bath since I'd left California. On several occasions, I had been *this* close to booking a room at the Grandover Resort just so that I could treat myself to a bubble bath, but so far, I hadn't cracked. It was one of the things I hated most about living in the dorm—showers only.

After running the hot water and filling the tub to capacity, I stripped down and submerged my naked body in the bathwater. I was used to listening to music while taking a bath, but since I'd left my cell phone out in the bedroom, I decided to just sing. The same way I couldn't dance, I couldn't sing, either, but it never stopped me from trying.

I belted out the lyrics to Trevor Smith's "What's It Gonna Be?" "Baby, just tell me just how you feel. We living it. I'm just giving it to you real, baby, c'mon."

Suddenly, there was a hard knock on the bathroom door. "Miss Paris, you all right in there?" Malachi asked from the other side.

"I'm fine."

"A'ight. Just checking, Mama. Sound like you crying in there."

"Ha, ha, very funny," I replied, wagging my head from side to side.

"And hurry up in there. The food's here," he said.

After spending a few more minutes in the tub, I got out and threw on a pair of pink silk pajama shorts and a cami to match. When I stepped out of the bathroom, Malachi was already lying back on the bed, shirtless, arms behind his head, with his eyes focused intently on the television screen. A gun, which I hadn't noticed before now, rested on the nightstand. Inadvertently, my eyes lingered on his muscular chest. I noted the blend of black and brown from the tattoos that covered nearly every inch of his skin.

Suddenly, the sound of him clearing his throat took me out of my trance. I looked up to see his bright hazel eyes smiling back at me. Teasing me. He'd caught me red-handed, and instantly, I could feel my cheeks flush from embarrassment.

Lifting my nose in the air, I flipped my curly wet hair back behind my shoulders. "I thought you were supposed to shower before you got in the bed?" I sassed, attempting to conceal my humiliation.

"I showered in the other bathroom," he said with a smirk. "You ready to eat?"

I nodded.

When Malachi got up from the bed, my eyes involuntarily traveled down to the bulge in his sweatpants. He smiled, almost blushing if he could, before pulling his bottom lip between his teeth. "Miss Paris, you all right over there?" he asked.

Moisture now accompanied a constant pulsation between my thighs, and I had to shift my eyes away. "I'm fine." I gulped.

As I followed him out into the hall, he looked at me over his shoulder, then shot a quick glance down to my bare feet. "A'ight, shawty, you straight." He nodded. "I forgot you had some pretty toes on you. If they were ugly, I'd have to lend you a pair of my socks for the night. Cover them bitches up," he joshed.

I gently nudged him in the back. "As if," I said, rolling my eyes.

As we descended the stairs, laughing and joking with one another, the doorbell rang.

"Who the fuck!" Malachi muttered in front of me.

As he jogged down the rest of the way, I stayed put, with my eyes honed in on the door. When he opened it up, Reese appeared with two small children standing in front of her. I instantly recognized them from the pictures Malachi had previously shared.

"Daddy!" they both screamed out in excitement, wrapping their little arms around his waist. Malachi reached down and hugged them both before kissing the tops of their heads.

However, when Reese tried to cross the threshold behind them, Malachi stood in her way.

"What's up?" he said, chucking up his chin before applying a firm grip to the edge of the door.

Her eyes immediately darted past him and shifted up toward me. Her eyes narrowed, and her neck momentarily stiffened. "Oh, I see what this is," she said, then twisted her lips with an attitude. "You're *entertaining* tonight."

I could see Malachi's head cock to the side. "What's up, Reesie?" he asked again, ignoring her comment. "What you and the kids doing out here this late?"

"I told you that I was flying out to Tennessee tomorrow. My granny in the hospital. Did you forget?"

Malachi groaned, swiping his hand over his face. "Damn," he muttered.

"Daddy, who's that?" his daughter asked, pointing up at me.

I gulped, suddenly feeling naked with everyone's eyes glued to me. Then I realized why I felt so naked to begin with. I didn't have any real clothes on. Immediately, I wrapped my arms around my chest, covering my stoned nipples, which were trying to peek through the fabric. Tilting my head to the side, I gave my onlookers a coy smile. "Hi," I said softly.

Although it was subtle, I could see Malachi clench his teeth. "Miss Paris, go wait upstairs for me," he said.

Feeling a little caught off guard by his command, I turned around and made my way back up the steps. When I got to the top landing, out of everyone's view, I leaned over the rail and listened.

Nosy Rosie, I thought, recalling one of the various nicknames Heather had given me.

"Mae, take Mekhai in the living room and cut the TV on," I heard him tell his daughter.

After a few seconds of silence, Reese said, "So, this young bitch done got your mind all fucked up, I see."

My mouth fell open. *Bitch?*

"Aye, watch ya' mouth," Malachi told her.

"No, I'm not gonna watch my mouth, because you're slipping. Forgetting all about your kids. That ain't even like you, Chi. And what is she? Sixteen?"

I could hear Malachi suck his teeth. "Mane, g'on head with that. You know damn well she ain't no sixteen."

"Well, she damn sure ain't far from it," Reese snapped back.

"She's just a friend, Reesie. Damn. That's it."

I didn't know why, but in that moment, I felt slighted. No, Malachi and I weren't in some exclusive relationship, but I damn for sure thought we were more than friends. Although not through sex, he and I had already shared quite a few intimate moments. To him, fragments of my most vulnerable sides had been revealed. I had opened up about my father and the depression I endured when he died. He knew all about my mother, who had deserted me at one of the most critical times in my life. The story of my very first kiss, along with the name of my first boyfriend, had already been disclosed. This man had the privilege of knowing things about me that not many could say they had.

Friends?

Not with the way my body ached when his lips were pressed up against mine. Nor the way his hazel eyes would sear into me, like he was searching the deepest parts of my soul. We had to be more than that, *right*? I mean, he acted like he didn't even want his children to see my face. Maybe I was overreacting, but somehow I felt wounded by his choice of words.

Without giving it another thought, I charged off to his master bedroom and immediately began packing. As I got redressed, I felt a concoction of emotions: hurt, angry, and irritated all at once. I just wanted to get out of there. After another five or ten minutes passed by, I was fully dressed, with my gym bag hanging from my arm. But just as I pressed the Uber app on my phone, Malachi came walking through the bedroom door.

"Where you going?" he asked with his eyebrow raised.

"You have your kids tonight. I don't want to intrude," I told him, forcing myself to sound mature.

"You ain't intruding. I was coming up to tell you that we finna eat."

I shook my head. "No, I'm not hungry."

He must have sensed that I was upset, because he stepped into my personal space and gently grabbed me by the hand.

"But I want you to meet my kids," he said lowly, pulling me into him.

"Are you sure?" I hiked my brow. "Because you acted like you didn't even want them to see me standing there just a few minutes ago."

He let out a light snort of laughter before wrapping his arms around my waist, drawing my pelvis to his. "You right. I didn't," he admitted. "You had all that ass and them thick-ass thighs hanging out of those little shorts." He shook his head. "My kids don't need to see all of that, Miss Paris. Especially . . ."

"Since we're just friends, right?" I said, finishing his sentence with an attitude.

The arrogant smirk on his face read like he had just been told the most scandalous secret. "That's not what I was gon' say, but we are friends, right?"

"Yep," I said curtly. Rapidly blinking my eyes, I tried to disguise my insecurities.

Without warning, Malachi dipped his head and positioned his lips to the side of my neck. Naturally, my eyes closed as I felt the tip of his warm tongue glide across my skin. "Friends don't do this," I whispered, feeling my legs go weak.

He didn't respond with words; instead, his hands slowly slid down to my ass, then gripped it through the tight jeans I wore. As he continued to kiss and suck all up and down my neck, a soft moan escaped me.

"Enough of that," Malachi said as he pulled back. He delivered a hard smack to my derriere. "Now, let's go downstairs and eat."

When the two of us got downstairs, his little boy was sitting on the couch, drinking from a sippy cup, and his daughter was on the floor, sitting Indian-style in front of the TV.

"You left them unattended?" I whispered.

"They straight. My kids know how to act," he said, bending over to pick up his son. "Ain't that right, big man?" He tickled his side. His son let out the most infectious giggle, exposing a mouthful of tiny Chiclet teeth. He was adorable, with his warm brown skin and bright hazel eyes. "Mekhai, say hi to Miss Paris."

Mekhai smiled and said, "Pai-wis."

"Hi, Mekhai." I cooed.

"Maevyn," Malachi called to his daughter, who was completely engrossed in cartoons.

"Sir?" she said, eyes remaining on the television screen.

Wow, what manners, I thought.

"Come meet my friend," he said.

Maevyn glanced back from her spot on the floor and allowed her eyes to land on me. She hopped up and smiled as she made her way over. The two pigtails in her hair bounced with every step. And like Mekhai, she was a beautiful child with warm chocolate skin and slanted golden eyes.

"Say hello to Miss Paris, Maevyn," Malachi told her.

"Hi, Miss Paris," she said bashfully. Clinging to her father's leg, she gave a little wave of her hand.

I stooped down to her level and said, "Hi, Maevyn. I'm Paris."

Gently, she yanked the leg of Malachi's pants and looked up at him with matching eyes. "She's pretty, Daddy," she whispered.

Malachi didn't respond to her remark; instead, he peered down at me. "Come on, y'all. Let's go eat," he said.

Over dinner, I was able to witness Malachi "the father," rather than Malachi "the hoodlum." It was a clear contrast to the man I'd been spending time with. His words seemed to come out gentler when he spoke to his children, and even his laughs and smiles were more abundant. It was evident that his children ignited a much tenderer side of him, reminding me of the memories I had with my own father.

After we ate, I told Malachi that I would clean the kitchen while he put his children to bed. As I was loading the last of the dishes in the dishwasher, because I absolutely refused to wash them by hand, Malachi came up behind me. His arms circled my waist as his chin nuzzled in the crook of my neck.

"Miss Paris?" he said.

"Hmm?"

"You 'bout done in here, so we can go upstairs?" he asked.

"Yep, totally done," I said. After turning the dishwasher on, I spun around and pecked his lips. "Come on."

As I closely trailed behind him up the stairs, I tugged gently at the back of his shirt to keep us connected. We tiptoed past the children's rooms before finally entering his master suite. I immediately went inside the bathroom to change back into my pajamas, and when I came out, he was already in bed, resting back against the headboard with the remote in his hand. For some odd reason, I didn't hesitate to crawl in bed next to him. As we both lay there beneath the covers, I felt like a little girl playing house, snuggled beside my husband while our children were deep in slumber in the very next rooms.

"What does eight-five-nine mean?" I asked, allowing the tip of my finger to trace the black ink on his neck.

"Eight-five-nine?" he repeated, almost saying it with pride. "It was eight niggas who started it all back in nineteen sixty-four," he began. "They all lived in a small town called Greenville, right in the heart of the ghetto, off Fifth Street. They were known for robbing, shooting, and killing niggas, until eventually, in the early eighties, they became known for moving weight."

"Moving weight?" I asked, having never heard the term.

"Yuh, drug trafficking. Crack cocaine," he clarified. "These niggas were into so much shit—murder, drugs, you name it—but never once got caught. They would go to trial but would get off each and every time. They'd go to war with some of their toughest rivals without ever once getting shot. It was believed back then that these cats had nine lives. And so that's where they got the name from . . ."

"Eight, five, nine," I uttered softly, finally understanding.

He released a soft snort of laughter. "Smart girl. I see that college shit is paying off," he joked.

I rolled my eyes. "And so, does all of that still go on today? The killing and the drug stuff?" I wanted to know.

"Nah," he replied smoothly.

I knew that he was lying, because I'd already heard some of the things Asha would say, but I didn't call him out on it. "What's this?" I asked, allowing my fingers to skim across a lump on his shoulder.

"I got shot. A couple years back."

My throat constricted at that. I'd never met anyone who'd been shot before. "I'm sorry someone hurt you," I told him.

I could feel his shoulder shrug next to me. "It's a'ight. He got the worst of it," he said.

I didn't exactly know what that meant or if I really wanted to know, so I quickly changed the subject. "So, whatever happened between you and Reese? Like, why aren't you guys together anymore?" I asked.

He let out a little chuckle and looked down at me. "Where the fuck did that come from?"

"I don't know. I'm just trying to figure out the deal between you two. When I first saw you at the nail salon that day, it seemed like you guys were together. But then, when we went over to Bull's place a few weeks after that, she could barely look you in the eyes."

He sighed.

"Then, like tonight, I could visibly tell that me being here bothered her. I just . . . I don't get it," I said.

"Mane," he groaned, dragging his hand over his face. "Reese and I got together when we just fifteen years old. Back in Northwest Guildford High. Used to cut class just to go down to Deedry Park. Drinking and smoking and shit. Then, when I got initiated into eight, five, nine, shawty followed right behind me a month later and got jumped in too." He let out a light snort of laughter and shook his head. "Surprised the shit outta me," he said. "Over the years, we grew tight. Real tight. Been through so much shit that honestly, a nigga thought we was gonna be together forever," he admitted. "But then, after she got pregnant with Mekhai, she fucked around with my nigga."

My eyes stretched in shock. "Your friend?" I asked as I peered over at him.

He pulled his lips between his teeth and nodded. "Yeah, she cheated on me with my homeboy Rich. Said I was never home, that we weren't getting along . . . a bunch of bullshit, basically."

"So, it's over now?" I asked.

With every second that ticked by, I could hear my own heart hammering inside my chest. My throat grew tight, and I was finding it difficult to breathe. It was like, all of a sudden, time had slowed, and the silence in the room was choking me. My mind started racing with thoughts of the two of them being an actual family unit with their kids. I was feeling something that I'd never really experienced before. *Jealousy*.

Malachi exhaled deeply before reaching over to cut off the lamp. Then he pulled my body in close to his and drew my thigh over his waist. "Yuh, it's over," he finally said. After tapping the remote to power off the TV, he tilted his head down and pressed his lips against my forehead. "Sweet dreams, Miss Paris."

"Good night," I whispered.

As I lay there in the darkness, the uneasiness I felt eventually melted away from my body. But with my mind running rampant, I couldn't help but stay awake for a while. I was honestly wondering what I was doing with a man like Malachi, someone so unrefined and so unlike my father. I didn't know if it was the thrill of being with a bad boy or those unnerving hazel eyes, but the two of us were like magnets, one positive, the other negative, but naturally drawn together by the laws of attraction. Granted, I was only eighteen years old, but Malachi made me feel things I had never felt before. He made me feel vulnerable at times I didn't want to be, and my heart beat differently in his presence.

We had to be more than just friends, right?

Chapter 19

Hope

Lost in Forever

"Well, it looks like we're all done here," I said, closing the textbook on my lap. When I removed the glasses from my face and stood up from the bed, Meeko gently grabbed me by the elbow. My body instantly stilled from his touch, and my eyes closed, fleetingly.

"You leaving already?" he asked.

I sighed.

Over the past few weeks, Meeko and I had been studying hard for final exams, meeting up at the library each time. But somehow, today he'd managed to lure me back to his room, claiming that Ty had his keys. He had said that he didn't want to leave his place unlocked. It was understandable, so after my classes were over for the day, I walked clear across the quad to Pride Hall.

"Yeah, it's getting late. I don't wanna have to walk to the bus stop in the dark," I told him.

"You already know I'll drive you home," he said, sweeping the pad of his thumb tenderly over my arm.

I peered down at him, as he was still sitting on the edge of the bed. "I thought you said Ty had your keys. How can you drive me home without keys?" I asked, narrowing my eyes.

Exhaling a frustrated breath, Meeko ran his hand over the top of his head. "Damn, Hope. Why you acting like you don't know a nigga miss you? Can't you see I'm just tryna spend some time?"

"Meeko," I sighed. "You know I can't." At this point, study sessions were all I was willing to give, and even that was against my father's wishes.

"Hope, I fucked up," he said, placing his hand to his chest. "Majorly. I should have been there to keep them bitches from putting their hands on you. I should have told Jazz flat out that you were off limits, because you were . . . You're mine."

In that moment, his words melted me like falling snow on a child's tongue. My eyes slowly connected with his. My chest instantly warmed at the sincerity I saw in them. Week after week, I'd been trying my best to play tough, keeping this thing between Meeko and me strictly professional, tutor to tutee. But today, he was truly wearing me down.

As if it hadn't been hard enough restraining myself from laughing at his jokes or from purposely inhaling the scent of his cologne, each time he'd flash that million-dollar smile of his, my brain would just fizzle into mush. I practically had to avoid looking at his handsome face altogether just to get back on track with our studies. And now, with him actually admitting that he missed me, claiming me as his own . . . *God*.

"I guess I can stay for a little while longer," I said softly, then chewed on the corner of my lip.

Meeko took the thick textbook from my hand and carelessly tossed it on the floor.

"Com'ere," he said, subtly tugging me by the hand.

Without warning, he brought me down on his lap and placed his hand at the nape of my neck. His thumb lightly feathered my cheek as he stared into my eyes. "I been missing the fuck outta you, Hope," he whispered.

As our faces drew near, my heart galloped like there were racehorses inside my chest. My mouth parted, allowing only shallow breaths to escape. "Why me?" I asked. Honestly, I just didn't understand why he missed *me* so much. Why was he all of a sudden wanting *me*? "You're popular. I'm not," I told him.

Meeko's lips grazed mine before he released a light snort of laughter. "This ain't high school, Hope. Popularity don't mean shit to me no more."

"Then, tell me what matters," I breathed, gazing into his dark brown eyes, our mouths only millimeters apart.

"You."

Unexpectedly, Meeko pressed his lips against mine, causing my eyes to flutter from shock. My hands went lax at my sides as his tongue pierced its way into my virgin mouth. Everything about this moment was wrong. I mean, he had been the root cause of my attack, and my father had warned me to steer clear of this boy more than once. But how could I? How could I not feel what I was feeling as our lips melded, tongues brushing over each other's in such perfect harmony? I couldn't.

"You so fucking beautiful, Hope," he said and pulled back, eyes surveying every inch of my face with adoration.

Although I felt like the most beautiful girl in the world in that instant, there was still this inkling of self-doubt. "I'm not your type," I told him. "The light skin, the green eyes, and the fancy clothes. I have none of that."

"And I don't want you to." He let out another soft chuckle and shook his head. "I only wish you could see what I see."

Meeko nudged me to my feet, stood up from the bed, and led me over to the full-length mirror on the back of his door. He forced me to face my reflection in the mirror. Then he planted himself right behind me before removing the bobby pins from my hair. As it slowly unraveled down my back, he sank his fingers deep into my scalp. Instantly, my eyes closed.

"Nah, shorty. Open ya' eyes," he said lowly.

My eyes flew open when I felt his fingers come around to find the buttons of my shirt. Slowly, he unclasped them one by one until the center of my tan bra was exposed.

"Meek, please," I whispered. But the sound of my voice fell on deaf ears. Carefully, he peeled my shirt back, revealing the smooth brown tops of my shoulders. I felt naked as he allowed the fabric to fall to the floor. When I felt his hands work themselves around my waist, then tease the zipper of my skirt, my breath hitched in my lungs.

"Breathe, baby," he said, placing a single kiss on the side of my neck. That one act alone caused goose pimples to cover my entire frame and a tremor to ease down my spine.

Before I knew it, my skirt was puddled around my feet, while I just stood there staring at my reflection, skin the color of a Hershey's Kiss and hair as black as midnight. One tan-colored bra, size 32B, and full brief panties that were made of cotton. How could Meeko, the star wide receiver of our school, Mr. When I Tell a Joke, Everyone Laughs—who had smooth brown skin, teeth white as snow, and the deepest set of waves I'd ever seen

on any man's hair—want me? Yes, I'd had a crush
on him for some time, but never, ever did I think
he would allow himself to feel the same about me.

As his fingers slipped beneath the elastic waistband of my panties, I felt a warm wetness seeping
between my thighs. His hand slid down slowly and
cupped the front of my hairy privates, inspiring my
lips to let go of a foreign moan.

"Mmm," I breathed.

"Shorty, open your eyes. I want you to see how
fucking beautiful you are," he whispered.

I followed his command, opening my eyes again.
I saw that the room was getting dim from the
slowly setting sun. When his finger dipped inside
me, my mouth dropped open from pleasure, and
I gasped. In the mirror, his eyes watched me
vigilantly, and a coaxing smirk played at his lips.
Normally, I would have felt embarrassed by this
whole scene, but it was feeling too good for me to
even care.

"Damn," he gasped, lips brushing my ear. "That
pussy's nice and wet for me."

As his finger drilled a little deeper, stroking
me at a steady pace, I felt a sudden tension in
my groin. "Meek," I moaned, wrapping my hand
around his wrist.

"That's it, Hope. Cum for me," he said.

Over and over, he rocked his hand against me,
palm teasing the very front of my clit. It was like,

all of a sudden, his hand and finger had found this perfect tempo that had me right on the edge. My head fell back against his shoulder, and before I knew it, something powerful was ripping through me. My eyes glossed over from tears as I whimpered out his name.

"Good girl," he said.

"Meeko," I cried out softly again, body trembling all over.

My legs gave out under me, but Meeko held me in place. Then he scooped me up in his arms and allowed me to wrap my legs around him like a child. After carrying me over, he laid me back on the bed and nestled himself between my thighs. As we lay chest to chest, he gazed into my eyes, and I could feel the beat of his heart. For some reason, it felt like he was just as nervous as I was.

"I just want to love you, Hope. You gon' let me love you?" he whispered.

I closed my eyes and grabbed the tiny cross that hung from my neck, body shivering from nerves.

"I know your beliefs, and if you're not ready, it's cool," he said.

"But what about all that stuff you, Big Mo, and Ty were saying about virgins? I don't want to be crazy over you, Meek. I don't want you to end up hating me when everything's all said and done."

"I could never hate you," he replied with ease. Gently, he pinched my chin between his fingers and kissed me on the lips. Then he sucked the bottom one into his mouth as he pulled back tenderly with his teeth. "A nigga could never hate someone as perfect as you."

My stomach fluttered as I peered into his eyes. "Promise me you won't hurt me."

Meeko positioned his lips at my collarbone and whispered against my skin. "I promise."

Without any more words exchanged, he deliberately slid down the straps of my bra. My chest heaved up and down from both excitement and fear. Suddenly, what felt like minor bolts of lightning shot through my entire body when he took my pebbled nipple into his mouth. My hands mindlessly slid beneath his T-shirt and swept across the flesh of his abs. I didn't know what I was doing, but I knew I wanted him. *I wanted this*.

As his mouth traveled farther south, his breath tickled my navel, and then I could feel his fingers tugging at the sides of my panties. I gasped when he slid them down over my hips.

"You're so fucking perfect, Hope," he said, his eyes wandering over my nakedness.

He removed his shirt over his head and leisurely tossed it to the floor. Other than a few tattoos sprinkled over his chiseled chest and arms, his skin was flawless like melted fudge. *Perfect*. His body was like an African warrior's, carved to perfection, and had me completely in awe.

In one fluid motion, Meeko's head dipped down between my thighs, and I could feel him spreading my lower lips with his tongue. "Sss," I hissed, quickly covering my face with my hands from shame as the tip of his wet tongue slithered down my folds. A warm tingle zipped through me, and I couldn't help but let out a moan. "Oh."

Meeko reached up and pried my hands away from my face. "Nah, baby. I want you to look at me," he murmured.

My eyes shifted down to see his head twisting from side to side, like he was right in the middle of a French kiss. As his tongue flickered over me, a natural arch formed in my back, and my thighs tightened around his face. "Oh God," I breathed. When his hands cupped by buttocks, permitting his tongue to travel deeper inside, I swear I thought I'd faint.

"Please," I cried out. A tension was starting to form in my core, the same one that just moments ago had me exploding on his finger. I didn't think I could endure it again.

"Mmm, sweet as fuck," he mumbled between loud sucks and kisses. The pleasure I was experiencing was overwhelming and intense, so much so that I had unknowingly begun to wiggle away from him. "Nah, ain't no running, baby," he said as he looked up at me. His grip firmed around my hips as he brought me closer. Then he pulled my hands down to grip the back of his head. "Push my face in it," he coached.

I didn't know why I even listened, because as soon as I pushed his head down, my body climaxed, like a bomb being detonated from within. "Oh, Meek," I moaned, quivering from exquisite pleasure.

As Meeko rose to his knees, mouth glistening from my sex, I watched as he slid down his shorts. Almost instantly his long, thick erection jutted out like a drawn sword. It had a slight curve to it, and I could already see that it was wet at the tip. Propping myself up on my elbows, I gulped.

"Is it going to hurt?" I asked.

He pulled a corner of his bottom lip into his mouth and gave a cocky smirk. "Not for long," he assured me. Then he hovered over me, sliding his shorts down the rest of the way until his foot was flinging them across the room. Finally, when his naked body lay on top of mine, he brushed my bangs back off my face. He was being tender. "I'ma go slow, a'ight?" he said, gazing into my eyes.

He reached down between us and placed the head of his muscle against my entrance. Instinctively, I closed my eyes and gritted my teeth, expecting the worst. However, it wasn't rammed in like I thought it would be. Delicately, he slid himself up and down my wet center before working his way inside.

"Fuck," he groaned and bit down on his lower lip to savor the feeling of our flesh becoming one.

"Meeko," I whispered. It was beginning to hurt.

He smothered my lips with his own and elected to push himself in a little more. As soon as I felt him fill me up, a piercing pain shot through my entire body. I yelped in his mouth.

"Ssh, I'm in," he said, then pulled back from my lips. Amid planting more light kisses on my face and neck, Meeko began traveling in and out of my body with slow, delicate strokes.

"It hurts," I whined, placing my hands on his abs to force some space between us.

"You want me to stop?" he asked.

I shook my head no, because at that point, it was too late. My virginity had already expired.

"You gotta say it," he said.

"Don't stop," I whispered.

He pulled my legs up farther around his waist and began to penetrate my soul. I had to squeeze my eyes and clench my teeth just to absorb the pain as his hips rocked into me. And then, out of nowhere, like a light switch being cut on in the middle of the night, my body began to feel pleasure. All of a sudden, I was inviting him in with ease, and the sounds of my moans were filling the room.

"That's it," he coached. "Open up for me." I lifted my hips and spread my trembling legs as wide as they could go. "Oh, fuck." Meeko closed his eyes and exhaled. "You feel too fucking good, Hope," he groaned.

As his slow, steady pumps gradually picked up speed, I could feel myself on the brink of another orgasm. "Oh, Meek," I breathed.

That seemed only to encourage him, because he kept the same pace, rotating his hips at an angle. And just when I knew I couldn't take any more, my fingers dug into his back and my body imploded from the waist down.

"Oh, fuck. Fuck," he breathed, body tensing as his throbbing muscle jerked inside me.

My legs and arms, weak now, fell to the bed, and Meeko's heavy body collapsed on top of mine, hearts beating out of control as our slippery sweat comingled between us.

"You love me?" he whispered into my neck.

"Yes."

"Let me hear you say it," he urged.

Gently grabbing the sides of his face as his head lay in the alcove of my neck, I forced him to look me in the eyes. "I love you, Meeko," I told him.

He let out a light snort, and in the shards of light streaming in from the blinds, I could see a lopsided grin on his face. "I feel it, baby. I feel your love." He pulled my hand up to his chest, right over his heart, allowing me to feel its steady beat. Then he threaded his fingers through mine and brought our hands up to his lips. I shuddered when his lips pecked the tops of my knuckles. He leaned down and planted a wet, sloppy kiss on my lips before snuggling back up against me. I was so caught up in Meeko, it didn't bother me when he didn't say "I love you" back. I figured that since we were so new, he might just need some time for his feelings to catch up with mine.

Eventually, in that exact same position, we ended up drifting off to sleep. It wasn't until three o'clock in the morning that I woke up in a panic. Through the darkness in the room, I reached over and hit the nightstand, in search of my cell phone. When my fingers finally retrieved it, I clicked on the glowing screen and saw that I had six missed calls from Aunt Marlene and one from my father. Knowing her, she had probably already called Deddy and had him on a red-eye flight back to Greensboro.

"Meeko," I said, struggling to push him off me as I shook his shoulder.

"Huh? What's wrong?" he asked, still half asleep.

"I have to go."

"What? You gotta go?" he asked groggily.

"My aunt's been calling me." I tried shoving him off me again, but his thick football player frame wouldn't budge.

"You not going nowhere tonight. It's three o'clock in the fucking morning, Hope. Just go back to sleep, and we'll deal with that shit in the morning," he said.

Meeko readjusted himself between my thighs and nuzzled back up against my breasts as if it were no big deal. But as I stared out into the blackness of the room, I began to worry. My stomach was literally in knots, and for the life of me, I just couldn't control all the thoughts coursing through my mind.

What lies would I have to tell to be with Meeko, and how would my father react if he ever found out? I didn't even want to know.

"I'm fine, Aunt Marlene," I said. Holding my forehead, I exhaled into the phone. "I just stayed in my old dorm and hung out with my old roommates last night. That's all." I felt awkward lying to my aunt, especially under Meeko's penetrating stare, but I had no choice. I certainly couldn't tell her the truth.

It was the very next morning after my deflowering that Meeko and I ended up in the café for an early lunch. Still basking in the events of the night before, we'd decided to skip our nine o'clock classes. I couldn't speak for him, but for me, the choice was easy. I didn't want to be away from him. Not yet, or *ever*, for that matter. We threw on yesterday's clothes and quickly decided on a bite to eat. Once we got to the café and sat down, I thought about calling Aunt Marlene, then decided to put it off until after lunch. But after sitting with an untouched plate in front of me for over ten minutes, my mind going back to Deddy and what I'd actually done, I mustered up enough courage to call my aunt.

"What's going on, Hope? Staying out all night and not answering the phone when I call. That's unlike you," she said. I could hear the concern in her voice.

I swallowed hard, suddenly feeling hesitant and a little scared. "Did you call my d-deddy?" I asked. My gaze shifted up from the table to Meeko, who was staring at me. I felt so embarrassed about sounding like such a little girl, especially after all the grown-up things we'd done last night, but I had to ask my aunt that question.

"No. But I was giving you only until noon."

I let go of a sigh of relief and pushed my glasses farther up on my face. "Thank you for that. I'll be there this afternoon, once all my classes are over."

"All right. I guess we'll talk more about it when you get here."

When I hung up the phone, Meeko scooted his chair next to mine, dragging its metal feet across the floor. He reached over into my plate to grab a fry before popping it into his mouth. "So what she say?" he asked.

"She didn't call my deddy. Just said that we would talk about it when I got home."

"So you gon' tell her?"

My head reeled back at that. "God no," I told him bluntly. "I don't want anyone to know."

"Anyone?" One of his eyebrows shot up as he grabbed a handful of fries this time.

I shook my head. "Well, I don't want my aunt or Deddy to know. That's for sure."

As we sat there and ate, it seemed like a lot of girls kept whispering and staring at us.

"Hey, Meeko," a petite, light-skinned girl sang, giving a little wave as she approached our table. She had dark, slanted eyes, and her shoulder-length hair was fire-engine red.

Meeko looked over and tossed up his chin. "What up, Reds?" he said, mouth still full of food. He turned back and placed the straw from his Coca-Cola between his lips while she just stood there.

"*So* . . . ," she started. "Why haven't you hit me up?"

He'd been oblivious to the fact that she was still standing there, and now he craned his neck back to look at her again. "Oh," he said, "I've been mad busy, yo. Studying for these finals and shit."

Her eyes lit up like she had suddenly been hit by the most brilliant idea. "I can help you study if you want. Maybe help you relax afterward." She whined the last part, making my stomach lurch at the sexual undertone.

Meeko shook his head. "Nah, my girl's been helping me study." He dipped his forehead over in my direction.

"Your girl?" she quizzed, narrowing her eyes. Her expression said she was clearly baffled. "This is your girlfriend?" she asked, looking directly at me. "But I thought you and Jazz—"

Meeko turned around halfway in his seat and faced her full-on at the mention of Jazz's name. "Yeah, this is my girlfriend, Hope," he said, cutting her off as he pointed back at me with his thumb. "Hope, this is Ra'chelle."

When the word *girlfriend* skated from his lips so effortlessly, I had to bite the insides of my cheeks just to keep from smiling. "Hi," I said, wiggling my fingers in a wave before repositioning the glasses on my face.

Ra'chelle rolled her eyes to the ceiling and let out a single chuckle.

Meeko turned back around in his seat and looked at the plate sitting in front of me. "Shorty, you gon' eat the other half of that turkey sandwich or what?" he asked.

"Well, I . . ." Before I could even get the words out, Meeko grabbed my sandwich and put it up to his mouth. "Was planning to," I said, watching him take an enormous bite.

"My bad," he said, laughing with his mouth full. Some people might have been grossed out, but to me, everything Meeko did was cute. Even the way the muscles of his jaw flexed as he chomped down on his food was sexy. "You going to the basketball game tomorrow?" he asked, taking me out of my trance.

Out of the corner of my eye, I noticed the girl Ra'chelle scoff before she finally walked away. I guess she finally got the hint. "No, probably not," I said with a frown. It was crazy how I had already reverted to my socially withdrawn self. "Well . . ." I twisted my lips, contemplating. "Maybe I should reach out to Paris and Franki. I feel like I haven't seen them in forever."

Meeko was nodding his head in agreement when, all of a sudden, Asha walked up to our table. She wore blue jeans that were practically painted on her lower half and a matching denim jacket. A pair of fancy sneakers were on her feet, and her braids looked new.

"Oh, hey, girl," she said. Her light brown eyes bounced between me and Meeko as she attempted a smile.

"Hey, Asha," I replied. I dabbed the corner of my mouth with a napkin before standing up to greet her with a hug. Although I hadn't seen Asha in almost two months and we had never really been close, I still felt bonded to her in a sense, even under the current circumstances.

She hugged me back, then allowed her eyes to fall on Meeko when I released her from my hold. I watched as her lips screwed into this weird kind of smile. "What y'all doing?" she asked, still looking down at him. I think that was her way of trying to engage him, but Meeko just ignored her and continued eating off my plate. The scene was definitely awkward, because she had no idea that I knew. I knew that not only had she slept with my boyfriend but with his friends, as well, before stealing their money.

"Just catching lunch with my boyfriend before my next class," I told her, then observed the reaction in her eyes.

She cleared her throat and nodded her head. "Nice," she said. I could tell she didn't know what to say. Suddenly, she sucked in a quick breath, and her eyes roved down the length of my hair. "And when did you start wearing your hair down?" she asked, touching the thick strands of my mane that were draped over my shoulders. "It's pretty," she said.

I could feel my face heat as I smiled. "Meek likes my hair down." I glanced down at him.

"Hmm," was all she said. "Well, I guess I'll see you around." She wagged her long, pointed nails and began to walk away.

Just when she got a few feet away, I remembered and called her name. "Asha."

She looked back, flipping her long braids over her shoulder.

"You wanna go to the game with me? I was gonna see if Franki and Paris wanted to go too."

One half of her mouth lifted in a partial smile. "Oh, I'm definitely going. My boyfriend's the starting point guard. Jaxon Brown." Her eyes shot over to Meeko, but he didn't budge.

"Oh, well . . . maybe we'll see you there. With Kiki?" I replied.

"Definitely," she said.

After she walked away, I returned to my seat next to Meeko.

"You need to stay away from her," he said.

"Who? Asha?" I asked, although I knew whom he was referring to.

"Yeah, shorty right there is as scandalous as they come. And if you trying to steer clear of trouble by worrying about me"—he pursed his lips mockingly as he shook his head—"you need to be running every time you see that bitch."

I released a heavy sigh and nodded. Although I was aware of Asha's checkered past and recognized that she wasn't always the nicest to me, I still wanted to be friends with her for some reason. Perhaps it was the God in me, the part that was always willing to forgive and forget. Or maybe it was the recollection of that night when Mark beat her down on the front lawn. I don't know, but either way, there was something about this girl that pulled at my heartstrings. I pitied her.

Looking down at the table, I realized that my plate was now empty.

"You want me to buy you another sandwich?" Meeko asked with a wide smile.

"No. I'll just get something later."

"You sure?" he asked.

I nodded.

"All right. Then, let's get you to class."

After we stood up from the table, Meeko grabbed my winter coat and began wrapping it around me. He proceeded to zip it up, as if I were a child needing his help. My eyes roamed the café, and I saw that the people gathered at nearby tables were beginning to stare at us. Some girls swooned with envy in their eyes, while others were probably wondering why Meek was with me in the first place. Either way, it didn't matter. He was caring for me, and although he didn't say it, I instantly felt loved and tended to.

When he reached behind my shoulders and pulled the hood of my coat over my head, I smiled.

"It's cold as shit outside today," he said. "Can't have you getting sick." He winked his eye, then leaned in to kiss me on the lips.

I knew there were eyes on us, because I could practically feel them, but I honestly didn't care. Nor did I care about the measly fifteen minutes

I had left to hike across campus to my next class. Everybody and everything else could wait. I puckered my lips and closed my eyes, escaping to all things Meeko.

Chapter 20

Franki

The Start of It All

I looked over at Josh and asked, "So, you really gonna read the whole way there?"

We were riding the train back to New York for Christmas break, and for the past two hours, his head had been buried in *The Souls of Black Folk*, by W.E.B. Du Bois. His legs were crossed, with a gap in the middle, and the book rested between his palms.

"Listen to this," he said. "'The Negro is . . . born with a veil, and gifted with a second-sight in this American world,—a world which yields him no true self-consciousness, but only lets him see himself through the revelation of the other world. It is a peculiar sensation, this double-consciousness, this sense of always looking at one's self through the eyes of others, of measuring one's soul by the tape of a world that looks on in amused contempt and pity. One ever feels his twoness,—an American, a Negro; two souls, two thoughts, two unreconciled strivings; two warring ideals in one dark body, whose dogged strength alone keeps it from being torn asunder,'" he read.

It was an excerpt that I had heard a time or two before.

Suddenly, his head lifted from the page. "That's deep, right?" he asked.

I shrugged. "I guess. I mean, I really don't think books written on race relations over a hundred years ago still apply to the world today."

"No?" He smiled. "Well, let me ask you this. Why did you come to A&T? I mean, you said you got a scholarship to William Paterson, right? And another one to go to the University of Connecticut, yes? Why didn't you just go to one of those schools?"

"Well, because I wanted to go to an HBCU," I said.

"But tell me why, ma? The education wouldn't be no different. Matter of fact, some would consider an HBCU to be subpar."

My shoulders hiked again. "Shit, if I'm being honest, I really just wanted to be around people who looked and sounded like me." I let out a little snort, thinking about Paris and Hope. *Epic fail.*

"But why does being around people that look and sound like you even matter? America is full of different types of people, black, white, brown, and everything in between. Hell, almost four percent of Americans consider themselves a part of the LGBTQ community. And more than three hundred and fifty different languages are spoken in US homes today. Why does it matter?"

I let out a sigh, hating when Josh goaded me with his over-the-top intellectual bullshit. "I just wanted to be somewhere where I could be myself, okay? Damn, yo." I tossed my palms in the air.

His dark pink lips spread into an even smile. "Exactly!"

My eyes lit up and then dimmed, since I did not fully understand. "Whatever," I sighed, hoping to end it there. Josh would carry on like this the whole way to New York if I let him.

Acknowledging my irritation, Josh snapped his book closed and slid it into the backpack beneath his feet. "I like politics and history, and you like science. It's all good, right?" he said, nudging me on the arm.

"I guess."

"So, tell me. What's Christmas gon' be like at your house?" Josh shifted closer to me and laid his head back on the seat.

"Well, it's just me and my muva, so . . ." My voice trailed off. "We'll probably exchange a couple of gifts, cook a small dinner, and then she'll go to church."

"You going with her this year?"

Scratching the back of my neck, I wagged my head. "Probably not."

When Josh stacked his hand on top of mine on the armrest between us, an unexpected warmth spread throughout my body. "You should come by my father's church. It'll be cool," he said.

I shook my head and twisted my lips. "I don't know. Going back to church brings back too many memories."

"Memories of what?"

"My father."

Over and over, Josh had prodded me for information on my father, assuring me that I could talk to him, but I just hadn't been ready to open up. The memories were too deep and too painful to communicate with words. At this point, I thought he'd just given up.

"Well, you did just fine when you went to church with me. You already know I'ma be right next to you." He curled his fingers beneath my hand, then gently squeezed. Another flutter stirred in my belly at that. *Fuck*.

"Why you always trying to get me to go to church, Josh? Ain't I done already went once?"

He tossed his head back in a laugh, showcasing the whiteness of his back teeth. "You right. You did go that *one* time."

"See?" I said, batting my eyes.

"But nah, fa' real. It's like something in my spirit keeps telling me to push you. Like I'm supposed to be the one that leads you back to the Word of God." He shrugged and shook his head. "I'on know. It's crazy."

"So, what? You wanna be a preacher now?" I asked sarcastically, cutting my eyes over in his direction.

He gave a one-cheek smile. "Nah, you already know I'm gonna be a lawyer."

And, boy, did I know. After politics, religion, and history, that was all Josh ever talked about, his wanting to be a lawyer and, most recently, his internship this summer. It was at some fancy law firm in Manhattan. He'd landed the internship with the help of some connection in his fraternity. Unlike me, Josh was a junior with just one more year of undergrad to go. He was already researching law schools that he would apply to in the latter part of the summer. He was leaving me.

After another four and a half hours on the train, our ride finally came to a stop. I woke up to see Josh's sleeping face, his head on my shoulder. "Wake up," I said, gently nudging his arm.

Once his eyes blinked open, he sat up and stretched his arms before wiping the drool from his mouth. "We here?" he asked.

"Yeah. We gotta go."

Josh stood up and retrieved our luggage from the overhead bin while I slipped on my coat. "You got that for me?" he asked, tipping his head down toward the book bag on the floor. I nodded and threw his bag on my back before following him down the aisle.

As soon as we stepped off the train, the New York frost nipped at my cheeks. I inhaled deeply, loving the raw, urban smell of home. Josh and I fought our way through the oncoming crowd until we finally reached the escalators that led to the main floor of the station. We'd already decided that we'd just share a ride, so when we made our way out front, Josh hailed us a cab.

He raised his right hand high and whistled through his fingers. "Ayo!" he shouted just a few feet beyond the curb.

When a taxi pulled up, Josh loaded our luggage in the trunk while I climbed inside. Then he scooted in beside me. As we pulled off, I stared out the window, taking in the bright lights of the city, the pedestrians walking up and down the pavement, the occasional barren tree, its branches like wild claws in the sky. Suddenly, I felt a tap on my arm, which took me out of my trance. I looked over to see Josh holding out a wrapped present.

"I got you something," he said.

"Josh," I whined, shoulders dropping from shame. "I didn't get you shit, yo," I confessed with a laugh, attempting to cover up the awkwardness.

"It's all good, ma." He cracked an asymmetrical smile and motioned for me to take the present.

Pursing my lips to the side, I hesitantly removed the gift from his hands. It was wrapped in glittery red paper and adorned with a large white bow. A slick comment about him being gay was on the edge of my tongue, but I held it. Carefully, I removed the bow and the pretty paper from the box. When I opened it, I had to pull out wads of white tissue paper. But beneath it all was a brand-new stethoscope. A Littmann 3200, to be exact.

My mouth fell open as I sucked in a huge breath of air. My eyes immediately flew over to Josh's, but I couldn't speak. I was fucking flabbergasted.

"You like it?" he asked.

Still unable to find my voice, I simply nodded my head.

"You sure? Because they had a couple other ones, but Dr. Urlich said that this one here was the best." Dr. Urlich taught freshman biology at A&T on the days he wasn't running his pathology practice.

"It's too much," I finally managed to say with a shake of my head. This stethoscope was a little over four hundred dollars. I just didn't see how he could afford it. Nor did I understand why he would want to spend that kind of money on me.

"Nah, I had the money and just wanted you to have it," he said with a shrug.

"But why?" I was confused.

"I just wanted to make you smile," he said. Then he scratched behind his ear, an uneasy smile on his face. "But, apparently, my plan backfired," he mumbled.

I placed my hand on his shoulder, causing him to look at me. "No, it didn't. I love it. Really."

When his eyes traveled down to my mouth, my heart began galloping in my chest as my clit pulsated inside my jeans. Josh leaned in slowly, and instinctively, I closed my eyes. My lips parted as I exhaled, and then I waited with bated breath. But then I felt an unexpected coolness skimming the sides of my neck. My body jerked, and my eyes opened. I saw that he was placing the metal stethoscope around my neck.

"Looks good on you, Doc," Josh said, winking his eye.

I licked my lips and gulped. "Thank you."

Narrowing his eyes at me, he smiled. Knowingly.

I'm such a fucking moron, yo.

Feeling like a complete fool, I sat back in the seat and continued staring out the window. He tried making small talk the rest of the way, but I was so embarrassed that I just kept nodding and giving one-word answers. When we finally pulled up to my place, Josh got out and helped the cabdriver with my luggage. I waited on the curb, watching as Josh rolled the big bag over.

After he approached me and placed all my belongings to the side, he tucked his hands in his jacket pockets. "So . . . ," he said, letting his voice trail off.

"I guess I'll see you in a couple weeks?" I asked, shrugging my shoulders. I didn't want to assume that we'd be spending time together back home. Hell, he'd already shot me down once by not kissing me in the car, and I didn't want to humiliate myself further by being too presumptuous.

A smile flashed in his eyes as he cocked his head to the side. "I'll call you when I make it home, Franki," he said.

I had to take another swallow as I watched the tip of his tongue wet his bottom lip. I simply nodded. "Yeah," I breathed. "Just . . . call me when you get in." I turned, grabbed my luggage, and started for the steps of my building, but then I had a thought. "Aye yo, Josh!" I called out, spinning around to catch his gaze.

"What's up, ma?" he asked. He walked back over to me.

I stepped into him, without warning, and planted my cold hands on the sides of his face. I didn't give him time to think or react; I just crashed my lips into his. Feeling the flanks of our noses rub against each other, I possessively eased my tongue into his mouth. His hands found their way around me and pulled me in before resting at

the small of my back. I melted into his embrace as
I further explored his mouth, tasting traces of the
Beech-Nut gum I'd seen him spit out earlier on
the concrete. His lips were so fucking soft that I
literally wanted to eat them off his face. We kissed
and kissed for what felt like forever, and I swear,
there was no other way to describe it than perfect.
With a final tug on my bottom lip, Josh shook off
the intensity, gripped me by the arms, and pushed
me back.

His breathing was ragged as he held me at
bay, staring drunkenly into my eyes. "Damn," he
whispered.

I couldn't help but blush at his reaction, because
Josh hardly *ever* cussed. "So, yeah," I said, with
a cool, nonchalant nod of my head. "Just call me
when you get in."

As I climbed the stairs of my building, heavy
luggage in tow, I could feel Josh's eyes attached to
me. I didn't look back until I reached the top step
and heard the cabdriver honking the horn. Josh
shook his head and cracked a boyish smile before
jogging back for his ride.

Once I stepped into the house, I laughed my ass
off. I couldn't believe that I had actually pulled off
such a bold move with church boy Josh.

Fucking church boy Josh.

"Ma," I hollered out, trekking farther inside.

"I'm back here," I heard her say.

I ambled toward the back of our two-bedroom brownstone apartment. When I got to the open door of her bedroom, I saw her kneeled down on the carpeted floor, putting clothes in her dresser. When she turned and saw me standing in the doorway, a smile opened on her face.

"Hey, baby, how was the train ride?" she asked, standing up from her knees.

"Long but good," I told her.

She came over and put her arms around me. "Let me look at you," she said. She looped her finger through one of my black curls and gently tugged. "Your hair's getting longer."

"You think? Since Thanksgiving?" I asked, unsure.

She nodded. "You ace them final exams?"

I sucked my teeth. "Why you asking questions you already know the answers to?"

She lifted her hand for a high five. "My girl," she said, her palm crashing into mine. "Come on in here. I know you're hungry."

"Oh, nah. Josh and I split a pizza on the train."

Her eyes crinkled from the corners as she flashed her teeth. "Josh again, huh?" she asked, remembering him from Thanksgiving.

"We're just friends, Ma."

"Mm-hmm. I saw you kiss that boy," she said. Pursing her lips to the side, she raised her left eyebrow.

My jaw momentarily dropped before realization hit. "I thought you was in here putting away laundry? Sneaky self," I said, constricting my eyes.

She giggled before tapping me on the arm. "Take your things down to your room and then come on out here so I can feed you a real meal," she said, then breezed past me out the door.

I continued on to my bedroom, flicked on the light, and immediately noticed a white envelope sitting on my bed. I went over and glanced at the sender's name and address on the envelope.

Pastor Warren Wright
15-15 Hazen Street
East Elmhurst, NY 11370

It was a letter from Rikers Island, from my father. With unsteady hands and a sudden rush of concern, I tore into the envelope without hesitating. My father hadn't contacted me or my mother in almost ten years, so I had no earthly idea what this could be about. Was he hurt, dying in there? Thinking about all the possibilities left me barely able to breathe. After pulling the letter out, I took a seat on the edge of my bed.

My darling Francesca,
I know it's been a long time since I've
reached out to you, but I promise that my

absence has not been in vain. I pray every night that you'll eventually be able to forgive me for what I've done and that one day you'll be able to move on from what happened that night. Back then, I realized me being present in your life would only be a constant reminder, a trigger of the horrible things that you experienced as a child. I can't put that burden on you more than I already have. But God, He came to me last week, one night in my sleep, telling me that you've lost your way. He said that there is resistance to Him dwelling in your heart. He asked me to deliver a message to you from Proverbs 3:5–6:

"Trust in the LORD with all your heart and lean not on your own understanding; in all your ways submit to him, and he will make your paths straight."

Never forget that I love you, Franki.
Forever and Always.
Your father,
Pastor Wright
P.S. See you in five.

I collapsed back on my bed, my head all of a sudden reeling from the haunting words my father had written. How could he possibly know?

Chapter 21

Asha

The Lowest Part

Today marked the fourth month that Jaxon and I had been so-called *kicking it*. No matter the countless number of times I'd fucked and sucked him, he still had yet to say the four-letter word in return. He hadn't even mentioned the possibility of our relationship being exclusive. As a matter of fact, he often referred to me as his friend. No special nickname, not his baby, not even his girl. I was just *his friend*. He even flirted with other women openly in my face, so it was safe to say that he was probably fucking them too. I'd been in the game long enough to have seen this shit coming, but I was so caught up, too in love with the idea of one day being Mrs. Jaxon Brown. The whole ordeal was starting to feel like Mark all over again, only this time I knew I had a plan.

"So, you really going?" I asked Jaxon over the phone.

"Yeah, I'm going to Cancún. Should be pretty dope," he said.

I rolled my eyes, wondering how he had been able to come up with two grand for a spring break vacation but couldn't even afford to buy me a measly Christmas gift. That's right. I bought him two Gucci shirts for Christmas, with a matching belt. I even threw in a pair of Jordans that ran me four bills, but Jaxon got me nothing in return. He said that he was completely strapped, on a scholarship and living strictly off his stipend check. At the time, I understood, but now . . . *Cancún*.

"Well, who's all going?" I asked. Tapping my long fingernails on the kitchen counter, I waited for his response.

"I don't know. Everybody. Most of the basketball team, and even a few guys from the football team, I believe."

"The frats and sororities, I'm sure," I muttered, more to myself than to him.

"But yeah, you should come."

Is that an invitation? Is Jaxon inviting me to be with him in Mexico?

The school was sponsoring this big spring break trip to Cancún, Mexico, and it was all the rage now on campus. The only problem was, I didn't have the money to go. The funds I'd saved from

Mark and the other guys I used to see had all been depleted. All the "dinner and a movie" dates and the mini shopping sprees I'd taken Jaxon on had run me completely dry. But now here he was, telling me that he was going. I was angry.

"I don't have that kind of money," I told him.

"Damn, that's a shame. I woulda loved seeing you out on that beach in a little bikini. Would have fucked you right there in the sand," he said.

I gulped, feeling the usual ache between my thighs. His sexy tenor, the memory of his muscular body and, of course, his massive potential to become an NBA superstar all worked against me. "I'ma see what I can do."

After hanging up with Jaxon, I hurried and called my mama. I knew she didn't have the money but could probably talk my daddy into giving it up. However, after pleading for five minutes or so, she shut me all the way down. She said that they just had to get their HVAC unit replaced and that they had no money to give. I thought about calling Malachi, because a couple of grand was like a couple of dollars to him at this point, but I quickly tossed that idea to the wayside. Malachi wouldn't even piss on me if my ass was on fire, so why the hell would he give me two grand?

After running down the list of everyone I knew who could possibly loan me the money, I came down to one name. *Mark Battle*. Honestly, I didn't want to betray my brother again by going back on my word, especially since he and Mark were now beefing. Malachi had already cut him out of whatever street business they had, and now he was just waiting for the right moment to catch Mark slipping. Unbeknownst to Malachi, I knew that he had killed niggas for less in the past. It would only be a matter of time before Mark came up missing.

I reached for my cell phone on the counter and took a deep breath before hitting Mark's contact on the screen. I was nervous as hell because I hadn't seen him since that day in Chili's.

"Well, well, well," he answered after the second ring. I cowered upon hearing the cunning little laugh in his tone. "What's up, stranger?"

"Um . . . hey, Mark. How you been?" I rolled my eyes at my phony attempt to break the ice.

"I've been all right, but what's up? What you calling me for?"

Shit. He wasn't wasting any time.

"Nothing. Just been missing you," I lied, voice extra syrupy sweet.

"Nah, you ain't been missing me," he chuckled. "Tell the truth, shawty. What you need?"

I drew in a deep breath and squeezed the pressure point between my eyes. I didn't want to ask his trifling ass for shit, but I had to. There was no way I could allow Jaxon to sex anyone other than me on the beaches of Mexico.

"I got a school trip coming up that's gonna cost me, like, three Gs," I told him, already knowing I would need spending money. I bit down on my bottom lip and squeezed my eyes, waiting for his response.

"Hmm, I see," he said in an even tone. As the seconds of silence rolled by, I knew that he was just trying to make me suffer. Finally, he asked, "Well, where you at?"

"I'm in my dorm room."

"A'ight, why 'on't you just pull up?" he asked straight out.

I rolled my eyes so hard that I was surprised those bitches didn't get stuck. "Nigga, you know I ain't got no ride," I huffed.

"Well, damn, shawty, I'on know how I'ma get you that paper, then." Now he wanted to play games. Any other time he would've just come and scooped me, but I guess this was his way of paying me back.

Clenching my teeth, I muttered, "Fine. I'll just call a Lyft."

"Yeah, you do that."

After catching a Lyft over to Mark's place on the other side of town, I found myself standing on his front porch, banging on the door. It was cold as hell out, close to forty degrees, but Mark seemed to be taking his sweet time answering the door. It took all of five minutes for him to come to the door.

When he let me in, I noticed right away that he was naked, with nothing but a towel wrapped around his waist. He smelled clean, like soap, so I knew he had just gotten out of the shower.

"Took you long enough," he said.

I didn't even bother answering him; I just peeled off my jacket and tossed it on the couch. When I started for the staircase that led up to his bedroom, he stopped me.

"Uh-uh," he said. I turned back, looking at the sinister grin on his face. He summoned me with a curl of his index finger. "Shawty, it ain't that type of party. Ain't no need to take this up to my room."

I released a deep sigh, planting my hands on my hips, ready and prepared for the degradation. "So, where's the money?" I asked, cutting to the chase.

He pointed over to the coffee table, where I saw hundred-dollar bills spread out like a wide fan. I sauntered over to him, noticed that the tip of his tongue was resting on the back of his teeth. He was obviously wondering where my head was at. After lightly running my fingernails down his abs, I reached for the towel and unwrapped it from around his waist. My eyes instantly traveled down to his long dick. He had always been hung like a thoroughbred, so while I really didn't want to be here, I knew I'd at least enjoy the ride.

Without warning, I pushed him down on the sofa and squatted between his thighs. I wasted no time taking his soldier into my mouth, dipping deep to wet his entire length. Tightening my lips, I began to suck him over and over until he was lodged at the back of my throat. I hummed over him, allowing my eyes to fly up to his face to see his response. Even though his head had collapsed back on the rim of the sofa, his heavy-lidded eyes were fixed on me.

When I widened my tongue to take him deeper, he fisted a handful of my braids. Then he lifted his hips from the sofa in an effort to finally take control. He drilled himself in and out of my wet mouth, going harder, deeper, again and again, until his eyes rolled to the back of his head from pleasure. Suddenly, his muscles tightened, and his body began to spaz.

"Oh, fuck," he groaned, voice strained, as he finally released. I caught everything, drained him dry.

Wiping my mouth with the back of my hand, I stood up from the floor and began pushing down my tights. But Mark shook his head.

"Nah, I'm good on that," he said, still out of breath and chest slightly heaving. He shot a quick glance over at the money on the table and flicked his chin. "You did yo' job. Now just take the fucking money."

My eyes bucked at that. In all the times I had slept with men for money, I had never been made to feel so low. Mark might as well have picked me up off the corner, fucked me right in his car, and handed me a twenty-dollar bill. That was just how cheap I felt, like a common whore.

With a deep swallow of embarrassment, I turned to gather the money off the table. After grabbing my jacket from the arm of the sofa, I started for the door. When I reached for the handle, I looked back, saw Mark retying his towel around his waist. He was relaxed and appeared not to have a care in the world.

"Shawty, lock my door on your way out," he said evenly.

He was doing all this to spite me, and to be honest, I just wanted to break down and cry. But I couldn't. I refused to give him the satisfaction. With the three Gs in my pocket, I turned the lock and walked out the door. When I finally made it back to campus, I saw Meeko and Hope sitting out on the yard. With her legs draped over his lap, he had buried his head in the crook of her neck and was making her giggle. I felt sick from jealousy.

Out of all the people for Meeko to choose, how in the world had he ended up with Hope? Meeko was our school's star wide receiver and one of the finest guys I'd ever seen. He had this bright, beautiful smile, even brown skin, and he always kept his hair in a fresh Caesar cut. His clothes hung on his muscular frame with ease. Never did he have to try too hard with anything when it came to his looks. He was just outright fine. If it hadn't been for the stunt I pulled a couple of summers ago, he would've been my number one target instead of Jaxon. But now, as I stood there watching the two of them kiss and cuddle from afar, I wondered exactly where I went wrong in my life.

After sulking past them on the stone-paved walkway, I headed for the dorm. That was when I heard Hope call out my name behind me. "Hey, Asha." Her voice was so fucking chipper and full of life. I rolled my eyes.

I kept walking, but I could still hear Meeko in the distance. "Man, fuck that bitch," he muttered.

When I got to Holland Hall, I rushed across the lobby toward the elevators, feeling a typhoon of emotions building in my throat. When I crossed the threshold and the mirrored doors finally closed, I burst out crying. Covering my mouth, I sobbed into my hands the entire way to the third floor, face flooded with tears.

How did this become my life? I wondered.

Chapter 22

Hope

A Million Pieces

The sound of light taps against my windowpane woke me from a deep sleep. Quickly, I shot up in the bed, startled by the noise. After hearing another round of what sounded like pebbles being thrown against glass, I rubbed my eyes and opened them to the dark.

"What is that?" I whispered to myself. Plodding across the hardwood floor, I made my way to the window. Not knowing what to expect, I peeked through the blinds with apprehension. That was when I saw Meeko standing on the side of the house, the streetlight shining down on his face.

I raised the window, allowing the cold night air to flow into my room. "What are you doing here?" I asked in a hushed tone, hugging my body to keep warm.

"The fuck you mean?" He cocked his head to the side and looked at me as if I should've known. "I came to see you."

My eyes bugged at his response. Not only had I made it crystal clear that Meeko wasn't welcome at Aunt Marlene's house, but I also had no clue as to how he even knew which room was mine. To my knowledge, he'd never been here before. "You can't be here, Meek," I said just loud enough for him to hear.

Making it known that he wasn't pleased with my response, he sucked his teeth. Then he tossed his head to the side, allowing his eyes to roll toward the street. "Come on, man. I need to see you."

Hearing the desperation in his voice, I gave it a quick thought. "Fine," I said lowly. "But just for a minute."

I pushed the window closed and went over to sink my feet into a pair of old slippers beside the bed. After removing the silk bonnet from my hair and tossing it on the nightstand, I quickly raked my fingers through the long strands. Hardly able to see without my glasses, I tiptoed down the dark hall. As I descended the stairs, hearing the wooden boards creak beneath my feet, my heart hammered inside my chest. I was just as nervous as Franki was a few months back, when she saw a rash on her inner thigh. Turned out to be just eczema, but still, she was scared out of her mind. I knew that if Aunt Marlene caught Meeko here at this time of night, she would surely call my father. The thought alone had me unnerved.

She'd already been suspicious of my behavior these past few weeks, my coming home late and not answering her calls. The last thing I needed was for my father to find out about me and Meeko. He would force me to come back home, and I couldn't have that. I liked attending A&T, but even more so, I loved being around Meeko. The mere thought of him was what motivated me to get out of bed every morning and made me excited to close my eyes every night just so that I could dream. If I had it my way, Meeko and I would never part, and given the fact that he'd shown up at Aunt Marlene's in the middle of a Sunday night, I think it was safe to say that he felt the same way too.

When I got to the first floor, I quietly made my way into the kitchen, where I knew I could easily slip out the side door. With only a nightgown on, I threw on my heavy winter coat and snuck out into the night. It was freezing cold outside, below thirty degrees, but Meeko didn't waste any time wrapping me up in his arms. He lifted me from my feet and squeezed me tight, as if he'd been missing me all day.

"Damn," he said with a light snort of laughter. Shaking his head, he placed me back down on my feet.

"What?" I beamed knowingly, seeing the fog float away from my lips.

He stroked his fingers down the length of my thick hair and licked his lips. "You got a nigga out here on some sucka shit right now. I had to see you," he admitted. Despite the cold, I instantly felt warm inside.

After taking me by the hand, Meeko and I jogged through the lawn and headed to his car, which was parked only a few houses away. At almost three o'clock in the morning, the neighborhood was completely dead, void of any noise or movement. Surprisingly, when we hopped inside his car, it was still pretty warm, but nonetheless, he cranked up the engine and turned on the heat.

He slid his seat as far back as it could go and summoned me with a tilting upward of his chin. "Com'ere," he said.

Without hesitation, I climbed over the console and straddled his lap. My palms gently grazed the sides of his face before planting themselves on his chest. As we sat there in silence, gazing into one another's eyes, I could hear a sappy love song playing on the radio. I smiled.

"What? Fuck you smiling for?" he asked playfully.

I shook my head and tucked in my lips. "Nothing."

He poked my side with his finger, causing me to squeal. "Nah, tell me," he urged.

I contemplated an answer for a bit and finally gave in. "How did you know where my bedroom was?"

Releasing a light snort of laughter, he rolled his head to the side and gripped the back of his neck. "You really wanna know?" he asked, allowing a boyish grin to play at his lips.

I nodded.

"After dropping you off that first time, I kept following you home."

My eyes ballooned. "You what?" I asked, completely shocked.

He nodded with a small smile. "Yeah, yo, I followed you. More than once," he confessed. Judging by his expression, I could tell he was a little embarrassed. "You kept dodging a nigga, talking 'bout we could get together only in the library to study." He shook his head. "I ain't like that shit. That one hour wasn't good enough for me. I'd already gotten used to hearing your voice every day. Seeing your pretty-ass face." He gently pinched my chin. "Having you in my bed."

"But that's when we were just friends," I whispered, more to myself, thinking about the handful of times I'd stayed over in his dorm just so that I wouldn't have to walk across campus in the dark.

He shook his head. "I wanted you. Even then," he admitted. "And when I'd follow you home, I'd see that same light cut on every time." He shrugged. "Shit wasn't that hard to figure out."

I released a soft snort of laughter. "Gosh, I never thought I'd have a stalker," I teased.

He grinned with a roll of his eyes. "Shid, you think I was stalking you then. I'm definitely gon' be stalking yo' ass now."

"Why?" I wanted to know.

"'Cause you done fucked around and gave a nigga the sweetest part of you, that's why."

My cheeks warmed. "I thought that I was supposed to be the one harassing you," I told him, recalling everything that he and his friends had to say about virgins.

"I mean you was, but . . ." He shook his head and smiled. "I'm fucking obsessed with yo' pretty ass now." He leaned forward and pressed his lips into mine. As we deepened our kiss, I began to feel his manhood rise beneath me. He pulled back. "You gon' ride it for me, Hope?" he asked in a whisper, staring at me with heavy-lidded eyes.

"Here?" I asked, glancing over my shoulder to peer out the car window.

"Yeah. Ain't nobody gon' see us."

Suddenly, I began to feel self-conscious, heart beating out of control. "I don't know how," I said lowly, avoiding his gaze. Meeko and I had been having sex for a couple of weeks now, but it had always been with him on top or behind me, taking the lead. I had no clue how to *ride*.

Softly guiding my head by the chin with his finger, he forced me to look him in the eyes. "I know. I'ma teach you," he said.

Without delay, he removed my coat and stuffed it behind me against the steering wheel. His hands gently slipped beneath the thin fabric of my nightgown and slid across the sides of my hips. Lifting his pelvis in a slow but eager grind, Meeko released a low groan. "I want you so fucking bad, Hope," he muttered.

My body quivered, and moisture formed in the seat of my panties. He lifted his hips again, but this time, he slid his sweatpants down below his waist. I didn't even have to peek, because I could feel his hardness immediately sprout up between my thighs.

"Gimme a kiss," he said.

Placing my cold hand against his face, I leaned in close to kiss his lips. Our tongues immediately danced, while his fingers played in my sex. Without warning, he inserted a finger inside me and then another, causing a moan to skate from my lips. As he dipped them in and out of me with ease, I closed my eyes from the pleasure.

Withdrawing from my lips, Meeko took his hand out of my panties and placed both fingers in his mouth without shame. "Mmm. You sweet as fuck," he said. Eyes locking with mine, he sucked his fingers like he'd just eaten the last hot wing on his platter. He was so nasty, but inwardly, I loved it.

He lifted me just enough to remove my panties from a single leg. As I hovered above his erection, Meeko slid the head back and forth across my slick folds. Then he gripped my hips and pulled me down on him. I gasped from pleasure-filled pain and closed my eyes. "Oh God," I murmured. Meeko was so big that it felt like he was planting himself inside my womb.

"Fuck," he breathed, biting down on his lower lip.

Leaning forward, I wrapped my arms around him and buried my face in the curve of his neck. As his hands palmed my lower cheeks, I could feel him start to guide me. Back and forth, up and down, until my hips found a steady rhythm of their own. Within a matter of seconds, the sounds of my wetness filled the car, and the windows were covered with a coat of steam.

As I rocked against him, feeling his strong hands slide to the top of my back, my body shuddered. Every time Meeko and I made love, it was like my body would reach new pinnacles of pleasure. This night was no different. Sucking in a huge breath, I allowed a powerful orgasm to rip through me. "Oh, Meek," I moaned, trembling uncontrollably.

Meeko gripped me tighter, pulling my body to him with more strength. Thrusting his hips in an upward motion, he continued to drive in and out of my limp body with ease. Then, without warning, his muscles locked up around me. The delivery of his strokes grew shorter and shorter. "Shit," he hissed, releasing inside me.

When he finally wrapped his arms around me, drawing me even tighter to his heaving chest, a lone tear trickled down my cheek. We stayed that way for a while, heartbeat to heartbeat, allowing our bodies to come down from their sexual high.

Then he pushed the hair out of my face and placed a soft kiss on the tip of my nose. "I love you, Hope," he confessed in a whisper. I cried harder.

After going around in Meeko's car last night, we decided to drive back to his dorm, where we made love two more times. My head was so clouded with being in love that I no longer cared what Aunt Marlene or my father would say. No longer did I find myself being concerned with rejection from the church or having to repent. I loved this man, and I wanted to be with him until the end of time.

Meeko groaned as I peeled back the covers from over his head. "Wake up, sleepyhead," I sang.

His eyes squinted, resisting the morning sun. "What time is it?" he asked in a groggy voice.

"Its eight thirty and time for you to get up."

"I'on got class till ten," he said, putting the pillow over his head.

After sitting down on the edge of the bed, I ran my hand down his back before placing a kiss on his arm. "I'm gonna miss you today," I told him.

He removed the pillow from his head and looked back at me over his shoulder. "I'ma miss you too. Don't forget to call me, a'ight?" he grumbled.

"Okay, and don't you oversleep." When I stood up from the bed, Meeko lifted himself up and gently bit my butt through my clothes. I had on a pair of his sweatpants, which I had had to roll at the top, and one of his old T-shirts. "Ow." I turned around and rubbed my behind in an attempt to soothe it.

"Sorry, baby." He smiled. "You want me to kiss it?" He puckered his lips.

I playfully tapped him on the arm and rolled my eyes. "Maybe later."

"Bet," he said, winking his eye.

After delivering a peck to his cheek, I slipped on my coat and quietly stepped out the door. Feeling a bit sore between my thighs, I plodded my way to the elevators. On the ride down, I hummed a little love song that stayed on repeat in my mind. I was literally smiling from ear to ear, because the joy I felt was practically oozing out of me. The way my body reacted to Meeko's touch, the way we held on to each other throughout the night—it was all I had ever dreamed of. Not even the fear of my father's wrath could take away from this type of bliss.

As I strolled across campus, wearing Meeko's baggy clothes and my slippers, I suddenly realized that I'd left my keys in his room. "Oh, shoot," I muttered, snapping my fingers, as I spun around on my heels.

It was a cold January morning, just above thirty degrees, but I didn't even care. Instead of being bothered by the fact that I had to walk all the way back, I got excited about the promise of seeing *his* face again. Truthfully, I wanted to shout his name to the hilltops and do cartwheels on my way there, but I knew how ridiculous that would look.

The entire elevator ride up to the fourth floor of Pride Hall, I kept telling myself that I was going to steal one more kiss before I left. When the elevator doors slid open, I stepped off and practically skipped down the hall. But then I saw Jazz banging on Meeko's door, and I stopped dead in my tracks. Suddenly, the pound of my heart began reverberating between my ears, and I stood immobilized, holding my breath.

When the door swung open, Meeko appeared shirtless, with my keys in his hand. Then his neck jerked back, and I could see his eyes widen with confusion. "The fuck, yo?" I heard him say to Jazz.

"Meeko, we need to talk," she told him.

He swiped his hand over his face, trying to clear the sleep from his eyes. "Fuck we need to talk about at nine in the morning, Jazz? I already told you that shit between me and you is dead. What else is left to say?"

"So what? You just gon' stop fucking with me for that little nerdy black bitch?" she replied, fuming, and placed her hands on her hips. "Be for real, Meeko. Look at me and look at her."

"I did, and that's why I can't fuck wit' yo' duck ass no more." His nostrils flared as he shook his head. "Yo, you lucky I didn't whip yo' ass fa' real . . . after all the shit you and ya' homegirls pulled."

"So, what? You can fuck me one day and flaunt that bitch in my face the next? When you're with her, you act like I don't even exist no more."

"'Cause you don't!"

Inwardly, I smiled as I heard him come to my defense. I wasn't going to approach the two of them; instead, I was just going to stand there and watch and listen from afar. Besides, our court hearing would be coming up soon from the charges I had pressed against her, and hopefully, the outcome would be more than enough justice served for me.

Meeko took a step back and attempted to slam the door in her face, but Jazz put up her hands to block the door from closing. "All of this over a stupid fucking bet!" she cried.

A bet?

"Man," he drawled, "you betta get the fuck off my door, yo."

"Nah, nigga. I ain't going nowhere. Let's lay all the cards on the table," she told him, holding her hand determinedly against the door.

Meeko exhaled a breath so loudly that I could hear him clear from down the hall.

"Yeah, nigga, that's right. You told me to chill out so you could win this quick five hundred dollars.

Remember that? The deal was to fuck that girl, get the money, and then come back to me!" she yelled, pointing to her chest.

My heart sank to the pit of my stomach as tears rose to the rims of my eyes.

This can't be right. She's a liar.

"Okay, *and*? It was a fucking bet!" he shouted, confirming the worst of my fears.

With trembling hands and unsteady legs, I somehow managed to walk down the hall and into their view. "I was a bet, Meeko?" I asked lowly.

His dark brown eyes fell on me before doubling in size. "Hope," he sputtered.

"Was it all a bet?" I asked, raising my voice this time. I didn't even give him a chance to respond. "Because you took something from me, Meeko. Something I can't ever get back." I shook my head just to keep the tears at bay. "Not only did I break the promise I made to my father, but I also broke the one I made with God," I said, more to myself than to him. That was when the tears finally fell.

How could I have not seen this? I thought.

His eyes immediately softened. "I swear, everything that happened between us is—"

"When?" I asked, cutting him off.

He looked at me, not wanting to answer.

"When, Meeko! When did you make the bet?"

"That first day in the café," he admitted lowly. "But I promise you, my feelings for—"

"No," I snapped, cutting him off again, shaking my head. "I don't want to hear any more of your lies."

When I turned to walk away, I heard Jazz talking a bunch of crap behind my back. "That's right, you ugly black bitch. Get to steppin'," she said. "Trash-ass pussy was only worth five hundred dollars anyway."

"Yo, Jazz, why 'on't you just shut the fuck up! Damn," Meeko seethed.

I twirled around so fast that I was surprised I didn't get whiplash. Without a second's thought, I charged over and pounced on Jazz like a leaping leopard. The powerful impact immediately brought her down to the floor. As my fists swung wildly in the air, sporadically connecting with her face, I screamed at the top of my lungs. "Argh!" I wasn't a fighter, by any means, but in this moment, I almost felt possessed. Every ounce of hurt that Meeko had inflicted on me, the burning anger I still felt from my attack and, even more so, the guilt I couldn't shake—they all were surging out of me.

Suddenly, I felt Jazz's fingernails dig into my face. Her legs locked around my hips, and in one swift motion, she rolled me over onto the floor. As she pinned me down with one arm, I felt her slap me hard across the cheek with the other. *Whap!*

"Ugly bitch!" she spat.

The sound of Meeko shouting for her to get off me played in the background. And in the midst of it all, I could see him hovering above us, trying to pry her body off mine. I kicked and screamed as my eyes flickered open and closed, but she just wouldn't budge.

Finally, I saw the muscle of Meeko's forearm wrap around her throat. He was choking her from behind. As her green eyes rolled to the back of her head, I felt her release the death grip she now had on my hair. With little struggle, he was able to lift her from the floor and, ultimately, free me from her arms.

She was coughing uncontrollably, rubbing the front of her neck where her fair skin had already turned a bright shade of red. "You put your hands on me for this bitch, Meeko!" she cried, tears streaming down her face. "You fucked me two weeks after we put that bitch in the hospital, and now you wanna sit here and play fucking hero!"

Wow.

"Nah, I let you suck my dick. Big fucking difference," he told her, trying to control his breath.

I looked at Jazz and right away saw that he'd wounded her with his words. Her eyes had glossed over just that quick, and her face revealed that she, too, was crushed.

When Meeko tried helping me to my feet, I drew my shaky hands back with disgust. "Don't touch me!" I screamed. Immediately, I covered my mouth with both hands to contain the cry that had mounted in my throat. In all my eighteen years, I had never known I could feel so much pain yet be so in love with the person inflicting it.

Devastated by it all, I grabbed my keys, which had fallen during the skirmish, and scrambled up from the floor. As I flew back to the elevators, almost tripping over my own feet, I could hear Meeko right on my heels. "Hope, baby, please, yo. Stop!" he begged.

But I couldn't. My heart had just been ripped from my chest.

Chapter 23

Paris

La Mexicana

"Mom!" I shrieked when I saw my mother standing in the hallway of my dorm. "What are you doing here?" I asked, looking at her in shock. Her blond hair freshly cut above her shoulders, she wore a mink fur draped loosely around her arms. A string of South Sea pearls had been placed perfectly around her neck.

"I wanted to surprise you, dear. For spring break," she said. Her blue eyes flickered back at me as she smiled.

Over Christmas break, my mother had explained to me why she hadn't been in contact. She'd said that she didn't want me to try to talk her into letting me come back home before I truly gave N.C. A&T a shot. I could sort of understand her reasoning. So, while things still didn't sit quite right with me, I felt a bit of relief knowing she hadn't completely forgotten about me.

"Well, I'm on my way to Cancún," I told her as I turned back to lock the door to our suite. Two large Fendi bags were already sitting beside me.

"Cancún?" she asked, perplexed. If only she would look at her credit card statement from time to time, instead of relying on her accountant, she would know that I had booked Franki's trip for her back in December. "Well, I already have reservations for La Garoupe Beach in the French Riviera," she said.

I shrugged my shoulders dismissively. "Sorry, but you should have called. I already have plans."

Her jaw dropped at my snarky reaction. "Paris, you can't be serious. You're gonna pass up seven days in the South of France for what? For Mexico?"

It was true that in years past, the French Riviera had been one of my favorite places to vacation. My father had taken us a handful of times, and before he passed, he had even mentioned purchasing a home there. The Mediterranean coastline was the perfect shade of blue and was known as the playground for the wealthy. Even in the middle of March, it was a beautiful sight to see.

"Sorry, but you're just gonna have to make the trip without me," I told her. As I grabbed the handles on my luggage, I heard Malachi and Franki coming down the hall.

"Damn, you taking both of those bags too?" he said, looking down at my rolling suitcases. He'd already carried two of my other pieces to his trunk.

When he walked up and my mother saw the tats covering his neck and the diamonds and gold encasing his teeth, she cleared her throat.

I looked at her, then cut my eyes over at Malachi. "Oh, Mom, this is my . . ." I hesitated, not knowing exactly what to call him. We still hadn't put a title on our relationship other than *friends*. And although we kissed and spent lots of time together, we still had yet to have sex. I was hoping for all that to change during spring break. "My friend Malachi, and that's my roommate Franki," I said.

Malachi reached out to shake my mother's hand, but she simply lifted her nose in the air and rolled her eyes. He let out a sarcastic snort of laughter before fixing the gold chains dangling from his neck. "A'ight, Miss Paris. I'ma see you downstairs," he said. He grabbed my luggage and took off down the hall.

"Nice to meet you," Franki mumbled before trailing behind him.

"So, is this what you're doing now? Following behind low-life thugs and ghetto trash?" my mother scoffed, a look of disgust on her face.

My neck instantly jerked back, as I was shocked by her words. "He is not trash!" I retorted, admonishing her.

"Well, you sure could've fooled the hell out of me. Your father and I worked too hard—"

"Worked too hard!" My eyebrows shot up at that. "You've never worked a day in your friggin' life!"

"You don't talk to me that way, young lady," she said sternly.

"And you don't talk that way about my friends. You sent me all the way out here just so I could get in touch with *my people*," I said, making air quotes with my hands. "Remember that? And that's just what the *fuck* I did. Now, if you don't like it, tough tittie." I shrugged.

Her jaw dropped to the floor. Never had I spoken that way before, especially not to my mother, but she had some nerve.

"Is everything all right, darling?" I heard someone say from down the hall.

My gaze shifted, and I saw a tall white man with chestnut-brown hair and bright gray eyes approaching us. He was dressed in an expensive suit, and his coat was folded over his arm.

"Yes, Leonard, I'm fine," my mother said.

I looked back and forth between the two of them before realizing that they were together. "So, this is what this is about? You wanted to take me on a trip just to butter me up about the fact that you're screwing someone else, huh? And what? Explain why you've been MIA for the six most important months of my life?"

"It's not like that, Paris. I promise. Let me explain," she replied.

"Don't waste your breath, Mom." Feeling my eyes burn with tears, I hiked my chin in the air and tossed my long hair behind my shoulders. "I've got a plane to catch," I told her, placing my shades over my eyes.

Leaving the two of them standing there, I rushed down the hall and saw Malachi waiting by the elevators. That was when I lost it. I darted into his open arms, buried my face in his chest, and allowed myself to cry freely. I couldn't believe he'd been waiting there for me all this time. More than likely, he'd heard all the ugly things my mother had to say.

"Shh," he whispered. Gently rubbing my back, he planted a tender kiss on the top of my head. "Come on, Miss Paris. Let me get you out of here."

When we got to his car, Franki was already sitting in the back, her wireless Beats covering her ears. Malachi's friend Bull was parked behind us in his car, with his lady, Nita, riding shotgun and Tee Tee and Nya in the back. Malachi didn't want to be the only noncollege student in Cancún, so he had invited his crew. Over the past few months, I'd hung with them numerous times, and now I even considered them friends, so it was cool.

Feeling helpless, I sank into the front seat and removed the sunglasses from my eyes. I wiped my cheeks and sniffed back the last of my tears.

"Everything a'ight with you and ya' moms?" Franki asked.

I glanced back, saw her headphones hooked around her neck. "No, but what's new?" I replied with a shrug.

"Y'all gon' be a'ight. Don't even sweat it, ma," she said. Then she looked down as she tapped away on her cell phone screen.

"Who's that?" I asked.

She looked up at me and smiled. "Oh, nah, this just Josh talking shit."

"Oh, it's Josh, huh?" I asked teasingly. She didn't catch the humor in my voice, and instead of reacting, she just kept typing on her phone.

A minute later, she looked up and announced, "Yeah, he's already at the resort with his frat brothers. Sending me pictures of what we're missing." She handed me her phone for me to see, and sure enough, it was a selfie of Josh, standing on a beach, blue water behind him, without his shirt on.

"Hey, since when did church boy Josh get muscles?" I asked, observing the peaks and valleys of his fair skin.

She snatched the phone out of my hand and smacked her lips. "I'on know. I don't look at Josh like that."

"As if," I mumbled. Franki could lie to me all she wanted to, but there wasn't a doubt in my mind that she had a thing for Josh.

Once Malachi finished putting the rest of our things in the trunk, he got in and reached over to grab my hand. Without saying a word, he brought it up to his lips for a quick kiss, letting me know that he truly cared. It was times like this that only made me fall deeper for him.

We drove for almost twenty minutes before we finally pulled up to the Piedmont Triad International Airport. After checking our bags, we had less than an hour to spare before they were boarding our plane. Malachi had sprung for first-class tickets, and we took full advantage of it by having him and Bull order us drinks the whole way to Mexico. By the time we touched down in Cancún, Franki and I were all giggly and feeling warm inside. Nita, Tee Tee, and Nya seemed to have held their liquor better.

When the shuttle dropped us off at the resort, we all decided to head up to our rooms, except for Franki, who took off to meet Josh by the beach. I could only shake my head and smile.

"Paris, you staying in the room with us?" Nya asked, then licked her lips to remind me that she went both ways. Both Nita and Tee Tee tittered.

Malachi snorted. "You stay wit' that playing shit, Ny," he said, warning her with his eyes.

I wrapped my arms around his waist and shook my head. "Nope," I slurred. Then I leaned over to her ear. "I'm hoping to finally get the big black dick this week," I whispered.

"Shawty, yo' drunk ass can't whisper for shit, you know that?" Malachi shook his head and laughed. "Come on."

After dapping up Bull, Malachi and I headed to our room. We were on the top floor, in a huge suite that overlooked the ocean. As soon as we entered, I went out on the balcony and took in the view while sobering up a bit. Malachi came up behind me and planted his hands on the rail.

"It's pretty, isn't it?" I said, keeping my eyes glued to the water.

"Yuh, but I've seen prettier," he said lowly, his warm breath tickling the nape of my neck.

There was a light wind in the air, so I tucked my hair behind my ears just to keep it from blowing in my face. "Can I ask you something?" I asked as I spun around. "And you not brush me off?"

"What's on your mind, Miss Paris?" he asked as he looked down at me.

"Why haven't you made a move on me?"

A half smile crested upon Malachi's face, exposing a hint of the gold in his mouth. Then he licked his lips. "We not ready for that."

"But you told me, when I get ready for the big black d—"

Malachi put his hand over my mouth and laughed. "Mane, you wildin'," he said, tossing his eyes to the side.

"I am not," I replied and pouted, folding my arms across my chest. "I just want us to be . . . more than friends."

Scratching behind his right ear, he sighed.

"Is it me? I know I've gained some weight, but . . ." My voice trailed off as I thought about the freshman fifteen I'd put on. It had taken me from a solid size ten to almost a size fourteen.

Malachi took his bottom lip in between his teeth and stepped back to allow his eyes a full sweep of my body. "Nah, baby, it definitely ain't you. You perfect," he said, approval apparent in his eyes. "You just don't need to be wit' a nigga like me."

"I'm not innocent, Malachi. I've had sex before, if you're thinking I'm some kinda virgin," I told him. Cringing, I thought about that one time with Brad in his parents' bedroom. I knew how desperate I sounded, but I was ready for us to take things to the next level. My feelings were growing stronger for Malachi by the day, yet his lack of sexual enthusiasm only left me feeling self-conscious and more confused.

"You're young as fuck, Paris, just barely eighteen, and I'm over here a grown-ass man with two kids. I've done shit . . ." He hesitated. "Things I'm not proud of. I can't just suck you into all of that."

"It's the gang, isn't it?" I asked, recalling the horrible things he told me he'd been a part of in the past. "Is that what's keeping us from moving forward?"

He let out a breath of irritation. "There's more to it than that. You gots to understand that I'm a no-good-ass nigga. You know only what I show you," he said, looking into my eyes.

"Well, then, show me who the hell you are, because I don't know how much more rejection I can take." I cupped my mouth with my hands, feeling more vulnerable than I ever had in front of him. "I'm falling for you, Malachi," I confessed softly.

He wrapped his arms around my waist and sighed. "Look, Mama, let's just enjoy this vacation."

"Is it someone else? Are you sleeping with someone else?" I wanted to know.

As he looked at me, I could see the torn expression on his face. He didn't want to answer that question.

"I don't want to lie to you, Paris," he admitted, immediately crushing me. "In the beginning, yeah, I saw a pretty face and a fat ass. I was just like any other nigga looking to fuck. I admit that shit. But now . . ." He paused, letting his hazel eyes float up to the sky. He sighed. "Now shit's done changed. I care about you. A lot. You're real fucking special to me."

We were staring at one another, trying to be with one accord without words, when suddenly a knock sounded at our door.

"I'll get it," Malachi said, eyes still locked with mine. I nodded as he released me.

As Malachi left the balcony and headed to the door, I turned back to take in the view again. The backdrop was picture-perfect with the palm trees, the white sand, and the sapphire water, but I was now in a sour mood. Malachi had been spending time with me but giving the big black dick to someone else. A part of me felt like he was only protecting me, but the other half believed he was playing with my heart.

"Malachi! Dude!" I heard a familiar voice shout out behind me. I turned around to see my BFF, Heather, giving Malachi a hug. They talked on the phone and even FaceTimed, so they were already acquainted with each other.

When I walked into the living room of our suite, Heather was already sprinting toward me. She practically knocked me down when she tackled me for a hug, but I wrapped my arms around her and held on. I'd missed her like crazy.

"Dude!" she let out again with a laugh.

"Bitch!" I said, mimicking her tone with a smile. I looked her over and saw that she was dressed in a hot pink string bikini and tiny jean shorts that barely covered her ass. A pair of Dolce & Gabbana shades were propped on her head, and her long blond ponytail swung in the back.

"Y'all ready to partayyy!" she sang, dancing with her hands in the air.

Malachi released a snort of laughter before looking over at me. "Now I see who you get your moves from," he joked.

I playfully smacked him on the arm and rolled my eyes. "What-evs."

"So, you guys ready to hit the beach, or are you two lovebirds gonna stay in?" she asked, bouncing her eyebrows obnoxiously.

I looked over at Malachi. "We're just friends. Right, Malachi?" I asked.

"Mane," he breathed, running his hand over the top of his head. "Y'all go on and do y'all thing. I'm about to go catch up with Bull. I'ma fuck wit' y'all later, a'ight?" he said, clearly being evasive.

Heather looked back and forth between us, obviously feeling the tension in the room. When her eyes finally landed on me, she gave me a broad smile. "Well, then . . . since we're both single and ready to mingle, let's go find us some *La Mexicana* dick," she said, using a fake Latin accent as she wound her hips in a circle.

Although I loved Heather like a sister, she was a complete fool. I couldn't do anything but laugh.

"Miss Paris, you be good, a'ight?" Malachi said with a penetrating stare. Although it wasn't out-right, I could hear the underlying threat in his tone.

I lifted my chin in the air and winked my eye. "And, Mr. Malachi, you be good as well."

He shook his head and let out a light snort of laughter before heading for the door.

Chapter 24

Hope

Hoping and Wishing

"Hope, are you all right in there?" I heard Aunt Marlene ask from the other side of the door.

I lifted my head from the toilet, barely able to speak. "I'm fine," I croaked. I'd been throwing up on and off all morning. My head was spinning, and I felt horrible.

"Are you sure you don't need to go down to urgent care?"

After pulling off a few squares of toilet tissue, I wiped the corners of my mouth. "No. Really, Aunt Marlene, I'm fine. Just go on to work," I told her.

"Well, I'm gonna leave the car here, just in case," she said.

I didn't even have the energy to respond.

When I finally heard her leave the house, I willed my feeble body up from the tiled floor. Not recognizing my own reflection, I stared at myself in the mirror. I honestly didn't know who I was anymore. That first day I moved into the dorm, I was simply Hope, the quiet church girl from Alto, Texas. But now, as I looked at the hair falling well past my shoulders, the bare spot where my glasses used to rest, and Meeko's old football jersey, which covered my nakedness beneath, I no longer knew who I was.

It had been well over a month since that whole Meeko and Jazz debacle, and still, I was heartbroken. Most days I found myself still wanting to be with him, even after all the pain he'd caused. Truth be told, I'd fallen for Meeko hard, and it seemed no matter what I did, I just couldn't shake him from my system. Up until a week ago, he had been calling and texting every day, but I had refused to answer. There had even been a couple times where he'd shown up at the house in the middle of the night. Although I cried like a baby, I couldn't allow myself to raise the window. And on those few occasions where he'd actually caught me walking around campus, I acted as if he were a mere stranger, ignoring his pleas and turning the other way. Even Big Mo and Ty had tried to apologize for the bet they made. I couldn't talk to them either.

Nevertheless, my rejection of Meeko and his friends was not an accurate depiction of how I truly felt. I missed them all like crazy, especially Meeko. I still craved his smile, his touch, even his sex. For just a brief moment in time, he had had me completely wide open, igniting and connecting with parts of me I never knew were there. But his betrayal had cut too deep. It was something I didn't think I could ever forgive and definitely not something I'd ever forget.

After a few minutes, I managed to brush my teeth before jumping in the shower. I threw my hair up into a messy bun and put my long khaki skirt on and a pair of canvas sneakers. With my glasses on my face, I made my way out of the house and over to Aunt Marlene's car. Although I wasn't ready to face the truth, I knew I had to. I cranked the engine and drove to the nearest Rite Aid.

As I was scanning the shelf, looking for the best pregnancy test to buy, I heard someone clear their throat behind me. Naturally, I jumped when I turned to find Asha burning a hole through me with her eyes.

"Hey, Hope. Long time no see," she said. Wiggling the long, pointed tips of her pink painted fingernails, she waved at me.

Like an admission of guilt, I opened my mouth, but nothing would come out. "Oh, uh . . . h-hey, Asha," I finally stammered.

"So . . . you're pregnant, huh?" she came right out and asked. Her eyes inadvertently gazed over at the pregnancy tests on the shelf as a cunning little smile graced her lips.

"Oh, who? Me? Um, no." Gosh, I was a terrible liar.

"Mm-hmm." She smiled knowingly. "Does he know?"

Crap.

I shook my head and sighed before letting my face fall into the palms of my hands. "I honestly don't know if I am or not, Asha," I admitted. The truth was, I had missed two periods and was now having spells of both nausea and vomiting. Even to my inexperienced mind, being pregnant was the only thing that made sense, especially since Meeko and I had never used protection. "And no, Meeko doesn't know anything about it," I told her, regretting it as soon as the words fell from my lips.

"Oh, don't sweat it, boo. You know your secret's safe with me," she assured me. "Anyways, let me go. I gotta catch a flight out to Cancún in a few hours. I'm meeting my man," she said, bragging. "I just came in here to pick up a few things to travel with."

My eyes instantly widened with recognition when I heard her mention Cancún. I'd been seeing the spring break flyers posted all over campus, and I remembered Meeko saying at one point that he was going. "Well, have fun," I told her.

She flipped her long braids over her shoulder and smiled. "Oh, you know I will," she said. Dipping her head toward the pregnancy tests, she added "And, hey, don't be cheap. Get the Clearblue. Shit's accurate as fuck."

I nodded my head and tucked my lips in my mouth. After Asha sauntered away, I grabbed a Clearblue box off the shelf and headed for the register.

Between my nausea and overwhelming bouts of nerves, the drive back to Aunt Marlene's was a long one. When I pulled into the driveway, I sat in the car for a few minutes, collecting my thoughts. *What if I am pregnant? Should I even tell Meeko? Will I keep the baby, or should I abort it, even though it goes against my faith?* My mind was reeling out of control. Before I could make myself any dizzier, I got out of the car and headed inside.

As soon as I entered the house, I ran up to my room and ripped the test right out of the box. I exhaled a deep breath. "Well, I guess it's now or never," I said to myself.

Walking inside the bathroom, I could feel my heart working overtime in my chest. At this point, I wasn't sure if I was feeling sick from being nervous or being pregnant. As I finally squatted over the toilet with the stick beneath me, I said a quick prayer. "Dear Lord, I ask in Jesus' name that you please let it be negative."

Just as I finished peeing, I heard my cell ringing from my bedroom. When I finished up in the bathroom, I carried the stick back down to my room, where I saw I had a missed call from my father. I hadn't spoken to him in almost a week, not since I'd first suspected that I was pregnant. I'd been avoiding him like the plague. Reluctantly, I took a seat on the edge of my bed and dialed him back. He picked up on the second ring.

"Well, hey there, stranger," he said cheerfully.

"Hey, Deddy."

"I haven't heard from you in a while. How's everything been going out there?"

I sighed. "It's been going pretty good," I lied.

"You on spring break this week, ain't cha?"

"Yes, sir."

"I thought you'd at least want to come home and spend some time with your old man, but I guess not." He laughed. "So, what's keeping you busy this week?"

"Um, nothing much," I told him. "Aunt Marlene asked me to help her do some spring cleaning around the house, and then I'll probably just catch up on some of my studying."

"Well, I must say, I'm very proud of you, Hope. After moving out of that dorm and getting away from that boy, you seem to have gotten right back on track. I know if your mother were here, she would be so proud."

I swallowed hard, allowing my eyes to fall on the word *yes*, which was more than apparent on the pregnancy test in my other hand. "Yeah," I murmured.

"All right, now. I won't hold you," he said. "I love you, and tell Marlene I said hi."

"Will do, Deddy. Love you too."

After hanging up the phone, I collapsed back on the bed and stared up at the ceiling. Almost instantly, I could feel hot tears trickling from the corners of my eyes. At this point, I had no one to turn to. Surely, I couldn't tell my father or Aunt Marlene that I was pregnant, and since I'd moved out of the dorm, I didn't even feel close enough to tell Paris or Franki. Weighing on my shoulders was the biggest decision I'd ever have to make in my entire life. I felt so alone and didn't have a clue about what I was supposed to do. And the one person who could help me figure it all out and ease all my fears was the one person I wasn't talking to.

As if everything were playing out like a movie on the big screen, my cell phone rang beside me. I picked it up, looked at the screen, and saw that it was Meeko calling. Just like the dozens of other times, I let his call go to voicemail, but this time, he decided to leave a message. I hadn't heard his voice in weeks. Half-heartedly, I played it back.

"I'm supposed to be on vacation right now, enjoying spring break in Cancún, but I can't. It's like one of the most vital parts of my heart is missing right now, Hope. The part that keeps the blood pumping through my veins. The part that wakes me up in the morning and puts me to sleep at night." I could hear him take a deep breath as he paused. He didn't even sound like himself.

"I swear, it feels like I'm dying without you, Hope. I can't eat. I can't sleep. I can't fucking *be*, yo." He sighed. "Shit, a nigga fucked around and broke his own heart when I broke yours," he confessed before letting out a light snort. "Look, I know I've asked you this about a thousand times before, but please, shorty, try to forgive me. Just call me, a'ight?" And just like that, he hung up.

If I hadn't been crying before, I was certainly crying now. My shoulders were trembling on the mattress, and as if I were in a room full of strangers, I put my hand over my mouth just to keep in the noise. Reality had hit harder than ever before: I was pregnant, alone, and brokenhearted all at once. All at the hands of Meeko Taylor.

Chapter 25

Franki

A Spring Breakthrough

Wearing an all-white bikini and a knockoff pair of Ray-Ban shades, I lay under an umbrella on the beach. Paris and her girl Heather were sprawled out beside me, greased up, trying to catch tans from the sun. We were all just relaxing, sipping on margaritas as we listened to the waves crash against the shore. Every so often, my eyes would float over in the direction of Josh. He and his frat brothers were playing a harmless game of football against Meeko and his crew in the sand. All of them were wearing nothing but board shorts, and sand covered their feet.

Although I hated to admit it, my attraction to Josh was becoming more apparent by the day. I loved the way his shiny black hair would curl at the top of his head just from the dampness of his sweat. And the way his lean, slender muscles would glisten out there as he hustled beneath the sun. It all thrilled me internally. There was no ink on his arms or chest, no nicks in his eyebrows, and not even a single scar blemished Josh's pretty boy face. Physically, he was everything I never knew I wanted, and I couldn't keep my eyes off him.

"So, is that what you're gonna do all day? Sit here and stare at Josh?" Paris teased, taking me out of my trance.

I snapped my head over in her direction, then gave her a screw face. "Ain't nobody checkin' for Josh's yella ass. I was just watching them play," I lied.

"Mm-hmm, sure," she said, rolling her eyes. "Why don't you just get it over with and tell 'im you like him? I mean, let's face it. Anybody with eyes can see that he likes you too."

Twisting my lips to the side, I gave her a cynical glare. "I seriously doubt that."

Well, that was somewhat true. Although Josh had made it known on more than one occasion that he was attracted to me, not once had he made a move. The last and only kiss we'd ever shared was the one back in Brooklyn, three days before Christmas. While we had talked just about every day thereafter, we'd never kissed again or even spoken about it. The only affection Josh would show me was when he'd drape his arm around my neck during our walks to class. To me, it was no more than a homeboy-homegirl relationship, but secretly, I now wanted more.

Suddenly, I could hear some of the guys heading our way. When I looked up, Ty was standing above Paris, his eyes roaming her half-naked frame.

"Damn, Paris. When you gon' stop playing wit' a nigga and let me take you out?" he asked.

I let out a snort of laughter. "Yo' corny ass," I said, shaking my head. "I don't know why you keep playing ya'self, son. You already know she got a man."

"Uh, no she does not," Heather said, lifting her index finger in the air.

I cut my eyes over at Paris for clarification. She had the tip of one of her nails between her teeth and was peering up at Ty with lust-filled eyes. "We can talk about it," she told him, hiking one of her bare shoulders up to her cheek.

My eyes stretched at that. I didn't know Malachi all that well, but I knew him well enough to know that he would've gone the fuck off had he heard Paris's response. Although I figured they probably weren't official yet, every other day Paris was claiming him as her man. However, since she was acting brand new today in front of Ty, I figured something must have changed.

"A'ight, cool. That's what's up," Ty said. He rubbed his hands together as he licked his lips.

I could only shake my head in response. "Malachi gon' fuck you up," I mumbled beneath my breath.

She looked at me with a deadpan expression. "Whatever. I'm sick and tired of Malachi having his cake and eating it too," she said, tossing her long hair back in the wind.

I didn't know what she meant by that, and given that I was on vacation, I honestly didn't care. It sounded like drama, and I was trying to steer clear of that. I wanted to use this time wisely to clear out everything that was plaguing my mind. The rape, my father, everything.

After hopping up from the beach towel I had arranged on the sand, I pulled my bikini bottoms out of my behind and made my way into the water. I was only knee deep before I felt someone gently hook their arm around my shoulders. I glanced to my right and saw that it was Josh. His pretty, dark brown eyes peered at me as a wide grin took over his face.

"You enjoying your time?" he asked.

I nodded. "Yeah, I am. Ain't neva done nothing like this before. Shit, before I left for college, the furthest place I'd ever been to was Jersey," I admitted.

Josh released a light chuckle at that. "Well, how 'bout this? From now on, no matter the year, we'll go somewhere new together for spring break?"

I sucked my teeth. "Boy, you know I ain't got that kinda money. I mean, Paris and her peoples paid for all this," I told him.

"Aye, let me worry about all that. All you gotta do is agree to go," he said, holding his hand out for me to dap up. Another one of his *buddy* moves.

Before taking his hand, I raised my chin and questioned him with my eyes. "What about when you go off to law school? You still gonna go on spring break with me?"

Josh didn't respond with words. Instead, he pressed his lips into a straight line and dipped his head toward his already extended hand. I smiled and dapped him up like I would one of my boys from back home.

"So, you swimming or nah?" he asked, nodding his head out toward the water.

I scrunched up my nose. "I don't even know how to swim."

His head reeled back as he let out a chuckle. "Well, what you doing out here in the water, then?"

"I like to get my feet wet. Among other things," I said, mumbling the last part.

"I bet you do. Come on. Let's go back."

With Josh's arm lying across my neck, we trekked through the blue water back to shore. Approaching the group, I instantly noticed that several beach chairs had been added and more people had gathered around, mostly Josh's frat brothers, and a few others, whom I immediately recognized as from the school's band. When I saw Ty sitting next to Paris with his hand on her knee, and Big Mo next to them, apparently rapping with Heather, my eyes went to find Meeko. I didn't see him right away, but as I gazed farther down the beach, I found him. About a quarter mile down, he was sitting off by his lonesome, drinking what appeared to be a double shot of something.

As we walked farther toward the crowd, I even noticed that Asha was now in the mix. It was funny how when we were back on campus, she never liked to hang, but here she was, with her ass sitting on my towel.

"Yo, get up outta my spot," I told her, not even bothering to say hello.

After looking behind each of her shoulders as if I was talking to someone else, she leaned back on her elbows. "Move your feet, lose your seat," was all she said.

Sliding my tongue across the front of my teeth, I shook my head, and then I gave her a pretentious smile. It was all I could do to keep myself from whupping her ass. "Yo, ma, if you don't get yo' funky ass off my towel, we gon' have a major fucking problem," I warned in an even tone, shooting blatant daggers with my eyes.

Josh gripped me from behind at the shoulders and placed his lips against my ear. "Chill out, ma. It ain't that deep," he whispered.

I didn't even respond; I just stood there with my arms folded across my chest, waiting for Asha to get up, silently daring her not to. After a few huffs and puffs, she got up and grabbed her beach bag, which was on the sand beside her. Suddenly, I watched as her eyes caught something down the beach. I followed her line of sight and saw Jaxon strolling hand in hand with a white girl in a Hawaiian-print bikini. She was thin, with large boobs and bleached-blond hair like a Barbie doll's. I looked back at Asha and saw an unexpected scowl on her face. I knew she would sometimes refer to Jaxon as her man, but to be honest, I had never seen them together.

"Ain't that ya' man?" I asked her, flopping down on my vacant towel. Josh quickly slid in next to me.

Before she could answer, Jaxon walked over and started dapping up all the guys. Although he played basketball and the other guys played football or were a part of a frat, they all seemed to run in the same circles. "This is my girlfriend, Brittany," I heard him say, gesturing toward the white girl at his side.

"Oops," I said, staring up at Asha. She looked like she was about to be sick.

"But I thought he was dating Asha," Paris whispered next to me.

I shrugged my shoulders.

As Jaxon approached us next, his girlfriend, Brittany, was all smiles. "What's up, Josh?" he said, leaning down to clap hands with him. "Ladies," he said, cutting his eyes over at me, Paris, and then Heather. When he stood upright, he looked directly at Asha. There was no fear or shock in his eyes, something you'd expect of a boyfriend who'd just been caught cheating. Instead, his lips curled at the corners. "What's going on, Ash? You doin' a'ight?" he asked.

Unable to peel my eyes from the crazy scene in front of me, I kept looking back and forth between the two of them.

"I'm perfectly fucking fine," she shot back with a venomous glare.

Before Jaxon could get another word out, Brittany came up and slipped her arm through his. Affectionately, she laid her head against his shoulder. "Oh, yeah," he said, glancing down at her. "Britt, this a good friend of mine, Asha. Asha, this is my girlfriend, Brittany."

Even from where I sat below them, I could see Asha gritting her teeth.

"So totally nice to meet you," Brittany said, beaming from ear to ear.

Asha just stared at Jaxon with a blank expression before finally walking off.

"Babe, what was that about?" Brittany asked Jaxon. He simply hiked his shoulders, and just like that, the two of them continued their stroll down the beach.

"Dude! Asha is so fucking pissed," Paris said with a laugh.

"Well, maybe this will humble her ass," I said.

Josh leaned over and nudged me on the shoulder. "Stop being messy, ma."

I rolled my eyes.

After another hour on the beach, we all headed back to our rooms to clean up for dinner. We ended up at a little Mexican restaurant called Lorenzillo's, right near the water. Surprisingly, Malachi showed up with his friends. Once we all ate, Paris invited everyone up to their suite to hang out before going to the club. I wasn't really up for it, but when Josh said he was going, of course I couldn't decline.

When we got there, it seemed like everybody and their mama was packed inside their hotel suite, which favored a small apartment. Malachi's friends Tee Tee, Rita, and Bull were all gathered at a table, sharing a blunt and playing a game of cards. While Paris and Heather were by the minibar, mixing drinks, Nya, Meeko, Ty, Big Mo, and Asha sat in the living room, talking.

"What's up, y'all?" I said, entering the living room with Josh. Both of us immediately sat down on the floor.

"So, I have an idea," Paris said, walking over with a tray of drinks in her hand. "Let's play spin the bottle."

"Yes!" Heather exclaimed, coming up behind her.

"Uh . . . no!" I said, mimicking Heather's and Paris's white girl voices. "I'm not playing no middle school games with y'all."

"Oh, phooey. You are no fun," Paris complained as she bent down to hand me a glass. "Well, here, go ahead and drink up. Maybe it'll loosen you up a bit." Then she leaned in closer to my ear. "Who knows? If you play right, you just might get a kiss from you-know-who," she whispered sneakily, a smile in her voice.

Although I smacked my teeth, her sentiments played in my mind. *Hmm, if only I could spin that bottle just right*, I thought.

"Well, I'm down," Ty said.

"Fuck it. Me too," Asha chimed in before tossing back a shot of something.

Heather clapped her hands and bounced on her toes. "Yay! We're playing spin the bottle," she sang. "We used to play this all the time back in high school."

"Exactly, high school," I said, rolling my eyes.

Paris walked over to the bar and retrieved a forty-ounce bottle that used to contain Dos Equis beer. She placed it down on the glass table that was in the dead center of the room. As we all gathered around, I looked over at Josh. He simply shrugged his shoulders, letting me know that he was game for whatever.

Let me find out church boy Josh is unpredictable.

While everyone sat around waiting for Paris to take the first spin, Malachi, Rita, Tee Tee, and Bull could be heard talking trash from across the room. "We 'bout to run a Boston on these niggas, Bull," Malachi said, fist covering his chuckle.

I noticed Paris rolling her eyes in his direction before nodding to Heather to go first. On her knees next to the coffee table, Heather leaned over and gently spun the bottle with her hand. It spun around six times before finally landing on Nya. With six cornrows braided to the back, Nya sat there with an eager expression on her face. She rubbed her hands together greedily before lifting herself onto her knees.

"Oh my God!" Heather squealed and laughed before covering her flushed face with both hands.

Big Mo licked his lips and nodded his head. "Yeah, let's get this thang poppin'," he said, sitting up in his seat, more than ready to see some girl-on-girl action.

"Hell yeah," Ty chimed in, clapping his hands.

"Don't sit here and act like this is your first time ever kissing a girl," Paris said, calling Heather out.

Heather's jaw dropped as she cut her eyes over at Paris. "I never said it was," she admitted.

"Hmm, let me find out," Nya declared with a smirk.

From opposite ends of the table, the two of them leaned in and shared a sloppy kiss. Nya was holding the back of Heather's head, and you could see her wet tongue slithering in and out of her mouth. Nya was so into it, but Heather was the first to pull back with a laugh.

"Girlfriend, you are wild," she told Nya with stretched eyes. Giggling, she wiped the corners of her mouth.

Nya simply shrugged her shoulders and pulled her lower lip in between her teeth.

Next up was Asha. She got up from the couch and tugged at the short shorts she had on before going over to spin the bottle. When it finally stopped and landed on Meeko, Ty had to nudge him in the arm. He was leaning back on the far end of the couch, staring off into space.

"It's on you, yo," Ty told him.

Meeko looked at Asha and shook his head. "Nah, man, I'm good," he said.

"What?" Asha sassed, placing her hands on her hips. "I thought you was playing."

"Nah, y'all go 'head," he said evenly.

Asha rolled her eyes and scrunched up her nose. "Well, you need to go sit over there with them, then." She pointed in the direction of Malachi and his friends. "You can't be sitting over here if you ain't playing."

"And who the fuck is you?" Meeko sneered. "You can't tell me where the fuck I can sit."

"Whatever. If you ain't gon' play, then you don't need to be over here," she said, lowering her tone.

Meeko sucked his teeth. "Bitch, just shut the fuck up and play," he spat. Obviously, he was annoyed by something more than Asha's ignorance, as he'd been distant and aloof all day.

"Bitch?" she questioned, snaking her neck. Her eyes immediately flew over to Malachi. However, he wasn't paying any attention to us. He was totally engrossed in the card game.

"Yeah, I'm talking to you. Bitch," Meeko snapped, standing up from the couch. "Fuck makes you think somebody want to kiss yo' ho ass. Shit, pussy been ran through more than a fucking high school track. Can't imagine how many dicks you done sucked."

Ty reached up and grabbed Meeko's arm. "Chill out, yo," he told him, cutting his eyes over at Malachi and his crew.

"Man, I don't give a fuck!" Meeko spat, violently yanking his arm out of Ty's grasp.

"Nigga, don't worry about my pussy or how many dicks I've sucked," Asha snapped. Then she paused, as if she'd had a sudden thought. "Matter of fact, what you need to do is worry about how you gon' take care of that baby," she added.

Both Meeko's lips and head cocked to the side from anger. "Baby? Man," he stressed. "Fuck is you talking 'bout?"

"Oh, that's right," Asha said with a sneaky smile. "You didn't know that Hope was pregnant, did you?"

My jaw damn near hit the floor at that. Sure, I knew Hope and Meeko had started dating a few months back, because at one point they had been inseparable. Just about every day, you could spot them eating lunch together in the cafeteria or walking across the quad to class. More often than not, if you saw one, you saw them both. But this . . . I had no idea. The thought of Hope finally having sex had never even occurred to me. That was just how pure and innocent her personality was. I had always joked around about how Hope would finally lose her virginity in college, but the truth was, I didn't think she'd actually do it until marriage. That was just how strong her faith was. I guess at the end of the day, she was only human, like the rest of us, trying to explore life and discover love to its fullest.

I glanced over at Meeko, saw a blend of both anger and confusion swirling around in his eyes.

"Judging by that stupid-ass look on your face, maybe the bitch's pussy is just as ran through as mine," Asha said, letting out a sarcastic snort of laughter. "Let me guess. You ain't the pappy?"

With a heaving chest, Meeko stepped forward like he was getting ready to beat Asha's ass. Everyone sat around quietly, just watching the scene unfold. It was apparent that nobody wanted to be in the middle of Asha's messiness or, even more so, to get caught up in the crossfire of Meeko's wrath. That was just how infuriated he was. But before he could make another move, Big Mo finally hopped up from his seat and grabbed him.

"It ain't worth it, bruh," Big Mo told him, hand palming Meeko's chest.

Meeko just stood there, jaw clenched, spearing Asha's face with his unflinching eyes. I was two seconds away from hopping up and saying, "Fuck this!" my damn self, but before I could, Meeko stormed out of the suite and let the door slam hard behind him.

"Tuh," Asha scoffed with another roll of her light brown eyes.

"Shorty, you wild as fuck for that," Ty said. "He crazy over that girl. Nigga ain't even been himself since she broke up with him."

That explained Meeko's recent disposition. Although Hope and I were no longer as close as we'd once been, my heart still went out to her. I knew better than anyone how your first breakup could really take a toll. After the rape and her attack, our friendship had become somewhat distant.

I didn't know if it was because she had moved out or because I hadn't been there for her when those girls kicked her ass, but either way, I was going to check on her when I got back to school.

Paris cleared her throat and clapped her hands, getting everyone's attention. "Okay, Asha, do you want to take another turn?" she asked, pointing to the bottle on the table.

Asha sucked her teeth with an attitude. "Don't nobody wanna play this dumbass game," she sneered. And just like that, with her eyes glaring at Malachi, she walked out onto the balcony.

"I—I'll go," Josh said and got up. I was caught by surprise. I watched him dip down to spin the bottle. When the neck landed on Heather, my stomach instantly twisted into knots.

"Ooh," Heather purred with a soft clap of her hands. "Your lips totally look soft," she said.

Josh cracked a boyish grin and shook his head.

As the two of them stepped closer, Paris looked at me with sympathetic eyes. No, I hadn't come right out and told her that I was falling for Josh. In fact, I had denied it every chance I could, but even still, she knew. Feeling the warmth of vomit starting to creep up inside my chest, I hopped up from the floor and ran into the second bedroom.

I couldn't just sit there and watch the two of them kiss, especially since he'd never made a move to put his lips on me. As I sat on the edge of the bed with my head hanging between my knees, I tried to calm my thudding heart. I knew it was childish, but I kept imagining the two of them kissing inside my head. Just the thought alone made me sick. I was flat-out jealous, and there wasn't a damn thing I could do about it. The fact of the matter was Josh wasn't my man.

Suddenly, the door to the bedroom swung open. I looked up and, my vision blurred, I saw Josh locking it behind him.

"What are you doing in here?" I asked as I stood up, blinking away the weak-ass tears that had surfaced in my eyes.

"I came to check on you," he said.

"Well, go on back in there and finish playing the game," I told him with an attitude. "I ain't tryna cockblock, if that's what you think." I swear, it took everything in me to say that shit.

"Look, man," he drawled, holding both of his hands up in surrender, "I'm not trying to upset you."

"Upset me?" I smacked my lips. "Man, you bugging. It's not like we're together or nothing. I know you don't look at me that way. Shit, you haven't even kissed me since Christmas." I snorted. "And I'm the one who made that fucking move!"

He ran his hand over his face and let go of a deep breath. "You know why I don't touch you that way?" he asked. "Why I haven't kissed you?"

Although my mind was telling me that it was probably because I was a used-up slut, I simply replied, "Nah. Why?"

He walked up close and slipped his finger under my chin. "Because if I touched you the way I really want to, Franki, I don't think I could resist taking things all the way."

Again, with my aggressive nature, I slinked my arms around his neck and boldly looked him in the eyes. "And exactly what's wrong with taking things all the way?" I asked lowly, pressing my breasts up against him.

Almost immediately, I could feel Josh's nature rise. Church boy was definitely working with a monster down there, and the mere thought caused a palpitation between my thighs. As he licked his dark pink lips, I could see his eyes studying my face with intensity. "I know it wouldn't be nothing for us to strip out of our clothes right now, ma. Get buck wild and have sex all night long," he said lowly. "But check it. You been there, done that. When you give yourself to me"—he pointed to his chest—"I want you to be able to bare your soul to me. I wanna be so deep in your spirit that I know your inner thoughts. I wanna be the one to ease away all your fears. That's when you're truly naked with someone." He shook his head. "Not that play-play shit you been on with all these other niggas."

I swallowed hard, feeling like both my heart and my pussy were about to explode. When he leaned in and allowed his hands to fall down around my waist, my breath caught in my lungs. Gently, he pressed his lips into mine, causing an unexpected shiver to ease down my vertebrae. The fine hairs on the back of my neck rose to attention when he slipped his warm tongue in my mouth. He groaned and forcefully pulled my body closer to his as we shared the most panty-wetting kiss.

Fucking church boy Josh.

When things got a bit too intense and I hiked my leg up and hooked it around his waist, Josh pulled back. "I'm not ready for us to take it there yet," he said. He gently grabbed my hand and led me over to the bed, where I sat on his lap.

"I know," I whispered, thinking about everything he had just shared.

Josh wanted me to bare my mind and soul to him before I granted him access to my body. I wasn't used to that. I was used to niggas wanting only one thing from me. Usually, something I could control. But now the tables had turned, and Josh had all the power.

"Did you know that I'm a PK too?" I whispered. "Or at least I used to be."

Josh's brows gathered in confusion. "Your pops is a preacher?" he asked.

"*Was* a preacher. He . . ." My voice trailed off.

Clutching my trembling hand in his, Josh interlaced our fingers. "Talk to me, ma. I promise I ain't gon' judge you. I just want to know who you are. In here," he said, pointing to my chest.

I sucked in a deep breath and closed my eyes. "When I was just eight years old, my father caught a dirty old man fondling me under my skirt, some shit he'd been doing to me for almost a year. Penetrating me with his fingers . . ." I shook my head and swallowed hard, recalling the unnatural feel of his touch. "He awakened my sexuality at such an early age, Josh. An age when I should've been thinking only about doll babies and cartoons. Not sex."

"Damn," Josh muttered lowly. His hand eased up my back and caressed me gently.

"I remember how livid my daddy was that Sunday after church. I don't think I'll ever be able to forget the look of anger and revulsion in his eyes when he walked down into that basement, catching us." I squeezed my eyes tighter, holding in the tears.

"Tell me what happened," Josh urged.

"My daddy didn't say anything. He just rushed over and punched the man so hard that he knocked him to the floor," I told him, voice quivering terribly. "And with his bare hands, he strangled that man to death. Right in front of me." When I said that part, I opened my eyes, allowing the tears to escape. I needed to see Josh's reaction. But as I peered deep into his dark irises, I didn't see any judgment, only sorrow.

His hand on my back continued to soothe me, moving in small circles at a slow yet steady pace. "Where's your father now?" he asked.

"Prison," I barely managed to say. More tears rolled down my face.

"Damn," he uttered again, thumbs gently swiping away the wetness from beneath my eyes. "I know that was hard for you to share, Franki, but thank you for trusting me."

As I held in a cry, my throat constricted almost to the point of pain. I could no longer speak, so I simply nodded my head.

Pinching my chin between his fingers, Josh planted a soft, closed-mouth kiss on my lips. "I promise we gon' get through this, Franki," he whispered. "You hear me?"

Although I nodded again, I wasn't so sure if that was true. Hell, this was a burden I had carried by myself for the past ten years. I thought about it every single day, tortured myself over and over, trying to decide if my daddy did me an actual favor or a disservice that day. Because after he'd killed that man, he'd never told a soul, not even my mother. No one knew that I had been molested. He had just allowed the police to haul him off to jail, leaving me out here to harbor this secret alone.

Chapter 26

Paris

Love's Deceit

My game of spin the bottle had turned into a complete disaster. Not only had Meeko and Asha left, but now Josh was running after Franki. I thought it was so sweet how he had refused to kiss Heather. Inwardly, I found myself a bit envious of the love I knew he obviously had for Franki.

Deciding to spin the bottle myself, I stepped back and watched it land in between Ty and Big Mo. Before Big Mo even had a chance, Ty shot up from his seat. I giggled to myself, knowing Ty had a huge crush on me. I glanced back over my shoulder at Malachi, who had a Corona bottle turned up to his lips while still engaged in a round of Spades.

I sighed. "All right, pucker up," I told Ty.

Rounding the coffee table in my direction, he eagerly licked his lips. I stood there waiting patiently, not really wanting to kiss him and, more so, just wanting to finish the game. When Ty stepped in close to me and we were less than a ruler's length apart, I could see lust dancing in his eyes. Feeling as if everything was in slow motion, I closed my eyes and leaned in a little, hoping that he would do the rest.

Suddenly, out of nowhere, I heard Malachi's voice cut through the room. "Miss Paris, you go 'head and put yo' lips on that nigga if you want to, but I swear fo' God, I'ma light this muthafucka up."

My eyes instantly popped open, and I turned in Malachi's direction. His eyes were still focused down on the cards in his hand. Only now there was a pistol sitting on the table in front of him.

"For Christ's sake, Malachi, it's just a game," I told him, slapping my hands against my sides. "And where did you get a gun from? I know you couldn't have gotten it on the plane."

Without warning, Malachi shot up from his seat, sending his chair flying back behind him. "Everybody get the fuck out! Now!" he roared.

Heather and I both jumped out of our skin, while Ty sucked his teeth and started for the door. Big Mo trailed behind him.

"Girl, you didn't know you was fucking with a crazy-ass nigga, did you?" Nya asked with a laugh.

"When you first mentioned playing spin the bottle, I was like, 'This bitch must don't know,' but then I thought about it again and was like, 'Nah, Paris know what the fuck she doin'.'" She laughed again, gathering her things from off the floor.

Unable to respond, I stood there and watched everyone scurry out of our suite. I didn't even hug Heather back when she put her arms around me to say goodbye. Asha came from the balcony, a lit blunt dangling between her lips. Attitude fully on display, she sashayed her way out the door. Bull, Rita, and Tee Tee followed behind her. Everybody was leaving so fast that I couldn't even get my thoughts together.

When the last person in the living room was gone, Malachi grabbed his gun off the table and headed for the master suite. "Bring ya' ass, Miss Paris," he said, not bothering to turn back.

With a lump of nerves in my throat, I began walking toward our bedroom. I heard the faint laughter of Franki and Josh coming from the other room, but I knew right away that I wouldn't tell Malachi. I needed witnesses, just in case he decided to kill me.

When I walked through the doorway, he was sitting on the edge of the bed. The gun rested on the nightstand. "Get over here," he commanded.

Feeling tension across the back of my neck and shoulders, I shook my head. "Not till you put that gun away," I said.

Malachi sucked his teeth. "What? You think I'm gon' hurt you?" he asked with a look of disappointment in his eyes.

I shrugged my shoulders.

He let out a deep sigh and put the gun in the nightstand drawer. "Now com'ere," he said again, still very much demanding, but in a much softer tone.

Slowly, I made my way toward him, hearing the loud beating of my own heart. As I stood in front of him, staring down into his bright eyes, neither one of us said a word. Then, without warning, Malachi got up from the bed. We were now standing so close together that I could no longer distinguish the sound of his heartbeat from my own.

"Take your clothes off," he said, not breaking eye contact.

"What?"

"I said take that shit off!" he ordered, wagging his finger up and down my frame.

Nervously, I peeled down the straps of my maxi dress and allowed it to puddle beneath me. As I stood there in a matching black bra and panty set, I timidly twiddled my thumbs. My exhales had become so soft and shallow, it felt like I was barely breathing. I watched as Malachi's eyes slowly journeyed along my body, taking in my curves.

"Take it all off, baby," he said, just above a whisper this time.

After reaching around and unclasping my bra, I let it slide down my arms and hit the floor. I had no idea why, given the fact that Malachi had just been acting like a jerk, but as I shimmied out of my panties, I noticed that they were wet. Regardless of the circumstance, my body had naturally responded to his presence.

As I stood there waiting, almost trembling in my nakedness, he slipped his hand down between us. Without delay, he ran a single finger down my slit, then in between my slick folds. I gasped and closed my eyes when it entered me.

"How you wet already, Miss Paris, huh? You wet for that nigga?" he asked with a hint of anger in his voice.

With my mouth still hanging agape from relishing his touch, I shook my head. "No," I whispered.

"You sure?" he asked, sliding his finger in and out of me.

I nodded and let out a moan.

"Nah, I need you to fucking tell me. Who got this pussy wet fa' ya like this?"

"You." I moaned again.

He removed his hand from between my thighs and roughly grabbed me at the hips. After laying me back on the bed, he quickly moved to hover above me. As he began roughly kissing my lips, stroking his tongue against mine, I couldn't help but pull at his shirt. I now wanted him naked in the worst way. My fucking clit was throbbing, and my heart was thundering out of control.

With his eyes still on me, he rose up and removed his shirt over his head. Instantly, my mouth watered at the sight of his brawny chest and chiseled abs. Tattoos covered almost every inch of him. I swallowed hard, eager for him to take me.

Leaning down, he traced each of my hardened nipples with his tongue, sending mini shock waves throughout me. When his trail extended down to my belly, tingles erupted in my groin.

"You spoiled as fuck, Miss Paris. You know that?" he said lowly, breath tickling my skin.

Panting, I propped myself up on my elbows and gazed down into his hazel eyes, watching as he dipped his tongue into my lower lips. "Fuck," I breathed, my head instantly dropping back from how good it felt.

Slowly, his tongue began to work against my swollen flesh. Up and down, in and out, until my hips began moving in the same rhythm. Possessively, he cupped my ass in his hands, burying his face deeper between my thighs. I moaned. And then like a hurricane in winter, my orgasm hit unexpectedly, jolting my body on the mattress. I could feel everything, each wave, ripple, jerk, and pull, coming from me all at once. And with a contented hum, Malachi lapped it all up with pleasure, not freeing me until my body had completely calmed.

As I lay there with quivering limbs, still whimpering, Malachi pushed down his shorts. I'd never seen a big black dick in the flesh, but here it was, just the way I'd dreamed, long, thick, and swollen at the head. Carefully, I studied the smooth chocolate skin of his erection, took in the distended veins, the one beauty mark on his right side. Although I was still recovering, I couldn't wait to have him pulsating inside me.

"You on the pill?" he asked, stroking himself with his hand.

I licked my lips and nodded with assurance, because I'd been on birth control since the eleventh grade.

With his dick still in hand, he wedged his thick body between my thighs. Slowly, inch by inch, he began to feed my sex. I could hardly breathe. With only one sexual experience in the past, I swear, it felt like I was losing my virginity all over again.

As he tilted my pelvis to finish filling me up, I watched as he bit down on his lower lip, eyes closed and muscles flexing all at once from pleasure. When his hips began to move, thrusting in and out of me, I naturally gripped his back. Fingernails lightly clawed at the surface of his skin. I was experiencing the most gratifying pain.

"This what you want?" he asked before kissing me on the lips, eyes filled with a passion I'd never known.

"Yes," I moaned, nodding my head at the same time.

"Shit," he hissed, closing his eyes again. "I swear, if you give this to any other nigga, I'ma have to kill you, Paris," he threatened in a whisper. Then came another drive of his hips. "Fuck," he belted from out of nowhere.

As he pummeled faster, I could feel my body begin to convulse. I was headed straight for another earth-shattering climax, but this time, so was he. Thickening inside of me, he growled against my ear and firmed his grip on my thighs.

I couldn't endure any more. From the inside out, my body imploded, seizing irrepressibly. "Oh God!" I cried.

"Fuck, bab . . ." Malachi's words faded into silence as he spilled everything he had inside me.

His heavy body collapsed down on top of mine, both of us breathless and spent beyond words. After a minute or two had passed, I found myself strumming my fingers up and down his back, enjoying the weight of his body between my thighs.

"Miss Paris," he finally said. "You mine now."

My heart instantly melted when I heard that.

Four days had passed since we left Cancún and returned to Greensboro. After dropping Franki off at the dorm, Malachi and I headed across town to his place. I didn't have class the next day and was desperate to spend more time tucked underneath him. However, we weren't even there for a good hour before Reese showed up with the kids. Thankfully, she didn't come in; she just dropped them off at the door. After eating dinner and getting the kids down for bed, Malachi and I made love in the shower. Ever since that first night we had sex in Cancún, only so many minutes could pass by before I yearned for his touch.

The next morning, we drove his children to day care. It was the first time I'd ever been. On the other side of town, we cut through a fancy neighborhood with homes almost as large as the one I'd grown up in. When we pulled up, I noticed that the day care was fancy too, a newly built all-pink brick building, with a freshly sodded lawn. It even had what appeared to be a state-of-the-art playground on the side. New Primrose Private Academy.

Malachi parked the car and killed the engine. "I'll be right back," he said.

With a loose-lip smile, I nodded before glancing in the back seat. "You guys have a good day at school, okay?" I told Maevyn and Mekhai.

"Bye, Miss Paris. I'ma miss you," Maevyn said with a smile.

An instant warmth spread throughout my chest as I watched her unlatch her own seat belt. "I'm gonna miss you, too, ladybug," I said, giving her the first nickname that came to mind.

Given that Mekhai was only two years old, he wasn't much of a talker. I simply kept waving at him until he finally gave in and wiggled his fingers back. When Malachi opened the back door to get them out, I gave him a quick wink of my eye. He threw one right back at me before scooping Mekhai up in his arms. Although I'd never pictured this for myself, especially not during my college life, watching the three of them walk away hand in hand made me love him more. That thug of a man, *my man*, was truly a good father, something I'd never expected.

Five minutes later, Malachi came out of the building and hopped in the car. He reached over the center console and grabbed my hand, then brought it up to his lips for a kis, something he did often. "IHOP or Cracker Barrel?" he asked.

"Definitely IHOP," I said.

He pulled off. We were driving back through the impressive neighborhood when suddenly, a police siren sounded at our rear. I looked in the passenger-side mirror and saw flashing lights.

"Fuck," Malachi barked, slamming his fist down on the steering wheel. He looked over at me with concern in his eyes. "Just be cool, a'ight?"

"Just be cool? What did you even do?" I asked.

He didn't say anything; he just pulled over to the side of the road. "Just be quiet. Don't say shit," he said.

"Malachi, you're scaring me," I whispered.

The first thought that came to mind was that Malachi might have drugs or guns in the car. *Surely, he wouldn't be so stupid. Especially not with his children in the car,* I thought.

Suddenly, two white police officers in uniform walked up to our windows, one on his side, the other on mine. One hand was already at their waists, with their fingers nervously strumming the pistols. My mouth abruptly went dry, and my hands began to sweat.

"Malachi," I whispered, my voice shaky.

"Don't say shit. Just let me handle it," he said.

Upon hearing the billy club tap against the glass, Malachi rolled both of our windows down, allowing the cool morning air to drift in.

"License and registration," said the officer on his side.

Reaching up to his sun visor, Malachi retrieved both items and handed them over. The entire time, the officer next to me inspected the inside of the car with his eyes. I remembered being pulled over for speeding in high school, with Brad behind the wheel, but I swear, it didn't feel anything like this.

Scanning Malachi's documents thoroughly, the officer asked, "You know why we pulled you over?"

"Nah," was all Malachi said.

"This car was spotted at a recent crime scene. A murder." His eyes quickly lifted, locked with Malachi's, like he was trying to read him.

I gasped out loud. "Malachi," I said, instinctively grabbing his arm. Immediately, I could feel the tension throughout his body.

"Nah, you got the wrong car. Wrong person," he casually told the officer.

"You got any drugs or weapons in the car?" the officer asked.

Malachi shook his head. "Nah."

"All right, I'm gonna have to ask you to step out."

Flexing his jaw, Malachi clenched his back teeth. It was evident that he was seething inside. Reluctantly, he stepped out of the car, leaving me scared shitless inside.

"This can't be right. He didn't kill anyone," I told the officer on my side.

"Miss Paris, be quiet and let a nigga handle it!" Malachi insisted, fuming, before walking to the front of the vehicle with his hands raised above his head.

The officer grabbed him by the arm and roughly slammed him down on the hood of the car. Instantly, I shrieked, every nerve ending inside me shaking to the core. As the cop brought Malachi's hands behind his back, the police officer at my window moved in and cocked his gun, aiming it in Malachi's direction. Without even thinking, I jumped out of the car.

"Put the gun down. He didn't do anything!" I screamed. Arms raised in the air, I trembled with fear.

"Get back in the car. Now!" yelled the officer who had been at my window.

"Paris, shut the fuck up," Malachi warned.

Seeing the cuffs being placed on his wrists as the officer read him his Miranda rights, I couldn't keep the tears at bay. Brutally, the cop jerked him upright with too much force, causing Malachi to flinch in pain. His pained expression and rigid movements were a dead giveaway of his discomfort. He was having difficulty walking at the officer's desired pace.

"Let's go, boy. Move," the officer ordered.

Just that quick, I could see Malachi's whole being fill with fury. He pushed back hard, causing the officer to lose his footing instantly. Quickly, the cop recovered and grabbed Malachi that much harder by the wrists. By the clenching of his jaw and the straining of his neck, I could see that Malachi was trying his best to ignore the pain. Then, without warning, the officer reached down, clutching his billy club in his hand, and struck him hard across the leg.

"Ahh! Fuck!" Malachi screamed out in agony.

"Don't hurt him! Please," I cried.

The officer near me still had his gun trained in Malachi's direction. "Ma'am, you need to get back in the car now!" he ordered.

As Malachi continued to be shoved in the direction of the police car, he took a quick second to look back at me. "Call Reese from my phone. Tell her to get in touch with my lawyer!"

"Call Reese?" I asked. I understood that this was the mother of his children, but I hadn't expected her to be the first person he wanted me to call. If it was about getting a good attorney, my father's old connections alone would do the trick. Hell, as far as I was concerned, we didn't need Reese or any two-bit lawyer she could provide.

"Do as I say, Paris," he said firmly from a distance.

"I'm not calling Reese." I shook my head stubbornly, sniffing back uncontrollable tears.

"You gotta call her!" he shouted, resisting the officer, who was practically pushing him into the car by his head.

"Why?"

"Because, Miss Paris, she's my wife."

To be continued . . .

Heartbreak U: Summer Vacation

coming October 2024